FINDING KYLE

FINDING KYLE

BY
SAWYER BENNETT

Find Sawyer on the web!
www.sawyerbennett.com
www.twitter.com/bennettbooks
www.facebook.com/bennettbooks

TABLE OF CONTENTS

PROLOGUE	1
CHAPTER 1	9
CHAPTER 2	18
CHAPTER 3	26
CHAPTER 4	37
CHAPTER 5	47
CHAPTER 6	55
CHAPTER 7	67
CHAPTER 8	74
CHAPTER 9	82
CHAPTER 10	93
CHAPTER 11	101
CHAPTER 12	110
CHAPTER 13	119
CHAPTER 14	136
CHAPTER 15	146
CHAPTER 16	155
CHAPTER 17	166
CHAPTER 18	179
CHAPTER 19	190
CHAPTER 20	198

CHAPTER 21   207

CHAPTER 22   219

CHAPTER 23   230

CHAPTER 24   241

CHAPTER 25   251

CHAPTER 26   266

CHAPTER 27   277

CHAPTER 28   287

EPILOGUE   298

Other Books by Sawyer Bennett   306

About the Author   309

PROLOGUE

KYLE

M Y ASS HITS the couch cushion, but no sooner do I twist the cap off my bottle of beer, then there's a knock at the door. With a sigh, I push back up, set my beer on the black lacquered tabletop, and move my way through the sparsely furnished apartment. It's done in whites, grays and blacks with plenty of leather, chrome, and glass. It's way too contemporary for my taste, but what do I know? I've pretty much lived the past three years in a shit hole.

After a quick look through the peephole, I'm unlocking the door to pull it open. Joseph Kizner stands there with a worried look on his face.

He's always fucking worried around me, and it's grating on my nerves.

"I'm fine," I say before he can ask, stepping aside to let him in.

"You look like shit," he returns casually as he shrugs off his heavy wool overcoat. Winter in Chicago is no fucking joke, but I wouldn't know as I'm not allowed outside this apartment. The walls are closing in on me, and all I can do is ride it out.

I don't address his comment on how I look. Instead, I walk to the fridge to pull out a beer for him. He follows me into the modernized kitchen, which is done all in stainless steel and granite, and accepts the bottle from me. He twists the cap off, setting it on the counter.

I wait patiently as Kizner takes a sip. After he swallows, he gets right to the point. "The wiretaps have been approved and are going into place as we speak."

I nod in understanding. That means shit's getting real.

"We're going to go ahead and move you," he says, and then watches me carefully for my reaction.

I've known Joe Kizner a long time. Over the years, he's lost a little more hair on top and gotten a few more wrinkles around his eyes, but, otherwise, he's not changed much. We worked together at the ATF on a very dangerous and high-profile case that started ages ago, but that doesn't mean we've spent a lot of time together. That's because I went deep undercover, immersing myself into a sinister motorcycle club named Mayhem's Mission. The club was long suspected of running drugs, guns, and sex slaves. Joe was my handler on the outside.

The case started just over five years ago after several informant tips started adding up to a plausible decision to go in. I volunteered and moved to Jackson, Wyoming, settling into a new life as nothing more than a motorcycle mechanic at a local shop. Over the next several months, I got to know some of the club members who would bring their bikes in for work. Eventually, I was invited out to some parties at the club. I went on some "charity" runs, which were nothing more than fronts to make the club look legit. I fucked club whores and snorted coke with my new buds. I devolved from my basic human nature, and I became just like them.

As time went on, I saw things.

I saw illegal shit go down at the clubhouse, and I kept my mouth shut. I did this all under the watchful eye of their leader, Zeke, until, after almost two years, he approached me to patch in with the club.

I'd been tested, of course, before the offer came to me.

A test that will probably continue to haunt me as it involved conveying a very direct message to one of Zeke's enemies, and while said enemy was a lowlife piece of criminal shit who had just gotten out of prison for raping a sixteen-year-old girl, I still see rivers of blood on my hands because I became his judge, jury, and executioner in one fell swoop just so I could pass Zeke's test.

That's when I became a real criminal as well.

For three years after that, I rode with the club. I facilitated drug deals, helped to transport women sold into slavery, and I hurt countless people who the club felt deserved to be hurt. I participated in gang bangs with my new brothers, and I lived without a single fucking regard for the law that I'd sworn to protect.

But I did all of this with the sanction of the U.S. government. As a deep undercover agent, I was given absolute autonomy in my actions to help solidify my position within the organization so that I'd be given a position of trust. It was sort of a "don't ask, don't tell" type of policy, and Joe will never know the true extent of the heinous things I did to play my part.

Thereafter, it was a matter of collecting evidence and information, and then passing it on as carefully as possible to Joe. We barely saw each other over the three years I was deep because it was just too dangerous, but I did my job and did it well. I garnered enough evidence that just a few short months ago, the ATF was able to bring down Mayhem's Mission and their operation, which was spread out over the entire western part of the United States.

This was one of the most remarkable take downs in ATF history because an agent had never been that deep before, or stayed that way for that long. But the real feather in my cap, which will earn me a hefty promotion, a pay raise, and probably some presidential medal or some shit, is that I was able to learn that one very high-ranking U.S. senator from Colorado was deep into business with the club. The senator had state-level cops in his pockets. They were able to pull strings all the way down to local police so that blind eyes were turned to most of the criminal activity. The club made millions of dollars on their enterprises, and that money surged upward to reward the senator.

While I was able to provide plenty of direct proof against Zeke and the club, I'd never been privy to any actual exchanges between the club and the senator. As such, the ATF was quietly moving to get federal wiretaps in place, because while Zeke headed the largest chapter of Mayhem's Mission in the United States, it wasn't the only one, and there was plenty of shit still going down.

Which brings me back to Kizner's visit to this apartment that I've been holed up in for almost three months now.

"Moving me?" I ask.

"We had to disclose you as a witness when we sought the wiretaps," he returns. "You're now officially a target."

"Not going into WITSEC," I tell him adamantly. No way am I giving up every last vestige of control to the U.S. Marshal's and their witness protection program.

"Stupid fuck," he mutters in return.

When the ATF took the club down back in October, I was still in deep. They were able to secure the compound and make their arrests without one Mission gang member knowing I was a rat. When they busted in with their flash-bangs and SWAT gear, I took off running as was the plan. I went out the back door, along with two other gang members, and we fled into the back woods, all three of us splitting up in various directions.

I stayed hidden until I was later extracted with such

secrecy that only three people in the entire ATF knew of my whereabouts. It later went down in the official report that I'd been executed by Zeke's right-hand man, a Mission gang member who had taken a bullet between the eyes during the raid and couldn't say anything to the contrary.

So, on October twelfth, I was officially declared dead and whisked away to hide out in Chicago until the ATF could finish building their case against the senator and the law enforcement officials who were on the take as well.

"WITSEC is your safest option, Kyle," Joe reminds me.

"It's a wasted resource on me," I counter. "I can take care of myself."

"But you'd have added protection until this gets to trial."

"You mean, I'll have watch dogs that will curtail my freedom," I tell him with a pointed stare. I'd been locked up here in this tiny apartment for almost three months, and I was going stir crazy. I wasn't about to stay in this type of situation going forward.

"To help keep you alive until trial," he again pushes at me. "And we need you for the trial. Every single fucking arrest hinges on your testimony."

"Well, gee, Joe," I say sarcastically. "I'm glad you're worried about me personally and not just as a valuable asset."

Joe sighs and rubs his hand along his balding head. "I'm not even going to address that. You know I'm worried about you personally."

I sigh as well, raking my fingers through my long, blond hair. It's taken on a few extra grays over the last few years with all the shit I've seen and done. "I know, and I appreciate it. If you'll just get me a new identity and send me somewhere remote, I'll handle myself. I can keep myself safe until the trial."

"There's more to it than just—"

"I know," I cut him off. "So set up bank accounts under my new name, move my monies in there because God knows I've saved a fuck of a lot of money over the last three years the ATF was paying me, and I don't know... get me a job or something, so I can stay busy."

Joe stares at me a long moment before he says, "You know if you don't go into WITSEC, you're on your own. And you know he'll send people after you."

"He" being the senator, and I nod... because yes, I know this is a distinct possibility.

"Then make sure you send me somewhere he'll never find me, and then cover my tracks," I say simply. The government's been hiding witnesses for decades, and they're good at it.

Joe takes a long slug of his beer before setting the unfinished bottle down on the counter. "Alright. It will take a few days to get everything set up. I'll be in touch.

Until then—"

"Stay in the apartment," I mutter.

It sucked donkey dick being dead and having to hide.

CHAPTER 1

KYLE

S*HE'S HAD ENOUGH.*

She sits on the cold concrete floor, slumped forward as far as she can because her arms are tied behind the four-by-four post and her legs are sprawled out in front of her. Her head hangs low, stretching her neck to its limits and causing her matted and blood-crusted hair to hang over her face, so I can't see the misery in her eyes. Yeah... she's had enough.

Kayla throws an icy bucket of water over the woman, but she doesn't even flinch.

Not satisfied by that lack of reaction, Kayla draws her foot back and kicks the woman in the thigh.

No reaction.

Bending over, I grab a hank of her gnarled hair and pull her head up. She's completely lax, eyes closed and mouth hanging slightly open, but she's not feeling anything at this moment. I slide my gaze over to Kayla, who looks at me expectantly.

"She's had enough today," I tell her.

"Maybe another bucket of water will wake her up," she

suggests pointedly.

I shake my head and release my hold on her. Her head flops back down, and I ignore the roil of acid gurgling low in my belly. Shaking my head, I tell her, "Nah. Try again tomorrow. Maybe using a knife on her again will get her to loosen her tongue."

Kayla gives a cackle of glee over my suggestion, and her eyes turn darkly clouded with wicked desire. Desire to continue her sick torture or desire for me, I can't tell. She licks her lips as she looks at me, and I have to repress the shudder that wants to overtake my body.

Instead, I lift my chin up at her as if I share her delight in tormenting this woman. Kayla gives me a mischievous wink and says, "Tomorrow then. I'll start with the knives."

My eyes snap open, but they don't see a damn thing. The room is pitch black at first, but then the soft glow of moonlight off the Atlantic Ocean starts to lighten my surroundings. I scrub my hands over my face briefly before kicking off the covers and rolling out of my bed. The floor is cold because I didn't bother turning the heat on last night. Even though it's May and spring is in full gear, it still gets chilly at night. My heart rate is only slightly elevated from that nightmare, but my skin feels like it's crawling with ants.

I don't dream of Maggie often, but when I do, it's that particular dream. I'm not sure why that dream plagues me because while it was definitely horrendous what we did to her, it's certainly not the worst thing I've done. On top of that, I broke every protocol in the book for an undercover agent by rescuing Maggie from that basement where Kayla was torturing her. I did it in the dark of the night when everyone was asleep, and I did it knowing I could be blowing three years of undercover work just to save one woman's life.

In hindsight, it worked out, but also in hindsight, it was probably a stupid decision. That is what I'm having a hard time reconciling. Probably why I keep dreaming of it.

I pad out of the small room to the bathroom just one door down, flipping on the light and momentarily blinking against the harsh glare. Bending over the sink, I turn the cold water on and let it run for a few seconds before cupping my hands under it. It's icy and abrasive and exactly what I need. I splash three handfuls on my face and give a hard rub to my eyes before I straighten up and look at myself in the dingy mirror above the sink.

Dead, bleak eyes stare back at me. The lightest of blues... practically colorless. They had never held much warmth in them to begin with, but coming out of the dregs of my memories, they seem to almost shimmer with a frostiness that matches the cold feeling inside my veins.

The man staring back at me is named Kyle Sommerville.

Well, that was his name as of last October, but then

he was shot, execution style, in the back of the head. That's the official story that was given to my only living relative, my sister, Andrea. She was told her brother was an undercover agent, a hero, and that he sacrificed his life to take down Mayhem's Mission. The day after I "died," I became someone else. I kept my first name because I was told it would make it an easier transition for me, but I had no say-so in my new last name.

And frankly, I didn't care.

It was just a name, so I became Kyle Harding.

The "new" Kyle who stares back at me looks nothing like the old Kyle. I've lost a little over thirty pounds over the past seven months—by design—and the gaunt angles caused by the weight loss and the removal of a fuck of a lot of my long, blond hair and beard left a new man in its place. Many people who go into hiding color their hair, but all I did was remove it, so nothing is left but very short stubble that actually appears dark against my pale skin. Put a recent picture against the old Kyle and nobody will see a resemblance. I'm hiding in practically plain sight.

My gaze drifts down past my jaw to halfway down my throat. Tattoos rise above the collar of the white t-shirt I'd worn to bed. Now those tattoos… those would identify me as Kyle Sommerville, so I keep them hidden as much as possible. I moved to Maine from Chicago in February. Those first few months were bitterly cold, and it wasn't a problem to hide my tats. But it's May now.

The weather is starting to warm, so they'll be partially visible.

Oh, well.

I seriously doubt anyone from Mayhem's Mission or, even worse yet, a certain senator who probably didn't take kindly to his arrest, are going to look for me here in Misty Harbor, Maine. This is about as far off the fucking grid as possible to get, and I trust the U.S. Marshal's office, in conjunction with the ATF, to have crossed all t's and dotted all i's when it came to creating my new identity.

I'd love nothing more than to return to bed and fall back asleep, but I've had that nightmare one too many times to know that won't fucking happen. With a sigh, I turn the faucet off and blot my face with the hand towel, deciding to head out for a late-night drink—or ten—and maybe for something else that will help me sleep.

♦

THE LOBSTER CAGE is a dive bar that smells like sea salt and fish. That's because most of the inhabitants work the numerous lobster boats that prowl the local waters by day. The jukebox is playing an old Johnny Cash tune, but it's turned down low. The men here aren't interested in loud music or entertainment. They want to get drunk, and possibly get laid, then they'll go to sleep before they hit the waters tomorrow for another hard day's work.

The pungent scent of cheap perfume hits my nose

before the scantily clad ass hits the barstool beside me. It's getting late—or rather, early morning—and there are only a handful of people still here. I've got a good buzz going as I nurse my fourth whiskey.

"Hey stranger," the woman purrs beside me, but I don't even bother turning my head. Her perfume identifies her clearly. "Haven't seen you around in a while."

That's true. I moved to Misty Harbor in February and since that time, I've only been here a handful of times. Still, I've come in enough times that I'm known by the bartender and a few of the other locals.

"What's up, Barb?" I return gruffly as I stare down into my liquor. If I were to look at her, I'd see a woman who has the potential to really be pretty. But she mars that up with too much makeup and too much hair frizzed up all over the place. She's got a decent body. Even in the winter months, it's always on full display with lots of cleavage and legs showing. She has no clue I've seen so much of that in my lifetime that it's sort of like looking at the same piece of art every day. No matter how fantastic or beautiful it may be, when it's seen over and over again, it just ceases to be special anymore.

She's nothing special at all.

"Looking for a good time tonight?" she purrs, her hand going to my thigh as her nails press down into the denim.

Good time?

Yeah, that is not what this will be.

A chance to bust a nut?

Absolutely.

I pick up my glass and toss back the last of the whiskey. Setting the glass back on the grimy bar top, I shoot a look at the old, grizzled bartender—a retired lobsterman named Gus—and give him a slight shake of my head to let him know I don't want another. He merely gives a short nod and lets his gaze go back to the TV above the cash register where an old black-and-white movie is playing silently.

Pushing off the barstool, I take Barb's hand. "Let's go."

I pause briefly at the door so she can nab her jacket off the rack, and then we head outside into the chilly night.

◆

IT TAKES LESS than five minutes to get my fix.

Less than thirty seconds to lead her around to the rear of the building that's completely darkened because Gus is too lazy to replace the back door light. If there was a light, I'd see that the gravel and hard-packed dirt are littered with empty beer bottles and used condoms.

After another thirty seconds, Barb's got my dick her in her hand and her mouth on my neck as she works me up. I lean back against the building and close my eyes, concentrating on the feel of a soft hand on my cock rather than my own callused palm.

It's nice.

I guess.

A few more strokes has me rock hard, then she's up against the dirty brick wall and I'm lifting up her short skirt. We've done this a time or two. With practiced hands, she gets a condom on me and then I'm inside, her long, skinny legs wrapped around my waist. She makes a move to kiss me, but I turn my head and bury my face against her shoulder.

I have no clue if she gets off, but, in less than five minutes, I do.

Over and done with.

I feel slightly better.

♦

BACK IN MY bed, just before I turn off the lamp, I note a few water stains on the ceiling. I'll need to check the roof boots to make sure they're adequately caulked. It's time to start getting the cottage and tower repaired for the summer tourist season. That will be good. At least I'll be busy.

This winter was harsh and there was nothing to do. While I am indeed hiding out, it fucking sucked being stuck inside most of the time because of the weather.

I start to get drowsy. Even though I don't want my attention to go there, it happens anyway.

Seven months ago was my death day.

I became Kyle Harding.

I started a new life.

I'm in hiding, waiting for the day that I might be able to resume my life again.

Turning my head slightly to the left, I locate the small bedside lamp and reach out to turn it off. When the room is plunged into darkness, I stare upward until my eyes grow heavy and my breathing turns slow.

The last thing I think about before I go to sleep is the look in Kayla's eyes when I suggested she use the knives on Maggie again, and I know, without a doubt, I'll be dreaming of that again.

That's okay.

I consider it to be a part of my penance.

CHAPTER 2

JANE

LEANING MY STOMACH against the counter's edge, I stare through the open plantation shutters as I sip my coffee. It should be a crime for a man to look that good. No, actually a sin. It should be a sin to look that good, and it should be addressed in the Bible. Or maybe it is, because I'm pretty sure the way I'm coveting my neighbor has probably been written about a time or two.

It's relatively mild for the middle of May in Misty Harbor, and I saw the forecast is actually going to hit the upper sixties today. It will still dip back down to the forties tonight, but, for now, I'm loving this weather. It means my window is open to let in the spring breeze, my shutters are thrown wide, and my neighbor across the private lane that separates our properties has his shirt off as he power washes the light tower.

It's a truly marvelous day.

Inhaling deep, I take in the smell of sea spray and the viburnum that's started to bloom under my kitchen window, and my lips curve upward. I love spring so much—the way it represents renewal and hope. The winter this past year in Misty Harbor was brutal, but it's over now. I'm looking forward to spending as much time outdoors as my schedule will allow.

My little cottage sits on the west side of Cranberry Lane, just across the dusty road from my new neighbor, a man I've yet to meet in person even though he's been here a few months. There'd been a rumor that the town council was looking to replace old man Boggs as the keeper of the Gray Birch Lighthouse, as he'd let the tower and attached caretaker's cottage fall into horrible disrepair. In addition, the council wanted to open the lighthouse up for tourists in the summer as a means to bring in a little bit of income into our small town. We didn't quite have the influx of people visiting the way Bar Harbor did across Frenchman's Bay.

The rumor was laid to rest when old man Boggs actually fell down the spiral staircase that led up to the tower in January and suffered a broken femur. A quick hunt was on to fill the position, and, before I knew it, I saw my new neighbor move in on a snowy night back in early February when his old pickup truck rumbled up to the caretaker's cottage. He had nothing but a large duffel bag that he carried in, and I know this because I watched silently from my kitchen window while I made a cup of hot chocolate.

Now that the cold weather is gone for good, I expect I'll be seeing him outside a lot more as he makes repairs to the property. I will not be averse if it's done without his shirt on like he's doing now. While he's a good hundred yards away, I can see that the top half of his back is covered with tattoos, as well as his ribs on his right side and most of both arms. He turned toward my house once to adjust the power washer, and I saw a large tattoo over his chest that crawled slightly up his neck. The details weren't ascertainable—it would require binoculars to see such a thing—but I'm not that much of a stalker at this point.

My iPhone rings and when I glance down to where it sits on the counter, I see it's Miranda calling. I pick it up and answer. "Good morning."

"Whatcha doin'?" she sort of mumbles, and it's clear she's eating while talking.

"Spying on my hot neighbor as he pressure washes the light tower," I tell her as my gaze narrows back in on said man. "Whatcha eatin'?"

"Corn Flakes." I hear her take another slurping bite, after which I think she asks, "What's he wearing?"

"Jeans," I tell her. "Faded. Well fit. Work boots. Oh, and tattoos. He's wearing lots of tattoos."

"I'm on my way over, Jane," she says, her speech now remarkably clear. I have to smile at her train of thought because while my best friend Miranda and I are about as opposite as night and day, we both share a healthy appreciation for a hot man in our little out-of-the-way town.

"Can't spy with me today," I shoot her down not so

gently. "Margery's going to be here any moment for her lesson."

"Piss on Margery," Miranda grumbles.

"She's ten years old," I chastise her with a laugh. "You can't say that about a kid!"

"I can when she stands between me and ogling hot, tattooed man candy," she retorts.

"You're so bad," I reprimand her, but she's all talk. Miranda loves Margery as much as I do. "Want to grab some dinner with me later?"

"Can't. I'm working tonight. But you could come hang out for a drink."

I wrinkle my nose. Miranda works three jobs, one of which is slinging drinks at a seedy bar here in Misty Harbor called The Lobster Cage. She only works a few nights a week there, but it helps to supplement her main job as a hairdresser. She is also a waitress at one of the popular restaurants when she can manage to pick up a few shifts. While Misty Harbor's population will swell somewhat in the summer months, it's hard to stay afloat doing haircuts and highlights for a town of less than a thousand permanent residents, particularly since she's not the only hair stylist around.

"Have you met him yet?" Miranda asks, turning the subject back to the man I'm still staring at.

"Not yet," I say glumly. I'd left a basket of baked goods on his doorstep a few weeks ago with a handwritten note welcoming him to Misty Harbor, but I hadn't heard a peep out of him. He didn't even have the good graces to return my basket. "I made some muffins and left them at his doorstep a few weeks ago, but he's not come over to thank me yet."

"Probably because he broke a tooth on one of them," Miranda says bluntly, and while most would be offended, I'm not. Sometimes my baking leaves a lot to be desired. Not even pausing to see if she hurt my feelings—which she didn't—she says, "Just go over right now and introduce yourself."

"Can't," I return quickly and remind her, "Margery's coming."

"Well, after Margery's lesson… go over there."

"Maybe," I hedge, because while there's safety and security in leaving a basket of muffins that may or may not have had the consistency of bricks, I'm not sure I'd have the guts to actually approach him.

"Okay," Miranda says firmly. "I'm coming over tomorrow. We'll *both* go over and introduce ourselves, okay?"

"Maybe," I say again, and I'm pretty sure my hesitation means I'm just content to ogle from a distance. There's something about the man that seems a bit dark and dangerous—which is probably just the large amount of tattoos he's sporting—and that is so not my type.

"Alright, chicky," Miranda chirps into the phone. "I'm going to go hop in the shower. Talk later?"

"Sure. Talk later." I disconnect and set my phone

down, resuming my lean against the counter. I watch my neighbor and wonder what his story is.

After he arrived in February, I hardly saw him emerge from that little cottage during the winter, although I know he must have as he needed groceries at the very least. I never saw him around town, though, and that was nearly impossible to do because Misty Harbor was tiny. Its entire length could be walked in ten minutes. Everyone knew everyone, and while the fishermen and lobstermen could be crusty bastards at times, most everyone was friendly and outgoing.

Miranda did tell me that she'd seen my strange neighbor come into The Lobster Cage on two occasions. By her accounts, he just sat at the bar and quietly drank, not engaging in conversation with anyone. He's definitely a loner and isn't here because of any ties to the area. This makes me wonder how he even got the job as the lighthouse keeper, because it's a pretty plum assignment from what I hear.

Tending the Gray Birch Lighthouse doesn't take much. The light that warns boats of the rocky jetty and shallows that must be traversed around before entering Misty Bay runs on electricity with a backup generator, so it's pretty self-sufficient. Past that, the keeper also has to keep the tower and cottage in good repair, but those are mostly patch jobs and spring cleanings that are done once a year. The job's pretty cushy. I imagine it doesn't pay a lot, but I've heard the rent on the cottage is super cheap.

A soft knock at my door startles me. With one last lingering look at the hot guy pressure washing the lighthouse, I set my coffee cup down and head to my front door.

When I open it, little Margery Dennison beams up at me with a bright smile. "Hi, Miss Cresson."

"Good morning." I beam back at her as she walks in. "You ready for your lesson?"

She nods enthusiastically. "I've been practicing."

My smile brightens because Margery has a lot of talent and takes her studies seriously. I started giving her private art lessons about three months ago when it was clear she was heads and shoulders above my other students at Schoodic Middle School. After I talked with her parents, they gladly sent her to me for a weekly private lesson. I was more than happy to supplement my teacher's income with the lessons, even though I also taught art at the junior and high schools as well. Our school district was so small that I had to teach at three schools, and I was still struggling to make ends meet. The private art lessons were the perfect way for me to have some breathing room, so I wouldn't have to work at The Lobster Cage with Miranda.

Margery shrugs her lightweight coat off and starts to tug at the hoodie she has on underneath. While it might get up into the sixties today, it's still a bit brisk.

"Keep your hoodie on," I tell her.

Her head tilts to the side in question.

"We're going to sit outside on my front porch," I tell her, hoping I'm not going to go to hell for using this time to continue to ogle my neighbor. "We'll work on a watercolor of Gray Birch Lighthouse today."

"Cool," she says in response.

I turn toward my studio, which is nothing more than my spare bedroom converted into a place I can work on my own stuff when I have time. "Come help me get all the materials, and we'll get set up."

And maybe... just maybe, if my neighbor sees us sitting out front painting the lighthouse, he might be inclined to come over and thank me for those muffins I left him.

CHAPTER 3

KYLE

I REST THE tip of the shovel into the ground, put my boot on the edge, and punch it down into the soil. Pushing on the wooden handle, I pop up a chunk of earth, lift it up, and turn it over to dump it back down again. I repeat this process down the entire flower bed that runs the length of my back porch, and when I'm done with that, I use the shovel to break up the clods of dirt.

Standing up straight when that's finished, I wipe the back of my gloved hand over my forehead and huff out a breath of frustration.

This fucking sucks.

While I didn't expect there'd be anything glamorous about hiding out from my enemies, I really didn't envision a life that consisted of gardening. And yes, while I knew the parameters of the job Joe had found for me, I guess I didn't realize just how much I'd hate some of the domestic shit I've had to do around this place. I mean, it was one thing to pressure wash and paint the light tower last week because that's a manly job, but come on...

planting a flower bed was not on my bucket list of things I wanted to try out.

I knew fuck about gardening, but because making the lighthouse grounds pretty and inviting to tourists was part of the job description, I had to man up and learn how to do it. I spent a few days watching YouTube videos because I didn't want to go to the local library to check out how-to books, and then I made a quick trip to a local gardening center and nursery that Gus recommended to me last night when I stopped in for a drink.

And here I am, fucking gardening, and the only thing that would make me look more ridiculous was if I were wearing overalls and maybe a straw hat.

Snickering to myself, I imagine what any one of my Mayhem brothers would do if they could see me now. Well, the obvious answer is they'd kill me since I was an undercover agent, but, outside of that, they'd probably stomp the ever-loving shit out of me to know that one of their tough, badass brothers was gardening.

What really blows about the work I'm doing is that, in a few weeks, the town of Misty Harbor is going to open up my home to tourists who want to see the lighthouse. It's only on Saturdays from ten to four, and I don't have to be here because one of the members of the town's historical society will give the tours, but still... this is my home and it's been my sanctuary. The thought of strangers trampling through pisses me off like nothing has in a very long time. On those Saturdays, I figure I'll be spending my time getting shit faced at The Lobster Cage.

My phone starts vibrating in my back pocket, so I shove the spade into the ground to free my hands. I don't even bother glancing at the caller ID because there's only one person who has my number, and he'll be calling me from a burner phone anyway.

My handler… Joe Kizner.

"What's up?" I ask as I connect the call.

"Just checking in," he says cordially. "Case has been set for trial to start on September ninth."

That's a little over three months away. Hopefully then, I get my life back.

"What's the scoop on Latner?" I ask as my eyes drift past the back of my cottage to the Atlantic Ocean that's as smooth as glass today.

"He's looking for you," Joe says softly.

This is no surprise. Senator Lyle Latner of the great state of Colorado had been impeached from office once he was arrested and charged with a list of crimes that involved conspiracy, collusion, money laundering, and a whole host of other charges that would ensure he went to jail for the rest of his life. If he's convicted, he's going down and never coming back up again.

Since I'm a key element to his conviction, I expected he'd put his list of criminal contacts in use to try to find me so he could eliminate me, which would solve most of his problems. While I was not directly privy to his dealings with Mayhem's Mission, I am the main witness who will bring the club down. Once they go down, the senator is going down as well, particularly because of the wiretaps.

"You good?" Joe asks, and I know what he's really asking. My thoughts go to the cache of weapons I've got hidden around my cottage, as well as to the security system I'd installed. I was as ready as I'd ever be if someone came after me.

Of course, they'd have to find me first. I wasn't sure how that could happen. Again, only Joe and two others in the ATF know where I am hidden, the two others being bosses above Joe's pay grade.

"I'm locked and loaded," I assure him, because I do know he worries. My refusal to go into WITSEC meant I was protecting myself with no other agents to watch my back. "You think the trial will start as planned?"

Joe huffs out a breath. "You know how it goes. Everyone's saying they're ready to go, but continuances happen all the time."

I can do another three months, but the thought of much longer here is not setting well. "Then you relay to the prosecutor not to agree to any continuances."

"You know that's not how it works, brother," Joe chastises.

My frustration boils over, which doesn't take much nowadays, and I growl back at him. "I'll give it a few more months here, Joe, but then I'm coming out of hiding. I want my fucking life back. I want Andrea to know I'm alive."

"Take it easy," Joe says in his attempt at a soothing voice. "There's a process, and we have to go through it."

"I gave over three years of my life to our government," I say in a low voice bristling with anger. "I want it back, and I want it ASAP. Don't let them continue it."

"It's out of my hands and you damn well know it," Joe retorts back, losing patience as well since I'm being a dick. "Besides… you're in a good place, Kyle. Think of this as a much-needed vacation. It's beautiful there, right? How about trying to enjoy it?"

Yeah, it's fucking beautiful all right. Beautiful ocean, beautiful spring weather, and a goddamn beautiful neighbor who never misses an opportunity to give me a cheery wave and a breathtaking smile if we happen to be outside at the same time. I never smile or wave back as that would encourage her, and I don't need any complications in my life.

I certainly don't need any more of her muffins, which were awful and had to be tossed. I should have kept them as weapons, but I figured they'd attract ants.

"I'll check back with you in a few weeks," Joe says, jarring me out of my thoughts. "Sooner if anything else happens."

"Yeah, man. Talk to you later."

After I pocket my phone, I head back around to the front of my house. My truck is in the gravel driveway, loaded with flats of flowers that I need. When I turn the corner, I stop dead in my tracks. Crossing the dirt road that separates our properties is my neighbor, and she's walking straight toward my cottage.

My motherfucking gorgeous neighbor, who, as she gets closer and closer, is even more beautiful than I was able to discern from a distance. She's got golden-yellow hair that hangs in loose curls past her shoulders. While she's dressed sort of primly in a flowered dress of pinks and yellows along with a white cardigan, it's offset by the fact she's wearing a pair of beaten-up gray Chucks without any laces.

I get all of that in a cursory glance, because I'm trained to absorb details quickly, and then I turn my back on her as I go to my truck. Maybe she'll get the hint and veer off her current path.

Determined to ignore her, I stalk to my truck and grab the first flat of flowers. My shoulders lock tight when I hear her say right behind me, "Hey."

I grit my teeth for a brief moment before unclenching them to mutter a return, "Hey" without even looking at her.

When I turn toward the back of my house, I hear a scraping sound behind me and immediately look over my shoulder to see her grabbing a second tray of flowers from my truck.

I curse under my breath and practically stomp around the house to the flower bed I'd just turned over, dropping the tray in frustration. When I turn around, she's right there, giving me a big smile that does nothing to diminish the fullness of her lips. "Need some help?"

"I'm good," I mutter as I pull the tray out of her hands and drop it beside the other one.

I start to brush past her, but she steps into my path and I come up short.

"I'm Jane Cresson," she says as she sticks out her hand. "Thought I'd introduce myself since we're neighbors."

My eyes flick down to her hand before coming back up again, but the only thing I give her is my name. "Kyle."

"Well, pleased to finally meet you, Kyle," she says cheerfully, and fuck... she almost emanates goddamn sunshine she's so perky and radiant. "And actually... I came over to get my basket back from you."

"Basket?" I ask dumbly.

"Basket," she affirms with a mischievous twinkle in her eye. "The one I left on your doorstep eons ago with homemade muffins. I'm sure you remember."

Yeah, I remember them. The miniature assault weapons.

"So I'd like to get it back if you don't mind," she prods me gently. "And then, I don't know... maybe you could ask me out to dinner or something?"

My entire body jerks. I blink at her several times, trying to figure out if I just heard what I thought I did.

"I'm sorry... what?"

"Well, you know," she says as she clasps her hands in front of her and looks at me sweetly. "I made you homemade treats to welcome you, and I thought you could thank me by taking me out to dinner. Or just coffee would be fine, too."

"I'm not following," I say, my mind actually reeling with the thought that she's essentially asking *me* out by goading me into asking *her* out.

Jane grins at me. "What we've got here is a failure to communicate."

I just blink at her.

"*Cool Hand Luke*, 1967," she says as she waits for me to recognize the movie line.

I ignore her attempt to win me over with her personality and cute-as-fuck quote of a very appropriate movie line by moving past her to head back to my truck. "Sorry. Not going to take you out to dinner. Or coffee."

If I thought that would put her off, I was sorely mistaken. She falls into step beside me as I walk, and Christ... I can smell her perfume. The scent totally fits her. It smells like coastal sunshine... salt air and sweet coconut oil.

"Well, I thought you might say that," she says slyly, and I don't dare look at her. Instead, I reach into my truck and pull out another flat of flowers. She does the same, and we both turn back to the cottage. "So I'm inviting you to dinner at my place tonight. I'm making a pot roast."

"No thanks," I mutter even as my stomach gives a slight grumble. I haven't had a decent meal since I've come here because I can't cook worth a fuck and I've not really ventured out much.

"Dinner's at seven," she says firmly.

I turn to her and glare. "I said... no thanks."

She beams that smile at me, and I note her teeth are white and her lips a delicate shade of pink.

Fuck... when did I start noticing or even caring about those things?

Jane steps into me, her smile still wide and dazzling. She leans up on her tiptoes and whispers, "This is the beginning of a beautiful friendship. *Casablanca,* 1942."

Goddamn it, she's cute. That makes her seriously dangerous to a man like me.

Taking a step back—for her preservation or mine, I'm not sure—I ask, "What's up with the movie quotes?"

She shrugs. "Just a hobby. I love movies. Some I love so much that I watch them over and over again, so I tend to memorize lines."

"Well, Houston," I drawl as I narrow my eyes and give her my fiercest glare. "We have a problem. I'm not coming to dinner. Now, if you don't mind, I've got a fuck of a lot to do today and I'd like to get back to work."

"Sure," she says sweetly with a nod of her head. "But dinner's at seven. Hope to see you then."

I growl low in my throat but don't respond to her. Instead, I toss the flat of flowers down and stalk to the side door of my cottage that leads into the small laundry room. It's just easier to leave the battlefield than continue to engage with her. I'll finish planting when I'm assured she's gone.

◆

A SOFT KNOCK at my door has me tensing up, and I close the book I'm reading. The prior caretaker had a pretty good collection of classics that he left here, and I've been reading them in the evenings. Tonight, I'm doing a re-read of *Call of the Wild* because it was my favorite in high school.

Setting the book down on the cushion beside me, I glance at the clock on the wall that sits adjacent to the fireplace.

Eight-thirty.

Leaning forward, I reach under the couch and grab my Ruger 9mm pistol, but I don't make a move from my seat. I listen and wait.

After a few minutes, with not another knock sounding, I push off the couch and go to my front door. I always leave the porch light on. As I pull the curtain away, I don't see anyone.

I unlock the deadbolt and pull the door open, leaning out slightly to look left and right.

No one.

As I start to shut the door, I notice something on the stoop.

A basket, covered with a red-and-white checked linen cloth.

Bending over, I pick it up and flip the cloth back. Inside is a plastic-wrap covered plate filled with what looks like pot roast, potatoes, and carrots, with another smaller plate beside it with what looks like chocolate cake.

I turn my head to look at Jane's house and can just make out her form moving across her darkened front yard.

With a sigh, I back into my house. Taking the basket with me, of course. I'm not about to pass up a home-cooked meal, though I can only hope she cooks better than she bakes.

CHAPTER 4

JANE

M Y ALARM CLOCK goes off, and I come out of a dead sleep. Reaching out, I slap at the "off" button, managing to silence the alarm on my first try. I'm not one who makes repetitive use of the "snooze" button, and that's mainly because I've always been a morning person. I've also got a very structured routine during the school year that lets me wake up, have a cup of coffee, shower, dry my hair and put on makeup, and get dressed—all in under an hour. The middle, junior high, and high school all sit on the same piece of property on the outskirts of town, so it's a fifteen-minute drive. I eat my breakfast—usually a toaster pastry—along the way.

I roll to my side and sit up on the side of the bed, arching my back and letting out a huge yawn. The sun looks bright outside my blinds, and I can almost taste the summer that's just around the bend. This is the last week of school, and I'm actually giddy over having the next few months off.

I'm in mid-stretch/yawn when I hear a weird clanking sound from somewhere in the house. This doesn't necessarily alarm me because this little house was built in the forties. There are usually clanks and groans from some pipe or vent that occur periodically. I'm renting the house for now because it has an amazing view of the lighthouse and the Atlantic Ocean, and I don't want to buy unless I can find something equally as charming. And there's always the possibility my landlord would sell to me at some point, but, for now, I'm content to just rent.

I pop up off the bed and ignore my robe, which is laid across the end of the bed. Even though it's the first week of June, the temperatures still dip low. I always turn the furnace on so I'm comfortable at night. After my shower, I'll shut it off, preferring to open my windows to the nice ocean breeze that will keep the place sufficiently cooled during the day. An air conditioner just isn't needed in these parts.

As I exit my bedroom, I hear the clanking sound again and turn left out of the hallway as it's clearly coming from the front of the house. With my head tilted to the side, I listen as I step into the kitchen, and there it is... I hear it again. A clanking sound that lasts for just a few seconds before it goes silent again.

I look toward the kitchen sink and wait.

And there it is again.

Except this time, the clanking doesn't stop. I watch in dazed amazement as the kitchen faucet actually starts to shake. The clanking gets louder, and I take a tentative step toward the sound. The faucet rattles in place, almost to the same beat of the clanking, and I hear a hissing noise. I take two more steps that put me right in front of the sink, and I reach out a hand to touch the spout. Before I can even make contact, the hissing noise stops, the clanking falls silent, and everything goes still. I let out a sigh of relief followed by a nervous little laugh, but it's cut short when a loud noise that sounds like metal being sheared pierces the quiet. A geyser of water shoots upward from where the faucet sits, blowing the damn thing clear off its mounting.

I let out a shriek of surprise as the faucet falls into the sink with a clatter. My hands go out automatically to try to stem the fountain of water that's spraying up so high that it's hitting the ceiling. I'm so discombobulated that my sink just exploded I can't think what to do, so I push my hands down onto the geyser of water like I'll miraculously manage to put it all back where it belongs. This only serves to shoot the water out at various angles, including straight at my face and chest. Within moments, I'm completely soaked.

Perhaps it's the icy water hitting my face, or maybe it's even the fact that I'm a naturally bright person with good reflexes, but it hits me all of a sudden that I've got a burst pipe and I need to shut off the water.

I immediately drop to my knees as water continues to shoot upward before raining down on my back as I pull open the cupboard doors below the sink and start pulling out the barrage of cleaning supplies I've got under there, frantically trying to clear a path to the shut-off valve. As I pull away a half-empty bottle of Lysol that I throw over my shoulder, my eyes go to the pipes and the shut-off valve that… is fucking missing the actual knob to turn it. All I can see is the end of a bolt-looking thing. I quickly process I'm not turning off the water this way.

But again, I'm a quick thinker. With a muttered curse, I surge upward, only to slip and slide my way across the wet linoleum as water continues to spew out of my sink. I turn into the hallway, using my hand on the casing around the kitchen door to keep my balance, and sprint to the back door. I burst through it, turning to my immediate left to a door that leads into an outside utility room. I open the door and immediately look to the red handle of the shut-off valve for the entire house. It's up high, but I also have an eight-foot ladder leaned against the far wall. I grab it, pull the legs open, and scramble up it. Grabbing onto the red handle, I pull downward with an expectant surge of relief that I've found a way to solve this problem in what was really only a few seconds. Less than a minute definitely.

Unfortunately, the handle doesn't budge. I try pushing it upward, but I know that's not right. It has to come down, and I dubiously eye the rust around the bolt that holds it in place.

"Fuck," I mutter, which is uncharacteristic language

from me, but it's warranted in this case.

I grab the handle again, lay my other hand on top for extra leverage, and literally start to pull with my entire body weight as I let my knees bend so I start to sink downward from my perch on the ladder.

I hear a creak, and this bolsters me.

I pull harder, giving an unladylike grunt with my effort.

With a scream of rust and metal, the handle moves so swiftly I almost fall off the ladder, but I manage to gain my balance. It takes me several dumb blinks of my eyes as I stare at the handle that broke off and is now sitting in my hands to register what happened. I lift my head slowly and gaze up at the valve, still wide open and now with no clear way on how to shut it off. I can still vaguely hear the hiss of water spraying from the kitchen that's filtering through the open doors, and I feel my mind completely shut down.

In an instant, I become a totally helpless female, and there's only one man close enough who could potentially salvage my house.

Without a thought to the fact I'm barefoot, soaked through to the bone, and looking like a drowned rat, I scramble off the ladder and jet out of the utility room. I run gingerly along the side of the house, the lawn starting to soften with new grass but also still having prickly winter blades beneath, and slow a bit further as I cross over the dirt lane that, while mostly dirt, also has rocks and some gravel mixed within. It's back to a cautious run across his yard and up his three porch steps.

I'm not surprised to see Kyle's old truck sitting outside his cottage because where else would he be at 6:45 in the morning? Neither am I reluctant in the slightest to start banging on his front door, frantic with the thought that every passing minute probably means another inch of water in my kitchen.

It's probably after only about seven bangs on the door, which are hard enough to rattle the small square panes of glass within, that I hear a very grumpy voice yell out, "I'm coming, for fuck's sake."

My hand falls away from the door. I bounce from foot to foot with anxiety as I wait for him to open it. I'm practically hopping with eagerness to get help at last when I hear the lock turning.

Kyle pulls the door open. His eyebrows shoot high when he sees me there. He holds my gaze impassively for a second before he looks slowly down my body, taking in my wet hair, soaked nightgown and dirty feet.

"Pipe," I gasp out, realizing how out of breath I am not only from the adrenaline coursing through me, but also from the mad dash over here. "Burst. Water everywhere."

His eyes snap back up to mine. "What?"

And then, complete lunacy bursts forth from my lips as I hold out the red valve for him to see. "Help me, Obi-Wan Kenobi. You're my only hope. *Star Wars*,

1977."

He doesn't laugh.

He doesn't smirk.

He doesn't roll his eyes.

But he *does* offer me aid. "Let me get my tools."

Kyle turns away from me and walks back into his house, leaving the front door open. I stay on the porch, continuing to rock from side to side on my feet while shooting cautious glances back at my house, afraid I'll see a geyser burst through the roof at any moment.

"Let's go," Kyle says as he reappears holding a tool bag. For the first time, I notice he doesn't have a shirt on. Just a pair of jeans—faded and well fit—along with a pair of unlaced work boots. I'm thinking I might have woken him up. While this would be prime opportunity for me to check out his tattoos, I can't even think about that now.

I don't wait for Kyle. I turn around, practically fly off his porch, and start running back to my house. I can hear Kyle's heavy boots hitting the earth right behind me, clearly impressed with the urgency of the matter. The minute my feet hit the dirt and gravel lane, I slow considerably and curse to myself when the rocks dig into my feet as I start to hobble across.

I'm surprised when an arm wraps around my waist and I'm lifted off my feet, which dangle just above the rocky dirt road as Kyle carries me across.

How gallant.

How very sweet.

He practically dumps me to the grass when we reach the other side.

How barbaric.

But still, he's coming to help, so I can't take him too much to task.

We jog along my house. Just when we near my back door, Kyle asks, "Did you try to shut off the water anywhere else?"

He clearly recognized that the main valve was broken off when I held it up for him to observe just a few minutes ago.

"Yes," I huff out at him as I point my finger toward the open back door. "It's the kitchen sink. The valve underneath doesn't have a knob on it."

"Let's start there," he mutters and heads into my house. I follow behind, but he doesn't need my directions. He just follows the sound of Old Faithful blowing steadily in my kitchen.

I cringe as we enter, particularly because there's a good two inches of water on the floor that's started running into the living room and partially down the hallway. Kyle doesn't hesitate. He just walks straight into the waterfall that's raining down, dropping to his knees in front of the cupboard. He peers in as he sets the bag on the ground. After only a moment's perusal, he's pulling out an adjustable wrench.

I know I should probably be doing something constructive. Like gathering towels and blankets to sop up water, or even calling the school to tell them I will most definitely not make it in on time.

Instead, I succumb to a case of the *stupids* as Kyle turns onto his back and scoots under the sink to manipulate the shut-off valve with his wrench. I get the stupids because his abs contract as he holds his head up and his thigh muscles bulge under his jeans. I get an absolutely unimpeded view of the tattoos on his chest, and now I have a moment to really look.

Well, really it's just one tattoo that starts in the center and spreads over both of his pecs. Frankly, it's a little terrifying. It's a hollow-eyed skull with sharp, pointed teeth that drip blood, and eye sockets with flames pouring out of them. The flames are pulled upward, almost as if by a silent draft of air, and then lick a few inches up his neck. Below the skull, which comes to mid sternum, the words "Fear Me" are written in capital gothic letters. To the left of the skull, running right along his collarbone, is the word "Mayhem's." On the other side, running along the right collarbone, is the word "Mission."

I wonder what that means. While I really know nothing about Kyle at all other than he's surly and rude in addition to being hot, I get the distinct impression that he's not a man to be trifled with. In fact, I'd bet he's not someone you'd want to cross paths with at all.

Kyle starts to scoot out from under the cabinet, and I

blink rapidly to dispel the images of washboard abs and scary, freaky tattoos. I also realize that the water has been shut off and is no longer spraying.

When he emerges completely from under the sink, he sits up and rests an arm on his knee. "You need to go get some clothes on."

"Huh?" I ask dumbly as I stare at him, trying to see if those tattoos perhaps make him a merciless killer that I've unwittingly invited into my house.

Kyle's eyes flick down to my chest, and then back up again.

I slowly lower my eyes and immediately flush hot with embarrassment as I see my very wet white cotton nightgown is absolutely see-through, and there is no room left to the imagination as to whether or not the cold makes my nipples hard.

My arms fly up and I cover my chest. Spinning away from Kyle, I mutter, "I'll be right back."

With my face flaming, I slide my way across the floor and scurry to my room. While I'd very much like to crawl into bed and hide away from that man until he leaves, since he just practically saw me naked, I forcefully push my discomfort aside so I can get dressed quickly. I still have a very waterlogged house to deal with.

CHAPTER 5

KYLE

C HRIST, SHE'S A mess.

A soggy, hard-nippled mess. I'm glad she's gone, so she doesn't see the fact I got hard the minute she showed up at my front door and I saw her like that.

As soon as she disappears down her hallway, I push off the flooded floor and pick my tool bag up. Tossing the wrench inside, I lay it on the counter and look around to survey the damage.

It's not overly bad. It appears she actually reacted pretty quickly, and with a straight head, by trying first to shut the water off under the sink and then attempting the main valve. There's a lot of water on the floor, but if it gets cleaned up quickly, it probably won't cause any floor damage.

I slide my gaze into the living room, seeing a quilt draped over the back of the couch. I slosh through the watery linoleum and nab the quilt before dropping it to the floor right where the open kitchen meets the living room. The water has already started streaming past the linoleum and onto the hardwoods, and those need protected the most. Luckily, the quilt is large enough that it quickly absorbs the bit of water that had reached the wooden flooring, while temporarily stopping the stream from going further.

I turn back into the kitchen, intent on raiding her drawers for at least dish towels, when I hear her gasp. I turn to see her standing just inside the kitchen—adequately dressed, so I can't see her breasts anymore—her arms loaded with towels, but her eyes are pinned on the quilt I'd just tossed down.

"You didn't just throw that quilt onto the water, did you?" she asks in disbelief, her eyes rounding in horror.

"Yeah, why?" I counter, quite grumpily because a thank you would have been nice.

Jane turns and stomps toward me, splashing water as she crosses the kitchen. She threw on a pair of gray sweatpants and a navy sweatshirt, but her feet remain bare. Her nails are painted a pretty light purple color.

She shoves the towels toward me, actually pushing them hard into my chest, as she snaps, "That's a quilt my grandmother made me."

Fuck.

Just… well, fuck.

I cautiously watch as she scoops the sodden quilt from the floor and just stares at it. I have no clue if I ruined it or not, but it looks okay to me. Just… wet.

Without another word, Jane turns to the front door and carries the quilt outside. I busy myself laying down the towels she unloaded on me, sopping up the mess, while throwing glances at her through the open door. She takes the quilt and stretches it across the front porch rail, which is already bright with the eastern sun that just rose above the Atlantic not long ago.

The minute I get all the towels laid out, I turn to the first one and pull it up. I take it to the sink and wring as much of the water out as I can before throwing it back down to sop up more. I repeat this process a few times, and then Jane comes back in and starts to do the same. We work side by side in silence, and I have to wonder why I'm still in this house helping her. I fixed her immediate problem, and she's well equipped to deal with the rest.

"Thank you for helping me," she says quietly, but I don't bother to look at her. I merely pick up another sodden towel and take it to the sink. "And sorry I snapped at you about the quilt."

"Did I ruin it?" I ask gruffly, not liking this feeling of guilt bubbling in my stomach.

"I don't think so," she returns, and I risk a look at her. She gives me an encouraging smile and says, "It should be fine."

"Good," I mutter and wring out the towel. "You own this place?"

"I rent," she says lightly. "I'll have to call the land-lord."

"The pipes probably need replaced," I observe. "This

place looks pretty old."

"That's gonna suck," she mumbles as she pulls up a wet towel and walks toward me. "But after all, tomorrow is another day. *Gone with the Wind.* 1939."

She gives me a cautious smile, filled with hope and optimism that this mess won't be as dire as it seems.

"Did anyone ever tell you that quoting movie lines is annoying?" I ask bluntly, because I suck at polite conversation with a normal person.

Jane chuckles at me as she puts the wet towel over the sink and wrings it out. "All the time."

I feel my lips start to curve upward, so I turn away from her before she can see. I should just throw the towel down and make my excuses to go, yet I find myself pulling another one up from the floor.

"I'm just glad it was confined to the kitchen," Jane says. It's clear she has no problem making conversation. "I'd be devastated if my art supplies had been ruined."

It's painfully clear she's throwing out information to me, probably in an effort to get me interested. I clamp my mouth shut and don't bother to inquire.

Jane's not daunted though. She continues right on, and honestly… her voice is sweet, cheerful, and not at all hard to listen to. "I'm an art teacher, by the way. Teach middle, junior, and high school, and I tutor part time. I also paint and sell some of my stuff, but you know how it goes… starving artist and all that."

No, I really don't know how it goes. Never met an

artist. Never been interested in art unless the quality of my tattoos counts.

There are several minutes of silence that seem awkward to me as we continue to work, but I bet Jane's not fazed. She seems the type to take things in stride with an unfailing well of optimism to bolster herself.

When we get up most of the water, I place the towel I'd just wrung out onto the kitchen counter and decide to make myself scarce. "I'm going to head out—"

"So what's your story?" she asks at the same time.

My body tightens as my walls go up. "No story. Just moved here seeking some solitude."

Jane throws a wet towel in the sink with a splat and shakes her head. Her eyes are knowing when she says, "No. There's a story there for sure."

"Don't know what to tell you," I say dismissively as I grab my tool bag.

"Where you from originally?" she throws out.

The words come out involuntarily, and I cringe over my lack of control. "Maryland."

"Did you always live there?"

"No."

"Where else have you lived?" she pushes at me.

"All over," I hedge.

"You're sort of vague," she points out.

"Exactly."

"And taciturn."

"Also true."

"Yeah," she says with a chuckle as her eyes sparkle with amusement. "There's a story there. But don't worry. I won't prod at you too much. I respect secrets."

I give a grunt of acknowledgment and nod my head. "Well, I got work to do at the cottage…"

"So there's an art and music festival in town this weekend," she says in an abrupt change of subject. I brace because I sense another one of her spontaneous attempts to go out with me. "You should come. I've got a booth there, and you can see some of my artwork."

"Not really my thing," I say, trying to sound gentle.

And why in the hell am I being gentle with her?

I'm not a gentle man.

I ease past Jane toward the front door, giving her a wide berth. I need some space from her.

"There's going to be some great music too," she calls after me. I don't ease up on my strides, because, in the last twenty minutes or so, I've come to learn that Jane is a very tempting woman despite all of my senses screaming at me to stay away from her.

"No thanks," I say loud enough that she can hear.

I'm at the door but still close enough I hear her sigh with something that borders between frustration and resignation. "Okay. Well, thanks again for helping me out."

I stop right in the middle of the doorway, my hand on the knob, preparing to pull it shut behind me. Looking over my shoulder at her, I make myself smile at her. It takes great effort and feels forced on my face. I'm sure she sees that as well.

"Thanks for dinner last night," I tell her. "It was really good."

She beams those pearly whites back at me, and fuck it to hell… I see hope blossoming in her eyes, which are a stunning shade of meadow green. "I'm glad. I'll make it again sometime for you."

Fuck.

I turn away from her and start to pull the door closed, but I'm stopped when she says, "Oh… and Kyle? I'll drop by sometime soon to get my baskets back from you."

Yeah, I have to shut this shit down. I cannot have her getting attached to me. I can't have her trying to worm her way into my life that's built upon dreadful deeds and a litany of lies. I don't know Jane at all, but I know she's way too good to get mixed up with the likes of me. No matter how much I'm attracted to her—no matter how intrigued I am by the very light that radiates from her personality—I cannot go there.

Ever.

"I'll leave them on my porch step when I get home," I tell her pointedly with a dull voice. "You can get them at your convenience."

And that totally worked. The smile slides right off her face and her eyes go flat. She gives me a slight nod and murmurs in complete resignation, "Okay, sure.

That's fine."

I nod back at her, content I've put her off, and yet oddly dissatisfied at the same time. I'm completely miserable here in hiding and want nothing more than to get back to my old life, but I've just managed to cut out the one thing I find to be good right now... and that sort of seems stupid as fuck to me for some reason.

CHAPTER 6

JANE

"**Y**OU TOTALLY UNDERPRICED that one," Miranda says lazily as she nods her head to the painting. It's a thirty-by-thirty watercolor in a simple wooden frame painted a distressed gray. I've got it propped on a tabletop easel. It's by far the biggest painting I'm displaying, and, frankly, it's my best one too. I have six others remaining on the display wall behind us, with the hope I can tempt some art enthusiast to give my work a shot.

The Misty Harbor Music and Art Festival is a great way to start summer and serves as the official opener to the short tourist season we have here. We're not big enough to have just a music festival. Even less people are interested in art than music so they got thrown together, but it's a pretty fun time. Various artisans set up booths where everything from art to cupcakes can be bought while bands alternate on an elevated stage on the town square.

I've participated in this event as an art vendor for the past six years—ever since I graduated from college. It was only then I felt I had the necessary chops to exhibit my work, because even though I'd been painting since I was a kid, it was only having an art degree behind my name that gave me the confidence to show my stuff to the public. Each year, I've made some money. Some years were better than others, but no artist truly does it for the money. I mean, it's great to have the extra cash because teachers make squat, but I know I'll never be rich from my art. And that's fine by me, as I never had those aspirations. For me, life is exactly perfect. I live in a community I love, have family and friends close by and a kick-ass job where I get to pursue my passion every single day. I couldn't want for more.

"Underpriced?" I ask as I turn my head to Miranda. "It's not even been seriously looked at all day. I should be cutting the price, particularly because I didn't glass it in and the frame is pretty cheap."

I had opened for business at ten AM. Miranda met me here at nine to help me set up, so now we're just relaxing in a pair of ratty beach chairs she'd brought along, waiting for my more potential customers to perhaps saunter by. I'd sold four paintings so far, but they were small and only thirty bucks a piece. It was getting close to dinnertime, though, and things would really start to get busy soon.

"It's magnificent and you know it," she returns dryly, her eyes flicking to the painting and back to me again. "And glass is easy to add. People aren't purchasing that frame. They're purchasing the art inside. It is merely for display so it can rest on the easel."

She's right about that, and it's a lot nicer looking than just the painting, which is done on watercolor paper taped to a board. Right now, it looks pretty nice as it sits on the easel at an angle, so I can clearly see it from where I'm sitting. And truth be told, it's probably my best work so far. It's of the Gray Birch Lighthouse. I did it a few weeks ago, inspired perhaps by the fact I'd stared at that old lighthouse a lot knowing that it was now inhabited by a sexy, mysterious man. But he really has nothing to do with the painting itself, for he's not in it. I just happened to catch it one morning as the sun was rising on the Atlantic, so there are swirls of orange, pink, and yellow stacked on top of a grayish-purplish ocean. That's all in the background. The focal point is the lighthouse as the white stucco exterior soaked up the colors of sunrise, even reflecting off the glass panes surrounding the light at the top. I made the frame myself, including the distressed gray paint job, and priced it for one hundred and fifty dollars, which I thought was reasonable. Sadly so far, no one was interested in shelling that out.

"I bet no one is even looking at it seriously *because* it's underpriced," Miranda suggests. "You need to give it a price that proclaims to the entire world that the buyer is getting a priceless piece of art."

I stare at her for a moment, seeing she's not bullshitting me, and I figure she might be on to something and I really didn't have anything to lose.

Scrambling out of my seat, I round the table and pluck up the little index card resting at the base of the easel where I had carefully printed the price in black sharpie. As I crumple the card up, I move back around the table, sit on my chair, and reach under the table where I'd put my purse. Nabbing my black sharpie and some extra index cards out, I carefully print out a new price after tossing the old card into my purse.

"How about... two hundred?" I ask just as I finish the last zero on the price.

"Still too low," Miranda says.

With a huff, I toss that card into my purse and poise the marker above a fresh one. Turning my head, I look to my best friend in the world and ask her, "What should I ask for it?"

"Three hundred and fifty dollars," she says earnestly. Firmly. With total belief that I can get that for my work.

It's one of the many reasons I love her.

Miranda and I went to school together from kindergarten up, but we hadn't been close from the start. I mean, we knew each other because our school was small, but she had her friends and I had mine. We were acquaintances, I guess.

That all changed in the middle of our eighth grade year when Miranda's parents went through a very bitter and nasty divorce. Worse yet, it was public fodder because Miranda's mom had cheated on her father... with another woman. Our town is so small that it wasn't a subject that would get swept under the rug. People whispered and hypothesized about what could drive her mom to become a lesbian, and sadly... all those whispers hit Miranda's ears because kids tend to be more vocal than adults.

Miranda got mercilessly teased. She got viciously bullied.

Then the worst thing happened. I found myself in a group of friends who started bullying her. I was quiet at first, usually awkwardly walking away when they started in on her, because as long as I wasn't saying those nasty things to her face, she'd surely understand I wasn't a part of it.

It wasn't until I walked by Miranda in the hall one day—alone and without my friends—that I smiled at her and asked how she was. She glared at me, tucked her head down, and sped past me. It was then I realized I was guilty by association.

The very next day during our lunch break, I spied two of my friends standing behind Miranda in the lunch line. They were clearly harassing her, as they were leaning in toward her and her shoulders were hunched forward almost protectively.

I didn't even think.

I just walked straight up to my friends and laid into them good. I did it loudly so everyone heard, and I did it with as much derision as I could muster so they would have the unequivocal realization that I was disgusted by this bullying.

That was the day Miranda and I became best friends. I could narrow it down to that exact moment and the way her eyes watched me warily as I told my friends off. It was also the day I lost those other friends and was shunned, but that was fine by me. Miranda was enough. She was a handful, in fact, and to this day... I still have no clue what those other girls were saying. As far as I know, they could have been discussing the weather at the moment I walked up to them, but I don't regret a moment of my actions.

The funny thing is... Miranda and I are like night and day. She's a pessimist, and I'm an optimist. She's wild and crazy, and I'm calm and sedate. My humor is quirky and adorable, hers is biting and sarcastic. She's got hair the color of midnight, while mine's the color of the sun. But the one thing we have in common despite all those differences is love and loyalty, and it's never wavered since eighth grade. Even when I went away to college—which was really only forty miles away so I was home often—Miranda and I never drifted apart. I made new friends at college while she went to cosmetology school, but we never let distance or new interests drive a wedge between us.

So when she looks at me and honestly tells me this painting is worth three hundred and fifty dollars, I totally believe her, because she believes it about me.

"Three fifty it is," I say as I neatly print out the new price and then rest it against the easel.

When I'm seated again, Miranda says, "This is pretty fucking boring, Janey. We've been here for hours and only sold four paintings."

Chuckling, I lean over and nudge her shoulder with mine. "I know, and I love you for keeping me company."

"Let's talk about Kyle then," she says, and my insides immediately go warm at just hearing his name. Of course, because Miranda is my bestie and I tell her everything, she's very much aware that I'm crushing on my elusive neighbor who I haven't seen hide nor hair of since he helped me with my pipe problem earlier in the week.

Obviously, I had to hear every dirty innuendo from Miranda, but my favorite was, "So Janey… did he really plow your pipes?"

Sadly, he did not, and I didn't learn much about him at all. The next morning, my two baskets were sitting on my front porch, so he effectively removed any reason for me to go over and knock on his door. This was disheartening, and I know it's foolish to even be thinking on these things. He's totally out of my league, as completely scary as he is sexy, and would probably hurt me very badly in the long run.

Still, I can't resist her offer to gossip like silly girls. "So, I told you about his tattoos, right?"

Miranda shakes her head. Clearly, I missed some crucial details. "Are they bad ass?" she asks.

"So bad ass," I tell her. "He's got this really scary-looking skull on his chest with the words 'Fear Me' written underneath, so I'm thinking that's probably a valid warning. I should stay away."

"No way," Miranda says knowingly. "As you well know, I've been with lots of men—"

I roll my eyes at her because she really hasn't… I mean, not comparatively to some of the looser women in our town.

"—and men who have tattoos just know how to fuck. And they know how to do things with their mouths. Oh, and they're usually really hung."

Just as Miranda says that, an older couple strolls by my booth. I give her a sharp nudge. We both turn our heads and give them a welcoming smile. They in turn glare at us as they walk right by, not even giving my paintings a glance.

"Okay, we are changing the subject," I hiss at her. "You're going to drive away any potential customers."

"Nah," she says dismissively with a wave of her hand. "Just the prudes. Anyway, men with tattoos are where it's at. Trust me on this."

"I trust you on most everything, but I don't know," I tell her dubiously. "It's seriously not normal for someone to be that reclusive and shut off from society. What if he has mental issues?"

"What if he has a big dick?" she counters.

"Okay, we are now absolutely changing the subject," I growl at her as I push out of my chair and turn to face her with a mock glare. She just looks back up at me with a knowing grin.

Knowing that I'll now be wondering about the size of his—well, you know.

"And what were you two just talking about?" I hear a distinctly male, distinctly annoying voice ask from behind me.

I slowly turn around and stiffen my spine as I lock eyes on my ex-boyfriend, Craig Bartles. My asshole ex-boyfriend, I should clarify.

And true to his sleazy form, he's standing there with Patty Dubois, the floozy he was cheating on me with. He's got his arm draped casually over her shoulder, and she's pressed into his side with her arm clinging tight around his waist. She gives me a nasty smile as she smacks at her gum.

We broke up over a year ago when I found him in my house, in my bed, giving it hard to Patty Dubois. When I gave him a key to use, I honestly didn't think he'd use it like that.

Weirdly though, it wasn't a difficult breakup. At least, not in the long run. While I had fashioned myself really in love with the man, it was about three days after our breakup that Miranda observed, "You know... you're not even sad that Craig is gone."

And I realized… she was right.

I was mad at what he did. And, as a woman, I was very hurt that he betrayed me. But I didn't pine for him. In fact, I almost felt light and free after we parted ways.

I moved on and didn't look back.

Craig couldn't seem to do the same.

Because this is a small town, we run into each other a lot. And every time, he has something nasty to say. Most times, he's with Patty, and he enjoys flaunting her in my face. I can't figure out what I did to deserve his ire, other than breaking up with him, but I always tried to take the high road.

So I lift my chin up and prepare to polite the two of them to death when Miranda sneers at them. "Sorry… you two are going to have to move it along. We don't serve patrons who have crabs."

Craig just smirks, but Patty takes great offense. "I do not have crabs."

"Yes, you do," Miranda says. "Henry over at the pharmacy told me that you routinely have to get a prescription medication for your problem. So, if you would just move it along… I don't want your creepy crawlies anywhere near me."

Patty screeches in outrage, but Craig merely removes his arm from her shoulder and steps up to the table. His gaze goes to the Gray Birch Lighthouse painting, and he studies it for a moment.

"Nice work," he says as he picks it up from the easel.

My body immediately goes tight as he puts his grubby fingers on my work. He turns to look at me, holding the painting up. "I'll give you five dollars for it."

I don't take the bait because he wants me to verbally clash with him. His tongue is sharper than mine, and he knows he'll cut me down. Instead, I step around the table, push past Patty, who's glaring daggers at Miranda, and I jerk the painting out of Craig's hands. The move is so forceful that he's caught off guard, and it easily comes free.

"It's not for sale to you," I tell him firmly.

And that should have been the end of it. But I'm completely stunned when his hand flies out and he jerks it right back out of my hands. He gives me a superior smile, and then purposefully lets it drop to the ground. I watch it tumble end over end until it falls facedown on the dirty pavement.

"Oops," he says with a shrug of his shoulders as he raises his eyebrows innocently. "My bad."

Normally, Miranda would be the one in this situation who would go apeshit. Instead, a wave of fury and frustration sweeps through me and I slam my hands into his chest, pushing him back a step. "You asshole," I hiss at him. "You motherfucking asshole."

"Tell him, girlfriend," I hear Miranda egging me on.

Craig's eyes narrow at me, but not so much that I don't see a glint of malice shining through. I'm unprepared when his hand shoots out and grabs me by my upper arm. He jerks me toward him and snarls, "Better watch out who you hit, Janey, because I'm likely to hit back."

CHAPTER 7

KYLE

I ARGUED WITH myself that there was no sound reason to go to the grocery store this morning. My freezer was stocked with enough frozen meals to last more than a week, and I had beer in the fridge.

I was good.

It absolutely had nothing to do with the fact that the Misty Harbor Music and Art Festival, that just happened to be set up on Main Street, coincidentally intersected with Haven Street where the grocery store was located.

I went in without so much as a glance over at the festival booths that lined the street for two blocks on both sides, all the way to the town square. Didn't care about it or anyone there. I bought some bananas and orange juice because I just happen to like both of those things and walked back out of the store. But rather than turn right to where my truck is parallel parked a few spots down, I turn left and scan the booths.

The one closest to me seems to be hawking wind chimes made of seashells and other various little knickknacks in a coastal theme. The one across from that has pottery.

And the one next to that one... has Jane Cresson.

I just stand and watch for a moment as she sits in a chair behind a table and talks to another woman who I vaguely recognize as maybe being a waitress at The Lobster Cage. Not sure.

The one thing I am sure about is that Jane gets more beautiful every time I see her. Or perhaps it's the more I stay away from her, the more beautiful she gets when I finally do see her again. I watch like a complete creeper as she seems to change her mind about something on her table. She pulls a card away from a painting, writes out a new one, and puts it back in place. I watch her sit back down and appear to have an amusing conversation with her friend, their bodies leaning in toward each other as they speak.

I'm a total creeper.

Then my hackles rise when some asshole and his woman go up to the booth and have words with Jane. I can't hear what's said, but I don't need to either. The guy's posture is cocky and Jane's is stiff. Her face is guarded, and I even notice her fists are clenched as they exchange words.

It's when I see her fists tighten that I decide to walk that way. I cut across Main on the diagonal, walking straight toward her booth. I walk faster when I see the guy pick up her painting. Jane takes it right back from him, clearly not wanting anything to do with him. I walk even faster when he jerks the painting back out of her hand, and I break into a trot when he drops it to the ground. I start charging by the time she slams her tiny hands into his chest. When he reaches out and grabs her arm, I'm on him.

My hand latches onto his scrawny throat and my fingers curl viciously inward around his windpipe, a move that's not only painful, but also breath-robbing. He immediately releases Jane, who stumbles back in surprise. I vaguely hear Jane's friend say, "Fuck yeah… this is going to be good."

In my days as a brother of Mayhem's Mission, I would have proceeded to beat the shit out of someone who would dare touch a woman such as Jane. Sweet, funny, and unbearably alluring. I would have beaten him to unconsciousness and never thought twice about it.

But those days are over, and I can't afford to call attention to myself. So I merely turn the douchebag around and march him backward down the side of Jane's tent, up onto the sidewalk bordering the street, and right into the brick wall of Chib's Hardware Store. Leaning in close to him, I say in a quiet but no bullshitting voice of menace, "Get your tramp and get out of here. If I see you even look sideways at Jane again, I will end you."

I release my hold on his throat, and the guy frantically nods his head in agreement. I watch as he leans to the side and holds his hand out. His woman runs up to him, takes his hand, and they start scurrying down the sidewalk together.

I watch until they round the corner and are out of sight before I turn back toward Jane's booth. I walk along the side and find her squatting down to retrieve her painting. Her hair has fallen forward as she leans over, and I watch as she turns the painting face up.

Jane lets out a gasp of dismay, and I let my eyes slide to the painting she holds. It's beautiful. I mean, stunningly beautiful. While serene seascapes aren't really my thing, I definitely have an affinity toward it since it's a painting of my current home.

I also happen to take in the fact that there's a hole in the bottom of the painting, probably from a rock, and dirt is smeared over the left side.

She stands up. As her gaze lifts to meet mine, I ask her, "You okay?"

"It's ruined," Jane murmurs as her eyes slide back down to the painting. "I should have taken the time to put glass on it."

"But are you okay?" I ask her, because I saw the way that dude grabbed her. It was done violently. Man, what I wouldn't give to have kicked the shit out of him. Hearing the despondency in her voice, though, maybe an ass kicking wasn't good enough.

Jane lifts a shaky hand and tucks her hair behind her ear. "Yeah. I'm fine."

Jane's dark-haired friend comes out of from behind the table. When she sees the painting, she coos, "Oh, honey… I'm so sorry. That motherfucking asshole."

I don't know this woman, but I really do like her. Couldn't agree with her more.

"It's no biggie," Jane says, but the tone of her voice says otherwise. She's devastated her work is ruined. "I think we should get packed up and call it a day, Miranda."

She doesn't spare me another glance, just turns to the table and tosses the painting on top of it next to the easel it had been setting on. My gaze goes to a white index card sitting there with the price of three hundred and fifty dollars.

Renewed rage sweeps through me as I realize that motherfucker not only hurt her feelings and her arm, but he just fucking hurt her livelihood with his malicious actions. I have to fight the urge not to track him down and give him a taste of my brand of justice.

Instead, I set my grocery bag down on the table beside the painting and reach into my back pocket to fish out my wallet. I open it up and flip through the cash, pulling out four one-hundred dollar bills. While this painting is a luxury I would not normally buy, particularly not in my immediate past life, it is certainly one I can easily afford. I was paid very well by the ATF while I was undercover, and every bit of that money was socked away into savings.

"I'll take the painting," I say gruffly as I set the cash down on the table and pick up the framed watercolor.

Jane spins around, her eyes wide with surprise. Her gaze flicks down to the cash, up to the painting in my hand, and finally up to meet mine. "Absolutely not. No way. It's ruined."

"It's got a little dirt on it," I say in a brush-off.

"It's got dirt on it and a hole in it," she grits out.

"It gives it character," I tell her with a shrug as I look down at the painting in my hands. It really is beautiful despite the dirt and hole, and besides… looking at it will remind me of the satisfaction I had by nearly crushing that guy's windpipe.

"Kyle," Jane says in exasperation. "It's ridiculous for you to spend money on a ruined painting."

I'm not going to sit around and argue with her. However, I do get the distinct impression that despite how sweet and bubbly she is most of the time, she'd be a hellion to argue with if she really got mad. On top of that, I had no intentions of crossing paths with Jane again, and this certainly went against said intentions.

I tuck the painting under my arm, grab my groceries, and turn away from her booth to cross back over to the other side of Main Street.

"Wait," she calls out.

I stop and look back over my shoulder at her.

"I need to get your change," she huffs at me in exasperation.

"Keep it," I tell her, to which I immediately get an eye roll back.

I turn my back on her again and cross the street. She calls out after me again, "Kyle… seriously… it isn't right for me to take this."

I don't respond, and I don't look back.

CHAPTER 8

JANE

I DON'T EVEN bother to unload my car. I leave the leftover paintings I hadn't sold and my pride sitting in there. Instead, all I take is my purse and the six pack of beer I'd picked up at Ernie's Grab-N-Go three minutes ago.

My driveway runs east along the side of my house, so after I close my door and lock it, I walk straight past my house and across my front yard. I cross over Cranberry Lane and enter Kyle's front yard.

But I don't go up to his front porch. I walk along the side of his little cottage, past the walkway that veers off to the right that leads to the lighthouse door. Before turning left to walk up his back porch steps, I notice that the flowers he planted the other day look really nice. At the top of the porch, he has a small, round wooden table flanked by two Adirondack chairs that face out toward the Atlantic Ocean.

Perfect.

I set my purse down on the porch, the beer on the table, and smooth my hands over my hair. I'd worn a summer dress to the festival today. I paired it with my standard white cardigan, which is appreciated right this moment as a chilly evening breeze is coming off the ocean.

Reaching an arm out, I sharply knock on his back screen door, then immediately clasp my hands behind my back to wait for him.

I hear movement inside and can see his form moving toward the door through the sheer curtain that covers the glass panes. Just like when I disturbed him a few mornings ago with my water pipe catastrophe, he answers without a shirt but in those really, really great-fitting jeans.

He doesn't say anything, just cocks an eyebrow at me through the screen door.

I tilt my head to the right, indicating the beer on the table. "I'm commandeering your back porch. I'm going to drink a few beers and enjoy the amazing ocean view that's blocked by your house when I'm on my front porch. Join me if you'd like."

I don't wait for an answer, just turn and serenely walk to the furthest Adirondack chair from the door. I ease down into it and perch my feet on the bottom of the porch rail, tucking my skirt in around my ass so it keeps my legs covered.

I have no clue what Kyle will do. If I go on past experience, he'll shut the door, lock it, and ignore me. But I can't worry about that. I truly am here to borrow his ocean view and drink a few beers because I fucking deserve them after what happened with Craig earlier.

Reaching into the plastic grocery bag, I nab a beer and twist the top off. I'm not a big beer drinker, and most definitely not a connoisseur, so I went with Miller Lite because it was on sale and I don't have all the money in the world. I would normally be drinking wine, but in deference to Kyle, who does not seem like a wine drinker, I bought beer.

I'm surprised when I hear the screen door open with a creak. I turn my head to the right to watch Kyle step through. Sadly, he put clothes on his upper body—a white t-shirt with a red-and-gray flannel shirt over it. Same thing he was wearing a little over an hour ago when he rescued me from Craig.

Kyle moves to the Adirondack and sits down with a sigh. He leans over, pulls a beer from the bag, and gives a slight grimace. "You have shit taste in beer."

"Beggars can't be choosers," I reply softly as I watch him open the bottle.

"So, you just thought you'd come over and share a neighborly beer with me, huh?" he asks, and I feel like that's amusement in his voice. And that's very nice, because he normally speaks in short, clipped tones that are completely lacking any humor. In fact, that could be the longest sentence he's ever said to me unprompted.

I reach into the breast pocket of my cardigan and pull the money out. Sliding my hand across the table, I hold it out to him. "Actually, I came by to give you your fifty dollars in change for that ridiculous painting you bought from me."

He ignores the money and looks out over the ocean. "I told you to keep the change, and it's not ridiculous."

"Kyle," I say in exasperation as I wave the money at him. He refuses to look at me. "It's a ruined painting. It should go straight into the garbage. I feel terrible—"

"Look, sunshine," Kyle growls as he turns and pins me with a fierce glare. "I'm not in the habit of throwing my money away. I bought the fucking painting because I liked it and I wanted it. It's hanging over my goddamn mantel right now if you don't believe me."

My jaw drops as I just stare at him in disbelief. First, because he sounds pissed and that scares me just a bit. But secondly, and more importantly, because he actually hung that stupid thing up. I mean, I just thought he was being chivalrous, but maybe he's being more than that.

"And put your fucking money away," he snaps at me as his gaze goes briefly to the fifty dollars in my hand before coming back to me. "And let me drink my damn beer in peace."

"God, you're grumpy," I mutter as I tuck the fifty dollars back in my pocket.

I don't miss the fact his lips curve upward over my sentiment.

We sit in silence for a few moments as we sip at our beers and watch the ocean. But I didn't come here to just sit quietly. And I really didn't even come here to make sure he got his change. I came here to try to learn more about him, and I did so on the hope—slim as it may be—that since he was so enraged over what Craig had done to me, that perhaps he's not as cold as he seems. Clearly, he has some capacity to care, and, unfortunately, that made me more curious about him than ever.

It also made him superiorly more attractive as well.

"So, bet you're wondering what the deal was with that guy, huh?" I ask out of the blue to make conversation.

"Not really," Kyle mutters before taking another swig of his beer.

I ignore that comment. "Well, it turns out we have a very sordid past together. We were together and really in love. Engaged to be married. But he got me involved in drugs. Soon after that, it was petty theft. My life was just spiraling—"

Kyle's head snaps toward me, his eyes narrowed. "You're fucking kidding me, right?"

"Yes," I say teasingly. "I'm just kidding, but it proves to me that you're at least interested enough to listen to my ramblings."

"Nutty as a fruitcake," he mutters, but his lips are definitely tipped upward as he turns back to the ocean.

And because he's at least listening, I do tell him the truth. "Actually, we broke up a long time ago, but he just can't stop being an asshole around me. I mean, I caught him cheating with that tramp, yet he has the gall to be pissed at me for breaking up with him. How's that not the definition of insanity?"

Kyle doesn't respond for a moment, but then he says in a low tone, "I imagine his insanity is in the fact he cheated on someone like you with that tramp."

And wow… just wow. That was really nice. And sweet. His voice was all kinds of sexy with that deep rumble, and it really sounded like he meant it.

I want to hear more, so I prod him. "You can't say that. I mean… you don't really know me or anything."

"Know enough," is all he says, which does nothing to continue to stroke my bruised ego.

"Well, I know absolutely nothing about you," I say, taking the opening that he just gave me. "Except that you were born in Maryland."

To my immense surprise, he asks, "What do you want to know?"

"Are you married?"

"Nope."

"Ever been married?"

"Nope."

"Do you speak in more than one-word sentences?"

"Sometimes."

I giggle and then ask, "Okay, serious question… how old are you?"

"Thirty-four," he says, and then actually extends his sentence. "How old are you?"

"Twenty-six," I tell him, pleased he's interested in something about me personally. "I'll be twenty-seven in November."

"A babe," he says gruffly.

"Not really," I disagree with him primly. "I know things."

For the first time, Kyle gives me a genuine smile as he turns to me and asks, "Oh, yeah? Like what?"

"Hmm," I ponder thoughtfully, tapping my index finger against my chin. "Well, you're a very interesting guy. You're dark and mysterious. Reclusive yet very intriguing. I'd say you've got a haunted past, and I'm kind of drawn to that."

Kyle's eyes burn into mine. "Why would you ever be drawn to that?"

I shrug. "Because I want good things for good people, I guess."

"You want to try to fix me?" he asks blandly.

"Maybe," I say with a grin. "Can I borrow your tools?"

The minute those words are out of my mouth, my face flames red at the innuendo I just innocently uttered. "Oh, shit… I didn't mean anything dirty by that. I mean… well, you have tools. You used them to shut off the water. I was talking about those types of tools, not like… *your* tool. And oh, God… I'm going to die right now from embarrassment."

I must be positively adorable in my embarrassment

because Kyle just shakes his head with a smirk on his face, and we lapse back into silence for a while.

I finish my beer and open another, because I've made real progress here tonight. He does the same.

The sun, which is behind us in the west, fully sets. Our view of the ocean gradually declines until we see only a faint glimmer along the water every time the light in the tower spins to alert boats of the jetty.

It's nice. Maybe a bit awkward since I like conversation, but I can't think of another place I'd want to be right now.

"Jane?" Kyle says quietly, and I let my head roll to the right to look at him. "Just so you know, I can't be fixed. So don't even go there, okay?"

"Okay," I murmur to reassure him of my good intentions, but now I'm committed more than ever to figuring out this mysterious man.

CHAPTER 9

KYLE

M Y SHOULDERS BURN and ache, but still I go harder, running the sanding paper briskly over the last picket on the fence that borders the walkway from my cottage to the lighthouse. The fence needs a new coat of paint. I could have taken the easy way out and just painted over the existing paint. It was in fairly good shape, but it definitely needed freshened up. But because I'm bored and feeling like a slug, I decided to sand the entire thing down by hand first. I could have also taken the easy way out and rented an electric sander from Chib at the hardware store, but it felt like a day where I should do something to expend all this excess energy I have.

I'm feeling restless from being cooped up for the few winter months I experienced here.

Anxious over the fact I've got a few more months left of hiding out. The days seem to go by slower than ever.

And I'm fucking wound up over my obnoxiously witty and drop-dead gorgeous neighbor who doesn't seem to be scared off from me and my surly ways. Moreover, she's managed to dig her way under my skin, not in a totally bad way, but in a way that makes me want to hand sand an entire picket fence.

Even though I doubt the temperature is past the mid-seventies right now, in between my vigorous sanding and the hot noon sun, I'm fucking roasting. I'd ditched my shirt less than an hour into the work, and then about thirty minutes ago I went inside and ditched my jeans, opting for a pair of old swim trunks I'd brought along with me when I heard from Joe my new destination was the coast.

Even though my muscles are screaming and sweat is pouring off me, I continue to scrub as hard as I can against the paint, operating under the theory that tonight I'll be too exhausted to think about the shit storm that is my life.

And about Jane.

Mostly Jane as I'm years into this shit storm and used to it by now. It is what it is.

But I'm not used to Jane. I've never met a woman like her. I've been surrounded by tramps and club whores for the last five years, so I'm not even sure I'd know what to do with someone like Jane in my bed.

But fuck… the things I'd like to do to her in said bed.

Goddamn it, you stupid motherfucker. Do not go there.

Which is exactly why she will never—and I mean ever—be there. I would tarnish her horribly, probably scare the crap out of her and traumatize her for life. I've become so roughened over the years—so criminalized—I feel like I barely resemble a normal human being. So what little bit of morality I've seemed to keep deep down inside is demanding that I forget Jane Cresson. Fucking bar tramps in back alleys is all I'm good for and I'll just have to be satisfied with that. Although, I can't explain to myself why I haven't been back to The Lobster Cage to take advantage of what Barb has to offer since I met Jane.

And as if just thinking about her causes her to materialize—

"I've been watching you work your ass off all morning from my porch, so I thought I'd come over to help," Jane says behind me.

My head drops forward, and I clench my teeth in frustration.

Temptation keeps putting itself in my path.

I don't stop sanding the last picket, even though I can't see a speck of white paint left. "Funny you show up when I just finished the last one," I mutter.

She gives a tinkling laugh that just two days ago would have annoyed the hell out of me, but instead, it sounds like music. "Well, of course I wasn't going to help you with the sanding, silly, but you still have to paint it and well… I'm a painter."

"You're an artist," I point out as I push up from my knees and turn to face her.

"Who paints," she says brightly.

And yep… she's glorious. White shorts that aren't

too short but still show a good bit of leg, a faded navy-blue t-shirt that's seen better days, and flip-flops. Her hair is pulled up into a high ponytail and her lips are shiny.

Why the fuck are they shiny?

"I made you lunch," she says as she holds out a brown paper bag that's neatly folded down at the top.

I blink at her a moment before my eyes drop to the bag. Just two days ago, that would also have annoyed the hell out of me, but for some reason, it fucking delights me.

Not going to let her know that, though, so I merely take it from her with a rough, "Thanks."

I walk over to my pickup truck that I'd backed up to the edge of the fence nearest to Cranberry Lane, and she follows me there. I open the bag up, reaching in to find a neatly wrapped sandwich that looks to be thick and piled high with turkey, lettuce, and tomato. Tossing the bag onto my tailgate, I unwrap the sandwich as I ask her, "Any chance our work can be done in companionable silence if I let you help me?"

"As if," she says with an exaggerated whine in her voice. I know she's quoting a movie, but I have no clue which one. She adds on, "*Clueless*. 1995."

"Never saw it," I say before I take a bite of my sandwich, and damn... that's good. Just a simple sandwich made for me, because she's kind and thoughtful, and I'm pretty sure it might be the best thing I've ever tasted.

I wonder what she tastes like?

I give my head a hard shake and swallow. She looks at me curiously, but I'm pretty sure she has no clue what I was just thinking.

"I could be very cruel, you know," she says with a sly grin as she hops up to sit on the edge of the tailgate, "and tell you that *Clueless* is a must-see movie for you."

"What's it about?" I ask before taking another bite, and well… sort of enjoying this conversation.

"Oh, trust me," she says with a laugh and a shake of her head that makes her ponytail swing jauntily back and forth. "You'd hate it."

I do nothing but grunt my acknowledgment and take another bite. I'm halfway through it and dying for another already.

I'm also strangely not put out by Jane's presence. Ever since Mayhem's Mission was taken down and I reentered the mainstream world, it's been hard for me to connect with normal people. Conversation was hard. Listening was hard. Just being in the presence of other people and looking at how very different they were from me, not so much on the outside, but mostly on the inside, and it's all sometimes too much to handle.

But with Jane… it's easy.

Well, easier.

"Since you don't seem to like to get into deep conversation, I thought I'd just entertain you while we paint with some random movie quotes. Really my favorite ones."

"Why would you do that?" I ask her.

"Because I don't think you can truly appreciate my talent based on the little interaction we've had. And since conversation with you isn't the easiest, I'll just toss some random ones out to you."

"For entertainment purposes only?" I ask as my lips do this very weird motion where they curve upward rather than downward.

"Totally for entertainment purposes only," she assures me.

"Okay," I challenge her as I point my half-eaten sandwich her way. "Let me see what you got."

Jane pinches her chin between her finger and thumb, and then looks upward in contemplation for a moment. Her eyes brighten, and she brings her gaze to mine. "Okay... this is seriously a good one."

I wait and watch.

She jumps down from the tailgate and clears her throat. Turning, she paces a few steps away before spinning back to me and saying, "My name is Maximus Decimus Meridius, commander of the Armies of the North, General of the Felix Legions..."

She turns, stalks back toward me, and in an imperious voice, continues, "...and loyal servant to the true emperor, Marcus Aurelius. Father to a murdered son, husband to a murdered wife. And I will have my vengeance, in this life or the next."

I smile in appreciation for her wit... her complete lack of fear in putting herself out there... for her absolutely nutty personality that got an honest-to-God smile out of me, and, trust me... those don't come easy.

"Very good," I praise her, and shit... I want to hear more. "*Gladiator.* Not sure what year."

"2000," she provides with a grin.

I nod my head to the back of my pickup truck. "How about you start to unload the paint materials while I finish this sandwich, and you can throw a few more movie lines at me if you want?"

"Sure," she says merrily as she reaches into the truck to grab the first gallon of paint. "And there's another sandwich in there too."

This day was getting better and better.

♦

THE SUN IS hanging low on the western horizon, and it's starting to cool off. We're on our last section of fence. I'm on one side and Jane's on the other. The sounds are relaxing. Brushes slapping against wood, seagulls crying, and the waves crashing against the jetty.

And Jane's voice.

"Okay, here's another one," she says without preamble. "Just keep swimming, just keep swimming."

She does this in a singsong voice and sort of bounces up and down a little from her kneeling position on the other side of the fence. I try not to notice the way her breasts move under that t-shirt of hers.

"No idea," I say.

"Seriously, your movie knowledge completely sucks," she says with a huff. "We'll have to rectify that."

"What movie was that?" I ask, because I've been silently committing these movies I don't recognize to memory to give them a try. Not even sure the last time I've seen a movie, as it wasn't a generally popular activity to do in a biker gang.

"*Finding Nemo*," she answers. "2003."

Hmmm. That was definitely before I went deep undercover, but it still doesn't ring a bell.

"What's it about?" I ask, because while Jane has indeed been quoting lines, it's led into other conversation, and that's been... well, nice.

Definitely comfortable since the conversation isn't exactly personal.

"Oh, it's awesome. It's about this fish, Nemo, who gets caught by a diver and put in a fish tank, and then his dad sets off to find him along with this really nutty fish named Dory that was voiced by Ellen DeGeneres. It's absolutely hilarious—"

"Wait," I interrupt her, my brush coming to rest against the picket. "Is this a cartoon?"

"Well, yeah. I mean, it's animated."

"I don't do cartoon movies," I tell her seriously.

She rolls her eyes at me. "Yeah, I kind of got that from you when the only movie line you've recognized in the last hour was 'Yippee-ki-yay, motherfucker."

I snort. "*Die Hard.*"

"1988," she adds as a reminder to me.

And I remember that movie well because it's one of my last great memories of my sister Andrea. She'd just graduated from the FBI Academy, and I went to visit her. Rather than go out to celebrate, we stayed in at her apartment and rented *Die Hard.* We did this because we hadn't seen each other in forever and with both of our parents gone, we'd only had each other and valued the little bit of time we had together. I'd already moved out to Wyoming to start the hard task of infiltrating Mayhem's Mission. In order to do that, I had to separate myself from Andrea a bit. She had no clue I worked ATF in special operations undertaking an undercover mission with the highest of stakes and the most extreme danger.

The trip to see Andrea for her FBI graduation was something I had to do, though, because she should have had a family member there to support her. I also needed to see her, because the chances were great that once I was in deep, I might not be coming out again.

We both loved that fucking movie, and that line has been tossed back and forth between my sister and me whenever we'd talk to each other on the phone.

It's a nice memory.

With just a few more dips of the brushes into the paint, some quick strokes on the last pickets, and we are done with the painting. I push up from where I was squatting and look down the length of the fence. It's shiny and white and looks pretty fantastic.

I turn back to look at Jane across the fence as she's also stood up. She arches her back a little in a stretch, and I know she'll probably be really sore tomorrow. "We did good work," she says with a firm nod of her head.

"That we did," I say as I take her in. She's got paint on her right cheek and above her left eyebrow, with a little bit in the end of her ponytail. Not even sure how that happened. "I really appreciate your help."

She beams back at me. "I was hoping you'd be appreciative. You owe me dinner."

"I can't cook," I tell her flatly, my walls immediately going up, blocking her out and pushing her away.

It's for her own good.

"Even better," she returns with an even bigger smile. "You can take me out."

"Jane," I say in a low, warning voice, intent on telling her that it is not going to happen, because as much as I've enjoyed this day with her and the ease with which it played out, dinner out together is an entirely different matter. It's too fucking personal. It's a date for Christ sake. "I don't think that's a good idea."

She just rolls her eyes at me and says, "Wait for it... frankly, my dear, I don't give a damn. *Gone with the Wind.* 1939."

"You did not just—"

"Pull out the most awesome movie quote ever?" she

suggests as her eyes twinkle with triumph. "Sure as hell did. Pick me up in an hour."

With that, she turns and starts flouncing back toward her house.

At least, I think it's flouncing. Isn't that the way Scarlett O'Hara moved in *Gone with the Wind?*

I'll call it flouncing, because her ponytail swings back and forth as she crosses back over Cranberry Lane and marches into her house. Only after her door closes do I start to clean up the paint.

An hour is plenty of time to get ready. In fact, I'll need about five minutes in the shower and I'll be ready to go.

I think about Jane and that smile, those perfect breasts that stared at me through the picket fence all afternoon, and… maybe fifteen minutes in the shower.

CHAPTER 10

KYLE

"**Y**OU CLEAN UP nice," Jane says as we meander down the sidewalk, heading southwest from her house and through a section of Misty Harbor I'd not seen yet. I drove my pickup truck to her house, but she advised me we'd be walking to dinner instead.

I didn't question her, because I'm terrified to even open conversation up with her. My repeated attempts to keep her at bay aren't working, so I'm thinking if I keep my lips sealed for most of the night, she'll finally get the hint I'm not interested.

Liar.

You're interested.

"Didn't realize you even owned something other than jeans," she says conversationally. And maybe just with a little challenge to get me to talk.

I remain silent, although I glance down at my outfit as we follow the sidewalk that takes us through a pretty residential area. I didn't bother to shave after my shower, but I did throw on a pair of khaki pants that had been bought for me after my "death." When I'd been put in that apartment in Chicago, I didn't have a stitch of clothing other than the outfit I'd been wearing during my supposed execution. That had consisted of a black Harley long-sleeved t-shirt, a pair of jeans, biker boots, and my leather cut. All of my pre-undercover clothes were in storage and wouldn't be fetched for me until my new destination was determined, so I'd had to make due with a variety of clothes that Joe Kizner bought me.

That included a pair of khaki pants and a light blue button-up shirt that I paired with a pair of dark loafers. I looked like a fucking moron, or at least I think I did. It had been so damn long since I'd worn anything other than biker clothes that I wasn't quite sure.

"And this is the time that would be appropriate for you to tell me that I look nice too and this outfit doesn't make my ass look big," Jane says with no small amount of snark.

"You look nice," I say automatically and with no change in my inflection, even though I'd like to tell her she looks beyond amazing. When she'd opened her door five minutes ago, the breath was almost knocked out of my lungs. She was wearing a white, gauzy-looking skirt with lace on the edges, and it floated around her legs to just below her knees. Her shirt was a pretty shade of light green and hung off one shoulder. With her hair loose and wavy, she looked like a beautiful gypsy. The entire look was sweet, but it was also most definitely sexy.

She truly deserves more than just "you look nice,"

and yet I can't make myself say it. Anything to draw her closer to me means I'll most likely be equally drawn back to her, and that's just not optimal with the fucked-up mess that is my life right now.

"Well… I'm just one stomach flu away from my goal weight," she mutters under her breath, but not so low that I can't hear her.

"What?" I ask as I tilt my head to look at her, not really sure what that even means.

"The Devil Wears Prada," she says as she glances at me briefly.

Devil? Prada? What the fuck?

"I have no clue what you're talking about," I say irritably, feeling completely out of sorts because she wants a true compliment from me and she deserves one, but I can't seem to give it.

"It's a movie," she murmurs as we continue to walk down the sidewalk. "2006."

And for some reason, this immediately lessens the tension for me. She's quoting movies and this is something she's done so incessantly since I've met her, that it actually feels comfortable. Oddly, it almost centers me and the feeling is so appreciated, I stop and reach out to touch her arm. She turns to look at me curiously.

"You look beautiful," I tell her truthfully, needing to give her something if only for the fact that she has the ability to make me feel okay in this strange world.

And your ass is slammin', by the way.

Jane beams a smile at me, tucking her hair back behind one ear. "Thank you."

"You're welcome," I say as I pull my hand back and turn to start walking again. Before I can even help myself or talk myself out of it, I open the door for conversation because I'm apparently a glutton for punishment. "This is a pretty neighborhood."

"It is," she says in agreement. I don't have to look at her to hear the fond smile in her voice.

To our left is the start of Misty Harbor, the actual body of water for which the town is named and the reason for a lighthouse. It starts on the end of the long jetty that separates it from the Atlantic and cuts into the mainland. To our right are houses that sit on tiny, well-manicured lots, their front porches facing the harbor waters with a view of the Atlantic just beyond the jetty. The houses are small, but I expect the prices are at a premium because of the views.

In between the water and the sidewalk is Front Street, and I'm assuming it's named so since it fronts the water. But I could be wrong.

We approach a white house with a matching picket fence around it. The porch has black rocking chairs that match the shutters and potted plants of various sizes. A tiny dark blur shoots down the porch steps and charges at us down a walkway that's lined on both sides by flowers. I realize it's a small dog as it starts yapping at us, running along the fence line as we continue to walk.

Jane… being Jane… turns to the dog and curls her hands into claws while she cackles, "I'll get you, my pretty, and your little dog too."

The dog is unfazed and continues to yap at her.

Jane gives a soft laugh, and then reaches over the three-foot fence as the little dog comes up on his hind legs. He stops barking and his tail wags back and forth as she scratches his head. "Hi, Bilbo. You protecting the neighborhood?"

The little dog's tail wags even faster. When Jane straightens and removes her hand from his head, he turns around and runs back up onto the front porch where he plops down on his stomach and watches us.

Jane turns toward me, and we start walking again. "That was the *Wizard of Oz*."

"Yes," I say dryly. "That I knew."

"1939," she adds on.

"That I didn't know."

Jane chuckles. As we start walking past the next yard, she throws her arm up and waves. I turn my head to see a couple sitting on rocking chairs on their front porch. It's a pretty two-story house with gabled peaks and gray shaker shingles.

The couple waves back, smiling. They look to be in their mid-fifties or so.

"Hey, Jane," the man calls out. "Where you going?"

"Over to dinner at The Black Swan," she calls back as we continue to walk along the front of their property, our pace slowing as she converses.

"Who's your fella?" the woman asks as she leans forward in her chair a bit.

Jane jerks her thumb at me. "Kyle. He's my neighbor. No clue what his last name is."

"Harding," I provide to her in a low voice.

"Harding," she calls back.

"How do you do, Mr. Harding?" the lady says with a wave at me.

I wave back and give her a nod of my head.

"You two have a nice dinner," the man says with a smile. By this time, we've reached the edge of their yard and are walking past the next house.

"See you later," Jane calls back, touching her fingers to her lips and blowing the couple a kiss.

When we make it past the next house, Front Street—and the sidewalk—starts to curve slightly to the right, and the rest of the harbor starts to open up in front of us. I'd not been to this part of the town, not having ventured past Main Street, which is where the grocery store sits on one end and The Lobster Cage on the other.

"You know everyone in town," I observe, thinking of her familiarity with the little dog and the easy exchange of friendly banter with the couple.

"Pretty much," she says merrily, and I can hear the love for her community in her voice. "That couple back there more than anyone as that was my mom and my dad."

I stop dead in my tracks and look back to their house, seeing that they're both still watching Jane and me. When I turn back to face Jane, I see her eyes sparkling with amusement.

"They're your parents?" I ask incredulously.

"Yup," she says with a grin.

I cock an eyebrow at her. "And they didn't want to meet or learn more about your neighbor whose last name you don't even know?"

"Oh, they want to meet you," she says with a nod of her head and mischief in her voice. "I'll be expected to call them later and tell them all about it. You see, I don't date a lot, and they'll be chomping at the bit to find out all about you. But they're also not intrusive, so they'll be content to wait for me to tell them the details."

"Of course you'll tell them that this isn't a date," I say gruffly as we continue to walk.

"Sure I will," she says as she loops her hand through my arm and grips me right in the crook of my elbow. She pats my bicep reassuringly with her other hand and says, "If it makes you feel better, I'll totally tell them this isn't a date."

"Because this is a thank-you gesture only," I say sternly, but even I can hear amusement seeping through in my voice, completely unwanted.

She just pats my bicep again. "Whatever you say."

"Seriously," I insist. "Not a date."

"Not a date," she agrees, but her lips are tipped up in

a way that clearly says she thinks she's on a date.

I resolve to myself that when I walk her back home tonight that I'm not kissing her. I'm going to show her that this is just a friendly dinner between neighbors and nothing more.

We walk along in silence. Jane's arm remains tucked into mine, but I don't make a move to dislodge it. It's the closest I've been to her physically, and I'm painfully aware it's been a long fucking time since a woman's touched me in such a sweet way. Despite every fiber of my being screaming at me not to get involved with her, I like her touch too much to push her away right now.

And the realization is almost shattering as it becomes clear I'm probably in a losing battle with myself.

CHAPTER 11

JANE

MY FINGERS DIG slightly into Kyle's arm as we step up to the door of The Black Swan, but then I release him. He hadn't uttered a word for the rest of our walk here, but he also didn't try to distance himself from me either.

To my surprise, Kyle reaches an arm behind me, his other hand coming to rest lightly on my shoulder as he gently pushes me to the side a bit so he can open the door for me. I step through and his hand drops away as he walks in behind me.

"Hey, Jane," the hostess, Kiley Grimmons, greets me from behind a podium. "Two for dinner?"

"Yes, please," I tell her with a smile. Kiley was three years behind me in high school, so I don't know her all that well, but her father owns the hardware store and everyone knows Chib. He used to be a deep-sea fisherman, but lost his hand in a tragic accident when it got caught in the gears of the winch system used to haul in the catch. He retired from that but wasn't deterred from making a life for himself. Instead, he opened up a hardware store on Main Street that's done surprisingly well for such a small community.

"Right this way," Kiley says as her eyes linger on Kyle curiously before she grabs the menus.

We follow her through the restaurant, and she puts us at a lovely table by a long wall of nothing but glass that overlooks the harbor.

"Miranda will be right with you," Kiley tells me with a smile, and I give her an appreciative nod. I knew Miranda was working tonight, which is her preference since she gets way better tips than at The Lobster Cage. Miranda would actually prefer this to be her "second" job, but it's hard to get on here as a part-time employee because the money is fabulous during the tourist season and return summer employees get preferential offers. Still, she keeps her foot in the door by covering people's shifts if they have an emergency come up, and Gus, who owns The Lobster Cage, never seems to get bent out of shape when she can't work there because she picked up an impromptu shift here.

I chose this restaurant tonight not only because the food was fabulous and I worked my ass off today to help Kyle so I deserved a great meal, but also because Miranda was working and I wanted her outside observing eyes to give me feedback later. Kyle's so damn hard to read, and Miranda is a great judge of character. She'll be eyeballing the hell out of him tonight to try to denote body language and such.

I snicker to myself over my devious ways, and that causes Kyle to prompt me, "What's so funny?"

"Oh, nothing," I say, smirking as I pick up my menu and open it. "The she-crab soup here is to die for so you should try that, and, of course, if you like lobster, that's a great choice too."

"Do you like lobster?" he asks, and I raise my eyes to him. I think that might be the first genuinely curious question he's asked about me personally.

"I love it," I tell him. "You?"

"Never had it," he says.

"What the what?" I ask dramatically as I close my menu and set it down. "You've never had lobster before?"

"Nope," is all he says.

"Then you have to try it," I tell him firmly.

"Okay." He puts his menu down and doesn't even open it.

"But it's expensive," I feel the need to provide, as he didn't even bother to look at the market prices for the day that would be printed on a piece of paper in the middle.

"Then you should have it too," he says gruffly.

"Well, okay then," I say, giving him a tentative smile, silently marveling to myself that for a man who doesn't want this to be a date, he sure is pulling out all the stops to impress me.

"If it isn't my favorite person in the entire world," I hear Miranda say from my left as she walks up to the table and pours water into my glass. I glance up at her, but she's staring across the table at Kyle, who sits to my right. Then she turns to look down at me and gives me a wink. "Oh, and hey, Jane. Good to see you too."

I grin at her, but then give her a mock pout. "I thought I was your favorite person in the world."

"No," Miranda drawls out as she puts her free hand on her hip and waves the mostly empty water pitcher at Kyle. "He's now my favorite person after that epic smackdown he laid on Craig the other day."

I purse my lips and give her an accommodating nod. "That's true. It was epic, and I can see how your loyalties would change."

Miranda laughs and blows me a kiss, then sticks her hand across the table to Kyle. "We weren't formally introduced the other day, but I'm Miranda. Best friend to Jane here, and well, she really is my favorite person in the world. But you're a close second."

Kyle smiles at Miranda, and I have to admit it's a beautiful smile. He shakes her hand and says, "I'd have liked to have given him more the other day, but didn't want to cause a scene."

Miranda laughs as she releases his hand, and then leans over to pour his water. "Okay, you're my favorite again. Jane will just have to be satisfied with second best."

And to my surprise, Kyle chuckles and that's even more beautiful. His face actually changes and his eyes lighten up. He actually looks approachable and I have to resist the urge to lean over and kiss him.

Instead, I look back up at Miranda. "We're going to both have the she-crab soup and full lobsters."

"What to drink?" Miranda says with efficiency.

"I'm fine with water," I say.

"Whatever you have on draft," Kyle says.

"We have a great summer seasonal from a local brewery over in Bar Harbor," Miranda tells him. "I'll go put your orders in and be right back with the soups and your beer."

I watch for a moment as Miranda walks to the next table to check on them before I turn back to Kyle. "And that crazy girl is Miranda Gale, truly my best friend in the world."

"She's funny," Kyle observes. "And she clearly adores you."

"Not as much as she adores you apparently," I say dryly. "But the feeling is mutual."

"Two peas in a pod?" he asks.

"Actually, no," I tell him as I cross my forearms on the table and lean toward him a bit. "We're almost like night and day. She's crazy, wild, and uninhibited. She doesn't have a filter on her mouth and can talk to any stranger. Miranda likes to fly by the seat of her pants and is completely spontaneous."

"Then that means you're sedate, cautious with your words, introverted, and goal oriented," Kyle throws at me.

"Something like that," I say as I pick up my glass and take a sip of water.

"You're not introverted though," Kyle says as he cocks an eyebrow at me. "You pushed your way all up in my business."

I laugh as I put my glass back down. Staring at it, I run a thumb over the condensation on the outside. "Well, I'm more introverted in crowds. Miranda would be the type who would dance on the tabletops at a party; I'd be in the corner by myself."

"Life-of-the-party type of girl, huh?"

"Let's just say I've had to pull her off a table or two at a party to prevent her top from coming off," I tell him with a laugh. "She's certifiably crazy, but I love her like a sister."

Kyle nods and then asks, "You have any siblings?"

I shake my head. "Nope. Just Miranda, who might as well be. She had a rough time growing up and spent most of her time at my house, so my parents sort of treat her like she's their daughter."

And because I want to learn more about Kyle, I add on, "What about you… do you have any brothers or sisters?"

I'm not sure if it's my imagination or not, but something painful flickers in Kyle's eyes before he lowers his gaze to the table as he plucks at the edge of the table-cloth. He shakes his head, "A sister, but we're not close.

We don't talk."

"What about your parents?" I ask, choosing to leave the sister thing alone. "Are they still back in Maryland?"

"They're dead." His eyes lift back up to mine, and they're clear. No hint of pain or anything. In fact, they are a little flat, and I don't like that.

"I'm sorry," I say softly as I reach my hand out to touch his.

"Don't be," he responds gruffly, quickly moving his hand away so we don't make contact. "It was a long time ago."

His message to me is clear. He doesn't want to talk about his family. I have to respect that, at least for now. But I'm not willing to give up on this opportunity where I have him pinned to that chair for the duration of this dinner.

"Why did you move here to Misty Harbor?" I ask him curiously. "I can't imagine it's because you've always wanted to be a lighthouse keeper."

I'm surprised when Kyle actually gives me a slight smile, causing him to appear relaxed again. "Just wanted a change of scenery and no… I didn't really want to be a lighthouse keeper, but it sounded interesting and I thought I'd give it a try."

"You said you've lived all over," I mention. "Where were you before here?"

"Chicago. Before that Wyoming," he says without giving any more detail.

"Never been to either," I tell him with a sigh. "In fact, never been much of anywhere. Went to New York City once for a class trip, but past that, I'm sad to say I've not strayed from Maine."

"Not even college?" he asks.

"Went to a school about forty miles away," I tell him with a laugh. "I'm not very adventurous, I guess you could say."

"I don't know about that," he says, his voice a low rumble. "You certainly kept poking at this bear. That's pretty damn daring.

"You're a bear?" I ask teasingly, my head tilted to the side.

He nods, his eyes pinning me in place. "I have claws and teeth, Jane."

"Is that a warning?' I ask, now more curious than ever, even as a small ripple of fear runs up my spine over his words.

"Would you heed it if it was?" he counters.

"Nope." I stare at him, refusing to let my gaze drop. He stares right back at me, his eyes flicking back and forth between mine, perhaps trying to figure out if I'm being brave or foolish.

Before I can answer, Miranda comes to the table, setting Kyle's beer down before him, and our gazes disconnect. Kyle looks up to her and says, "Thanks."

"Sure thing, hot stuff," she says back to him with a grin, and then proceeds to lay our bowls of soup down before us.

When she leaves, Kyle picks up his spoon and gives the creamy soup a try. I watch him carefully, wondering how I can get the conversation back to where it was, because I want to test him. I want to see if he really wants to push me away or perhaps if he wants me to disregard the warning bells to keep after him.

But the moment is clearly broken when he asks me the most dreadful question imaginable after he swallows his bite of soup. "So, what's your favorite movie?"

Really?

We're going to talk about movies?

We're going to have a boring, lame, and non-invasive discussion? He wants stupid details about me that don't mean anything?

I suppress an eye roll as I pick up my spoon before telling him, "*Forrest Gump*. What's yours?"

And I wait to see if discussing movies will provide an opening so I can try to learn more about him.

To find out if he's really more grizzly than teddy bear, but I suspect I already know the answer to that.

CHAPTER 12

KYLE

I DON'T WANT it to be, but this is definitely a date.

I came to this brutal realization about ten minutes after we finished our lobsters. Somehow, while I was busy cracking the shiny red shell of a huge claw, it hit me that Jane had managed to completely captivate me with some good fucking conversation.

Despite my best efforts to keep us talking about impersonal shit, Jane managed to make me more and more curious about her. Learning her favorite movie led into a conversation about the fact that there wasn't a decent movie theater in this area. Like a dumbass, rather than ask about where she would go to see her movies and keep the conversation impersonal, I made the mistake about asking what she liked to do in her free time. That started an avalanche of information flowing toward me at a breakneck speed.

And I was fucking hooked.

I already knew that Jane was quirky, funny, and I'll even admit, practically irresistible. It goes without saying that she's gorgeous and sexy. But I also found out, through stories she told me about her life, that she has an amazing sense of self. If you don't look too deep, it would be easy to believe that Jane is merely comfortable in her quiet life here in Misty Harbor. There would be many people who would look at a young woman with all of her natural beauty and clear gifts and wonder why she would be content to live in a very small town with no real possibilities to be anything other than a favorite daughter, a wonderful best friend and a well-loved art teacher.

But by the time we had finished dessert—which was cheesecake for Jane and another beer for me—I knew without a doubt that Jane was more than just content in her life here in Misty Harbor. Rather, she adored everything about it and it made her insanely happy. I learned she's incredibly close to her parents, has a completely fulfilling relationship with Miranda that resembles more of a sibling nature than just best friends, and she has a career that brings her such joy, she would never think to do anything else with her life.

Some would call her simpleminded and lacking goals, but I see someone who is incredibly centered and has achieved everything she could ever want in life.

This fascinates me.

This more than fascinates me, because despite the fact that I almost single-handedly brought down a major criminal organization, which is an accomplishment most people could never even hope to imagine, I'm sitting here in Misty Harbor wondering how I've wasted so much of my life. I'm in a town, hiding out, and removed from everything important in my life. As I reflect back on the last five years I gave up so I could bring a pack of criminals to justice, I feel strangely unaccomplished.

I look at Jane Cresson and realize I've been missing out on the reality of life. I've been completely without those little things that make life worth living. Good friends and family, a sense of belonging, and a joy-filled life. My life so far has been nothing but subsistence, and not a very fulfilling one at that.

While I admit this is a date, I still don't have a fucking clue what I'm going to do with this revelation. If I was a kind and gentle man, I'd drop Jane off at her house with a handshake and wish her well in life. I'd then barricade myself in my cottage and make sure I never crossed paths with her again.

But I'm not kind or gentle. More often than not, I've been called a supreme asshole by many people, and they wouldn't be wrong in their beliefs about me. It would be completely repugnant to encourage Jane. It would be almost morally deviant of me to do anything other than chase her off.

And yet, I'm debating right this very minute as I walk her back home whether I'm going to kiss her or try to fuck her when we get to her house, because at my core, I'm a selfish bastard. I've got so many years of living life as amorally and sinfully as possible, I almost believe it's within my right to dirty Jane up. It's certainly all I really know anymore.

"So, what did you think of your first experience with lobster?" Jane asks as she nudges her shoulder into my arm playfully. The push doesn't move me off course, and I keep my hands firmly tucked in my pockets as we walk along the same path back to her house. Up ahead in the distance, I see her parents' house, the porch light glowing but the rocking chairs thankfully empty. I breathe a little easier not having to face her mom and dad again, or, God forbid, receiving an invitation to come in for coffee or something. While I've conceded this is a date, I am not going to be meeting her parents.

Ever.

"It was fantastic," I admit about the lobster. "Outside of being a pain in the ass to eat."

"You can order them to be cracked and the meat pulled out for you," Jane tells me. "But you'd look like a total pansy ass at that point, and I don't think that would be a good look on you."

My lips twitch as she'd be totally right about that, but I don't respond. Despite Jane's knack for keeping conversation flowing, I also find that moments of silence with her are just as comfortable.

So comfortable, in fact, I almost trip over my own feet when she startles me with her next crazy proclamation. "I think this was a nice date, and I'm wondering if you're going to kiss me when we get to my house."

"It's not a date," I say automatically and way too vehemently, and Jane just snickers at me.

"Of course it's a date," she says. "You picked me up, took me to a nice restaurant, we had amazing conversation, lingered long over dessert, and we're taking a totally romantic walk back to my house."

"It was a thank you for helping me paint," I state firmly.

"That would have been beer and a pizza, not a romantic restaurant," she counters.

"You picked the restaurant," I remind her.

She ignores that very pointed reminder. "So are you going to kiss me?"

"Jesus Christ," I mutter, completely wanting to tell her, *No, I'm not going to kiss you. Not now. Not ever.* But nothing else comes out.

She snickers again. "You totally want to kiss me."

"Wring your neck more like it," I growl at her.

She laughs at me again, and my lips twitch… again.

"Seriously though," she says solemnly as she stops mid-stride and curls her hand around my forearm, which causes me to stop and turn to her. Her gaze is troubled, all traces of amusement gone. "I'm giving you a hard time. You don't have to kiss me."

I stare at her a thoughtful moment, my eyes moving over her beautifully innocent face. Her head tilts to the side, almost as if she's trying to figure out what's lurking inside my head.

"I'll think about it," I finally tell her. "And let you know when we get to your house."

She beams a smile up at me. It causes my stomach to tighten and my skin to tingle, in a not wholly unpleasant way. So I'm guessing I already have my answer.

Jane moves her hand down my forearm, past my wrist, and slides her palm against mine. Her fingers curl around my own as she says, "The suspense is killing me. I hope it lasts. *Willy Wonka*, 1971."

Smiling internally but never showing her that she amuses me, I don't bother pulling my hand away from hers because it feels too damn nice. It's soft and warm and secure against mine, unlike anything I've felt in my grasp before.

Instead, I just start walking, this time a bit quicker and with our hands firmly clasped together.

We walk past her parents' house in silence, and the yappy dog the next house down is thankfully inside. Otherwise, Jane might be tempted to pull away from me to pet that ridiculously loud thing.

When we reach Jane's house, she lets go of my hand and reaches into her purse to pull out a set of keys. Rather than unlock her door, she turns to me with her chin lifted in challenge. "Do you want to come in for a drink?"

"Not really," I tell her truthfully, because, in my mind, if I step through that door, it's going to be more than just a kiss. I'm not a gentleman, and I'm used to taking what I want. Jane will be in very real danger if I take her up on her offer.

She cocks an eyebrow at me skeptically. "I know no man who won't accept an invitation in for a drink."

"Is that really what you're offering me?" I counter in a low voice.

She blinks at me in surprise. "Well, of course that's what I'm offering. Is that wrong?"

"I thought you wanted a kiss," I remind her.

"I do," she says with her chin tilting higher. "But I figured we could have a drink… talk some more."

God, she can't be that fucking naïve. And if she really is, I need to educate her a bit on the dangers of assuming nice things about me.

I step toward Jane, crowding her space and forcing her to step backward until her back flattens against the door. I take another half a step until our bodies are separated by just a few inches of air and vibrating tension. As I peer down at her, I take in the fact her breathing has gotten faster and her eyelids have dropped slightly. Her gaze lowers slowly until she focuses on my mouth, and fuck it all to hell… she licks her lips.

It takes a massive amount of sheer willpower not to touch her.

Grab her.

Fuck… maul her.

I want to fucking maul her like a damn savage, but that's not me anymore.

I swear it's not me.

Taking in a slow breath through my nose, I let it out quietly through my mouth before I tell her, "Jane... in my world, you invite a man inside your house, and he expects you to spread your legs for him."

I hope to shock her and piss her off, so she'll do what I can't do in this moment, and that's to realize this has disaster written all over it. I want to offend her notions of romance and sensibility, and send her scurrying away from me.

Instead, she raises her gaze to meet mine and whispers, "That wasn't what I was offering, Kyle. Maybe later... after I get to know you a bit more, but for now... I really only want a kiss."

Goddamn it.

I fucking want it too. And I'll be more than happy with just a touch of her mouth on mine with the promise of nothing else in return. I can be satisfied with that.

I think.

I'm overwhelmed with a burst of anger toward her for her tenacity and ignorance of the ways of bad men, and I'm turned on beyond measure that, despite my scary attempts, she still wants something from me.

I bring a hand up and touch my fingers to her cheek in a move so gentle I don't recognize myself. She lets out a small gust of air that sounds appreciative and accepting, but it turns into a tiny gasp when my hand slides back into her hair and I grip it in my fist. It's not enough to hurt her, but it holds her tightly in place as I lower my face toward hers.

"I'm not a nice guy, Jane," I warn her.

"You seem nice enough," she says in a low murmur, but there's enough sass there I have to suppress an involuntary smile.

"I'll hurt you," I say ominously.

"Right this very moment?" she inquires sweetly.

"Eventually," I mutter.

"I'll take my chances, Kyle," she whispers. Those five words seal her fate.

"So be it," I say on a regretful sigh, and then I give her what she wants.

CHAPTER 13

JANE

WASH MY hands in my bathroom sink and glance into the mirror. I'm pretty sure the look on my face is just as dopey as it was this morning. I've felt it all day. The way my cheeks pull up a little, the way my mouth has been curved in a smile, and the slight flush to my skin.

I went to bed last night thinking about that kiss with Kyle at my doorstep, and I woke up thinking about it. Hell, there's even a slight tingling to my lips that hasn't gone away.

Turning the water off, I dry my hands on the cute little hand towel done in lemon yellow with white lace edging, and look into the mirror one last time. Yup... bright eyes that I may have accentuated with some smokier than I normally wear eye shadow, along with a volumizing layer of mascara, and decide that I'm really going to do this.

I head into the kitchen and said dopey smile remains. I can feel it. If anyone had seen me today, they would have looked at me with knowing eyes—that girl was kissed and kissed well. But I'd been at home by myself today, doing some cleaning and a little bit of painting for purely pleasure purposes. It was a casual, summer day off for me, one of the things I loved about being a teacher.

I'd relaxed today, ruminated about that kiss, and around three o'clock this afternoon, made the decision that I'd see Kyle tonight. This may or may not be a surprise to him. When he walked off my porch last night, he left me without a single innuendo or hint that he wanted to see me again. Perhaps he thinks he's made things clear. On the other hand, I've never really let Kyle put me off, and that seems to be a good play right now.

I cook dinner—a roasted pork loin, candied carrots, and fresh baked bread. Granted, the bread feels like a rock, so I throw it away and pack the rest up in a basket. After I top it off with a red-checkered linen cloth, I'm going to bring it to him and insist we eat it together.

Maybe I'll get another kiss, although I'm not sure it could top the one he gave me last night.

Kyle told me he wasn't a good man. He pretty much assured me he'd hurt me at some point. So when his lips came down on mine, I actually braced for him to be rough with me. Let's face it… he's crude, withdrawn, gruff, and anti-social. He's all angled planes and tattooed skin with scary designs. I'd watched him grab Craig by the throat and single-handedly dispatch the creep without breaking a sweat.

And even though I wanted the kiss, I knew there was a slight possibility that Kyle could, in fact, be a dangerously dark man. Even more so, I knew I could have been in actual danger. After all, he pretty much told me he considered an invitation into my house to equate to a spreading of legs.

Oh, but that kiss.

He was none of the things I had some reservations about.

It was so soft and gentle. His mouth moved so slowly over mine without any rush, but with the intent to seek everything I had to offer. Kyle was absolutely unhurried. If I had to guess, I'd say he was savoring it as much as I was. He was content to just roam at a leisurely pace, and it drove me absolutely bonkers with needing more. So I made the next bold move by letting my tongue hesitantly reach out to touch his.

And I got a reaction.

A soft growl from deep in his chest as his hand tightened slightly in my hair, and it so turned me on that my body involuntarily leaned into his.

But then… he was gone, releasing me suddenly and taking a full step backward. His eyes were hooded and his face impassive, and I would have thought he was unaffected by it all, except his voice was very hoarse when he said, "Good night, Jane."

Without another word, he spun around, bounded down my porch steps, and jogged across my yard to Cranberry Lane. I watched him—lips in full tingle mode—until he went inside his house and shut the door behind him.

I didn't struggle all that hard in my decision to cook and bring him dinner. I know I should heed his warning that he's a "bad" man, but I'm sorry... that kiss was way too gentle for that to be true. As such, I'm going to see what else is lurking under his carefully layered facade that's designed to keep people away.

After picking up the basket, the dopey smile on my face remains as I head over to Kyle's house. I have to concentrate to wipe it off, putting on my charming, quirky smile when I knock on his front door at six o'clock on the dot.

When Kyle opens the door and stares at me, he doesn't look surprised to see me, but, truthfully, he doesn't look happy about it either. One could argue that he doesn't look pissed off or put out. Not curious or resigned. He just stares at me without giving me a single hint as to what he might be feeling.

And that's okay.

I'm standing here, pushing myself into his life, because something happened last night when he kissed me. It was an epiphany of sorts because my entire life has sort of been settled. I had a charmed life growing up, followed my dreams to go to college and became a teacher, and I wake up every day living in a town that I adore with wonderful family and friends. But when he kissed me last night, the realization was clear that I had truly been missing something I had not realized I was missing until that moment. Kyle Harding presents more than just excitement and intrigue into my ordered world. He is an absolute puzzle, and I'm enjoying the process of figuring him out. Perhaps he's even a bit broken, and while I don't want to be the one to fix him, I do want to be an integral part in peeling away the outer layers so I can find out who he truly is. I've seen enough goodness and gentleness in him to know that he's not who *he* thinks he is. While he acts like he wants nothing to do with the world as it exists, I've seen enough curiosity within him to consider the possibility that perhaps he could have things he'd never thought were possible.

"Hi," I say with a shrug since my hands are full. But then I nod down to the basket in my hands. "Brought us dinner."

His gaze drops down to the basket, and then back up to me. "Us?"

"Well, yeah," I chastise. "I didn't cook all this food just for you to eat it by yourself. I get some of the rewards too."

"Are there any baked goods in there?" he asks dubiously, and I know I'm moments away from him opening the door.

Good thing I threw that bread away. "Nope. Just a pork loin and some candied carrots. I'm a good cook."

"But the baking leaves a lot to be desired," he adds on, and I can't help but grin—not over his backhanded slight that was said all in good fun, but because his arm shoots out and he opens the screen door to let me in.

I push past him, taking in the rustic decor of his cottage. It's totally a man's place as there's minimal decorative touches. The living room is small and boasts only a love seat and a ratty-looking recliner that's crowded around an old wood-burning fireplace with a red brick mantle. My heart warms when I see my painting hanging over it.

Beyond the living room is a small kitchen. I walk into it, setting my basket on the old, chipped countertop. As I pull out the two casserole dishes—one that contains the pork loin I'd already cut into thick slices and the other holding the carrots—Kyle wordlessly pulls out plates and flatware before turning to the fridge and pulling out two bottles of water.

I dish up our dinners. By silent agreement, we both take seats at his kitchen table that has seen better days. It's battered wood with nicks and scratches surrounded by four mismatched chairs.

I watch him carefully as he cuts into the pork, takes a bite, and chews slowly, his eyes focused on his plate. But I'm not going to sit here in silence when this is prime opportunity for conversation.

"Any good?" I ask, and he tilts his head to look at me.

He swallows as he nods. "Very good."

I beam a smile at him. "Thanks. I'd actually made some bread, but well… you'd be throwing me out of your house right about now if I'd offered it to you."

"You more than make up for the lack of baking skills," he mutters before spearing a carrot.

"My mom's a good cook," I say by way of explanation.

"How is she at baking?" he asks.

"Sucks like me," I admit.

He gives me an amused smile as he cuts another piece of pork loin. I use this opportunity to go for it.

"So you said you lived in Wyoming," I say as I work at cutting my food up into bite-sized pieces. "What all did you do there?"

I expect sullen silence, so I'm surprised when he says, "Worked various jobs here and there, but did a few years working in the oil fields. Eventually, I became a mechanic."

"Wyoming has oil?" I ask curiously.

He nods. "Mostly in the western part of the state."

"And what type of mechanic were you?" I ask as I punch my fork down into a piece of pork.

"Motorcycle," he says, and I'm surprised when he elaborates without me being pushy or nosy. "Started out as a hobby. Bought an old Triumph and fixed it up myself, then realized I liked working with engines. Eventually moved over to the eastern part of the state and became a full-time motorcycle mechanic."

"I can totally see that," I observe thoughtfully.

"How's that?" His expression is doubtfully curious.

"Well, I mean you're handy," I tell him. "Good with your hands. Knew exactly what to do when my water pipes broke. Some people are naturally gifted with stuff like that. I also saw you working on your truck's engine a few weeks ago, so I figured you knew what you were doing."

"Engines sort of make sense to me," he mutters as his gaze goes back to his plate. "But as good as I am with mechanical stuff, I totally suck at electronics."

"But aren't most modern engines full of electronic components?" I ask, enjoying this simple and unstilted conversation where he's not holding back.

"True," he says. "Always learning something."

I nod. "Pretty big change you've made, going from a motorcycle mechanic out west to a lighthouse keeper on the East Coast."

"You could say that."

He doesn't offer more, and the silence becomes instantly oppressive. So I veer off the path a little and try for something a bit more personal.

"So what do you like to do for fun?" I ask as he continues to eat. "I mean, you came in the dead of winter. There's not a lot to do around here unless you're into winter sports like snowmobiling or skiing. You had a few months where you were holed up in here all by yourself."

He raises his gaze from a piece of carrot on his fork to me and gives a half-hearted shrug. "I don't know... I read a lot."

My eyes brighten. "Really? I love to read too. What type of books?"

"Crime stuff," he says.

"Like real crime or fiction?"

"Both actually," he says. "I like the classics too. The guy who lived here before me left a nice collection, and I've read through all of them already."

You know, for all of Kyle's gruff ways, I can totally see him reading the classics. I've learned enough about him to know he's a smart guy.

"Did you go to college?" I ask curiously.

His gaze drops quickly to his plate, and I sense an immediate vibe of discomfort in the air. I wonder why that's a sore subject, but then he looks right back up at me. "Yeah, I did. Worked my way through at night. Took me six years going part time."

"Wow," I say, completely impressed but not surprised. Kyle seems to be a goal-oriented type of man. "What's your degree in?"

He hesitates only slightly, as if it might go against the rules to admit it to me, but then offers up. "Criminal justice."

I smile in understanding. "Hence you liking crime books. So why didn't you ever do anything with that degree?"

"What makes you think I didn't?" he challenges me, and yes... his eyes flash with something I can't quite describe.

"Did you?" I ask bluntly.

He holds my gaze steadily for a moment before he says quietly, "No. Found out I was more apt to commiserate with the criminals rather than catch them."

My jaw drops. He sounds serious, and yet... there's an untruth in that statement. I can hear it and it confuses me, because I also hear some elements of truth as well.

"I don't believe that," I say softly.

"Why would I lie?" he counters, his eyes continuing to bore into me.

"Are you a criminal?" I ask, not answering his last question.

He shakes his head without hesitation. "I have a spotless record. I'm sure you can look it up."

"No, I trust you," I say automatically, and I have to wonder why that popped out so easily. I don't know him at all, but, for some reason, I believe what he just told me, despite the fact he's clearly a secretive man.

Kyle merely grunts at me, and I'll have to assume that means he takes me at face value. But he doesn't offer me anything else, and I'm suddenly feeling off kilter. I feel like he was telling me something important about himself, but I can't figure out the deeper message.

♦

KYLE FINISHES HIS meal well before me, and that's merely because he focused on eating. I think that was a calculated move to discourage any further personal conversation, and I respected that.

So instead, I thought about that kiss we'd had, and I wondered if it would happen again tonight.

Then I became obsessed about it as I ate a piece of pork, then a carrot.

Pork. Carrot. Pork. Carrot.

When I finish the last bite, I look up at Kyle and find his plate empty. He's watching me across the table with his arms crossed over his chest. His chair is pushed back a bit, one leg cocked with his foot flat on the floor, the other one pushed out straight with heel to the floor, so he's slouched a bit lazily. "Dinner was great. Thanks."

And that totally sounds dismissive.

So I try to stall. "I'll help you clean up the dishes. After that, maybe we can watch a movie or something."

He's shaking his head in the negative before I even finish my sentence. "Don't have a TV."

"You can come to my house," I offer, and then I blush, because I remember what he thinks about a woman who invites a man inside. "You know… I mean, I've got a lot of DVDs and such."

He's still shaking his head. "I'm sort of beat. Going to call it an early night."

And yep… that was a total brush-off because it's barely six-thirty. I've been here a grand total of thirty minutes and he's had his fill of me—and well, my food. My heart sinks as it's clear he wants nothing more to do with me, and I'm thinking that kiss last night may have felt amazing only from my perspective. This embarrasses me greatly, giving me incentive to make a quick exit.

"Well, okay," I say as I push up out of my chair. Kyle does the same and shoves his hands in the pockets of his jeans, just staring at me. "I'll… um… get the dishes from you later."

I expect him to fight me on that. Perhaps insist I take them right now. But there's still more food in them, and that would require me to stay a bit longer to pack it all up, so I'm not surprised when he nods in agreement.

This heartens me slightly as I realize, at the very least, I'll see him again when he returns my stuff.

Unless he just leaves them on my porch, which causes my stomach to sink.

The tug-of-war this man plays on my emotions from second to second is disorienting to say the least.

I turn and head through the living room, Kyle's boots thumping softly behind me on the wood flooring. When I reach the door, he reaches past me and opens it. My mind races with something to say.

Anything that will keep an opening between us as my pulse fires on all cylinders.

I'm surprised when he pushes open the screen door, his shoulder brushing against mine, and when I step onto his porch, he follows me out.

Looking over my shoulder, I give him a tentative smile. "Well, good night."

"Good night, Jane," he says softly, and that right

there… it's regret in his eyes. I see it clearly and it causes me to freeze in place. Is that an opening?

Should I press an advantage?

But before I can even think what that might look like, he says, "Thanks again for dinner," and then turns back toward the screened door.

My shoulders sag at the cold brush-off and I turn away, telling myself with absolute certainty I need to give up on him. He's just not interested.

I get no more than two steps toward the first porch step before Kyle's hand clamps on my wrist and he's spinning me back toward him. My mouth falls open in a gasp of surprise, only to be covered with his as he pulls me roughly to him.

He puts a hand to the back of my head, another at my hip where he squeezes once before pulling me flush against his body, and then he kisses me like I've never been kissed before.

Never, ever kissed like this before.

Certainly not like last night, which was gentle and exploratory, hesitancy a barrier. But this is a full-on assault on all of my senses. His mouth is urgent, rough, and demanding. His tongue immediately claims mine, and I give it up to him without a second thought.

My hands reach blindly to grip into his t-shirt, and then claw inward so I can hold him tightly so he can't get away and I can't fall down because my knees are so weak.

Almost as if he's satisfied that I would never in a

million years think to pull my mouth from his, his hand drops from my head to take my other hip and he presses me into him.

And I feel everything.

Every inch of his hard body.

Most importantly, I feel his erection pressing into my stomach, and I go dizzy from how quickly this has escalated.

A tiny moan flutters up from my throat and doesn't even hesitate before it slithers into his mouth. Kyle's fingers dig harder into my hips as I press my body tightly against his, my arms now snaking around his shoulders. My fingers touch the back of his neck, sliding upward to the back of his head where they rub against the stubble of his shorn hair briefly before gliding back down and around to lie against his chest.

I can feel the mad hammering of his heart, and mine seems to gallop at the same speed within my chest. My entire body is on fire, my limbs feel like jello, and an ache throbs between my legs. In this very moment, I've never been more turned on in my entire life by a man, and if we were in my house, I'd indeed be spreading my legs for him.

Not a doubt in my mind that's what I'd be doing.

But then Kyle hesitates, his mouth pausing and his grip loosening. His forehead touches mine as he mutters almost painfully, "You need to go."

"No," I say automatically, my fingers dragging over

his chest, down his stomach, and pausing at the waistband of his jeans.

Kyle lifts his head, and his troubled eyes bore into mine. His words are clipped and harsh. "You need to go, Jane."

"No," I say again. Okay, it comes out almost like a whine, and my fingers boldly skim downward to brush over his erection in a very desperate and perhaps pathetic move to keep him in the moment.

To not lose him.

Kyle hisses and his body jerks when I press my palm against him, and holy mother of God, it's huge. I want to feel more, so I start to curl my hand around him, assured he won't be able to resist.

I'm wrong though, probably about everything.

Kyle's hands shoot upward, roughly grabbing my shoulders so he can push me away. It's not a hard push, but in a nanosecond, he puts two feet of space between us and then drops me like a hot potato.

I stare at him, my chest heaving with hardened nipples. A silent plea on my mouth for him to touch me again.

He shakes his head, but his voice is surprisingly gentle when he says, "You need to go, Jane. This isn't happening."

"But I don't understand," I whisper.

Kyle scrubs a hand over his head and huffs out with frustration. "There's nothing to understand. I'm not good for you and I just can't go there, okay?"

"No, it's not okay," I argue, and even though my body is starting to cool, I feel more drawn to him than ever. I feel absolutely compelled to admit to him, "I like you."

Kyle's eyes gentle as he gives me a sad smile. "I like you too, Jane. But it can't go past friendship. I really shouldn't even take that, but…"

"But?" I prompt him.

"But nothing," he says firmly. "I'm not going to be here long, so I'm not about to start anything with you. So it's just friends, Jane, and frankly… I won't make a very good friend so take that for what it's worth."

My eyes drop to the porch, and I try to make sense of the emotions warring within me. So much disappointment, and a huge pool of sadness, that Kyle feels the need to stay so closed off.

"I'm sorry," he says, and my eyes snap back up to his.

And he is sorry. His gaze is filled with regret and pain, not for me, but for himself, and it crashes into me hard.

"Me too," I murmur with a nod of my head. "I guess it's just friends."

"Just friends," he agrees. He even attempts a smile that's completely lackluster, causing my heart to squeeze like it's been locked in a vice grip.

"Well, good night," I say with a smile back at him.

"Good night, Jane," he says and turns away from me.

I watch him walk through his door and shut it behind him, the memory of his regretful gaze burned vividly into my brain.

Most women would take him at face value and give him what he just asked for. But I'm not most women, and I'm sure Kyle has that figured out. I know he thinks he needs space, probably to protect himself and me at the same time.

I see something different though.

I see a man who wants something for himself but is too afraid to take it. He's afraid of failure.

So I throw my shoulders back, determination forging my spine into steel, and I vow to myself I'm going to get through those walls he just put up around himself, no matter what it takes.

CHAPTER 14

KYLE

I TAKE ONE last glance around the living room, my eyes purposely avoiding Jane's painting, and I'm satisfied. I've always been a bit of a slob when it comes to my living quarters, and I guess that comes from the last three years pretty much living in the shit hole of the Mayhem's Mission clubhouse.

But in this little house that attaches to the lighthouse by a covered walkway, I have a duty to keep it neat and clean, not only because it doesn't belong to me, but also because the stupid fucking historical society wants to give tours during the summer. I'm not sure why a tour includes my cottage, because it's just that… a cottage. I'm guessing for the five dollars they charge for admittance, they have to include something other than the thirty-three steps of spiral staircase that leads up to the rotating light. Probably want to show the charm of coastal seaside living or some shit like that.

Today is the first tour and I've got to get lost, which is fine by me. When Joe arranged for this "job" for me, I was asked to be the one to give the tours. I think my answer was something like "no fucking way." However he got this job nailed down... however he got it all worked out... all I have to do is ensure the cottage is clean and tidy every Saturday for the rest of the summer. I figure that's the least I could do since this job is a cakewalk anyway. Outside of the repairs and maintenance, which are all pretty much done, all I have to do is ensure the light stays on. With a backup generator, that pretty much ensures I have squat to do while watching the lighthouse.

Patting my back pocket, I note my wallet is in place and I snag my car keys off the small table by the front door. No clue how to keep myself busy all day away from the cottage, but figure it will include multiple beers at The Lobster Cage. Pulling the front door open, I start to push at the screen door and come to a dead halt when I see Jane standing on the other side, her hand raised and poised to knock.

"Hey," she says in surprise, and I'm struck for a moment just staring at her beauty. Hair in a ponytail, a pair of cutoff jean shorts, and a vintage orange Crush t-shirt. She's got a satchel-like purse hanging on the diagonal across her chest, the canvas strap cutting through her cleavage, and I have to force my eyes upward.

She smirks at me when they land on her face.

"What are you doing here?" I ask as I push through the screen door. She takes a step back to give me room.

As I turn to lock the door, she says, "Thought I'd

come see what you were doing today. Figured maybe you'd like to take a ferry ride across the bay to Bar Harbor."

I secure the lock and turn back to her, stepping to the side to let the screen door swing shut. "I was on my way to The Lobster Cage to have a few beers."

She holds her wrist out and glances down at her watch. "It's 9:30 in the morning."

"They open at eight," I point out. I found since moving here that fisherman like to drink and that means Gus keeps the bar open most of the time.

"Seriously, Kyle," Jane says in exasperation, and I'll admit… it's cute. Even that eye roll she just gave me. "You totally don't want to waste your day in a bar when you could be spending it with me."

I raise a dubious eyebrow.

"Because," she finishes with an impish grin. "As I'm your only friend here, it's my duty to show you the surrounding sights. Bar Harbor is amazing, and there's a great bookstore there I thought I'd show you, and then, if you wanted, we could hike a bit over in Acadia National Park."

And fuck if that doesn't sound a hell of a lot better than sitting in a drab bar all day.

But still… I have to consider this carefully. First, I don't want Jane to get the wrong impression if I agree to spend the day with her. It will have to be just as friends. And second, I have to weigh the risk. While there's no proof that anyone is really looking for me, there is safety in being in a small town. If someone had located me and were watching, they'd be a lot easier to recognize here than in Bar Harbor.

"Come on, Kyle," Jane says with an exaggerated whine. "I don't want to go over there by myself. Miranda's working and my parents are doing yardwork, so if you don't go, I won't, and I'll be stuck planting petunias all day at their house."

Hmm… well, it does sound like she's only viewing me as a friend. And apparently a friend who's low on the list, as she'd considered spending the day first with Miranda and secondly with her parents.

Now I'm not sure how that makes me feel. I should be relieved, but part of me is a little put out by that. I mean, it was just four days ago she'd her hand pressed up against my dick and it felt so good I was afraid I'd make a fool of myself.

Whatever.

"Alright," I grudgingly say, although I'd be lying if I didn't admit to at least myself that I was excited about the prospect of spending the day with Jane. While I still believe I made the right call in pushing her away the other night, it didn't mean I was happy about it. Jane has brought a tremendous amount of brightness into my life the last few weeks, and she has made the hiding out and waiting at least bearable. As long as I can keep my hands to myself, why not take advantage of that brightness today?

♦

I PEER OVER the edge of the book I have opened in front of me and look at Jane. She's sitting across from me in a big, mushy-looking chair with her back pressed up against one arm and her legs thrown over the other. She's reading a book she'd bought about fifteen minutes ago. After we both purchased coffees, we decided to have some quiet time to read in this pretty amazing bookstore she brought me to. It's massive with rows and rows of books, but it has little alcove sitting areas all around where you can enjoy your spoils or peruse potential purchases. Jane had also bought a big cinnamon roll, and I will admit it may have been a little torturous watching her lick her fingers when she was done, but then she settled into her chair quietly and she's been ignoring me ever since.

It does appear that she took me at face value and is accepting the friendship boundary I put in place. She seems to be her usual quirky self, throwing movie lines at me when the situation presents. The first one came on the ferry as we got out of my truck that was parked with several others that were catching the ride across French-man's Bay to Bar Harbor. She'd put her sunglasses on her face, pushed them up the bridge of her nose, and said, "Roads? Where we're going, we don't need roads. *Back to the Future.* 1985."

I couldn't fucking help it. Of course, I laughed. She gave me back a sparkling grin, and I thought perhaps this might be a very good day.

But sadly, the more I'm around her, the more I'm hating the boundary I put in place. I can smell her subtle perfume, which is as light and airy as her personality, and I can see the bare skin of her legs and how it glows, and I know damn well it would be as soft as silk if I touched it, and Jesus fucking Christ… this just sucks.

Jane's head tilts to look at me, and she totally busts me staring at her over the edge of my book, which is some crime thriller I'd picked up.

Before she can even say anything to try to embarrass me for my blunt perusal, I nod at her book and ask, "What are you reading?"

Keeping her thumb inside the pages to hold her place, she turns it around and shows me the cover. It's of a bare-chested man giving a smoldering look to the camera.

I look back to her and smirk.

"What?" she asks defensively. "I like romance books. So what?"

I hold one hand up, palm raised to her in defense. "Hey. I didn't say anything."

"No," she mutters. "But you had *that* look."

"What look?" I counter, but I know damn well what look I gave her.

"That totally judgey look people give you when you

read romance," she huffs.

"I have no clue what you're talking about," I tell her truthfully. I merely thought it funny she was reading a book with a half-naked guy on the front. "Why do people judge you for reading romance?"

Jane swings her legs off the chair arm and plants her feet, leaning toward me a bit. "Many people think this stuff is just fluff. It's not literary. Waste of time to read and it's for simpleminded people."

"You are in no way simpleminded," I point out. That's the honest fucking truth as I think Jane's about as bright as they come.

Jane holds the book out and waves it. "I read this because it makes me feel good. It transports me out of my reality and gives me all the feels."

I eye the cover dubiously. "All the feels?"

"About love and romance," she says dreamily, and I have to force myself not to grimace. "I know that's a girl thing, but the authors who write this stuff? They really know how to reach you down deep into the center of your chest."

"If it's all about love and feeling emotion," I have to ask, "then why does it look like it's about porn on the cover?"

Jane's eyes flick down to the cover, and she gives a shrug as she looks back up to me. Holding the book out for me to inspect the cover again, she says with a grin, "You got to admit. It's eye catching."

I give a short bark of a laugh, cognizant though that I'm in a bookstore, so it's not overly loud. "I could see why it caught your attention."

Jane leans a little closer to me and says in an almost conspiratorial tone, "While I read these books for the romance and the relationship, not going to lie... there are some smoking hot sex scenes in some of these books."

And if that's not a punch to the fucking gut. Thinking about Jane reading about sex. About hot, sweaty, dirty sex. And wondering then what she might do when she's alone, reading about hot, sweaty, dirty sex.

I shift uncomfortably in my chair and give another nod toward the book. "I've never read a romance, and without a doubt never will, but really... how many ways can a love story be told?"

"Oh, hundreds and hundreds," she says quickly. "No, probably thousands and millions. I mean, the characters are different, settings different, plots are different."

I'm betting the sex is different too, as I personally know there are hundreds of ways to have an orgasm.

"You believe in that stuff?" I ask, another nod to the book.

"You mean love?" she returns, her head tilted in confusion.

"Love, romance, soul mates," I say in a dismissive tone.

"I do," she says simply. "Don't you?"

"Nope," I answer quickly and with utter honesty. My views on relationships are so fucking whacked based on what I've been immersed so deeply in over the last several years. I don't have much faith in people or in love.

"Ah," Jane says knowingly, her eyes turning soft. "You've had your heart broken before."

I blink at her in surprise and sit up straighter in my chair. "Actually, I haven't."

Never had my heart broken... but it had absolutely turned to stone fairly early on in my days with Mayhem's Mission. It was a necessary means to survive because I'd have never been able to make it through all those years of crime and depravity if I left open any soft spots to knock me off course.

"You've never been in love?" Jane asks softly, pity written clearly on her face over my suspected answer.

But I decide to deflect. "Why? Have you?"

Her mouth opens to answer, then it snaps shut. Her eyes seem confused, and she glances down at the book.

"Jane?" I prompt, because she looks like someone kicked her best puppy.

Her gaze slowly slides up to mine, and she looks at me sheepishly. "I was going to say 'yes,' I have been in love before. With Craig—that creeper you helped me with that day at the festival. But then I just realized... what I felt for him is nothing like what I feel when reading these books."

"Maybe because what you're reading is fiction," I

suggest. Because that makes the most sense to me.

Jane shakes her head adamantly. "No. I mean… yes, this is fiction, but it's also real. This is what love's supposed to feel like, and it just hit me… that's never what I felt with Craig."

While it is absolutely none of my business what Jane had with her ex-boyfriend, for some weird reason, I feel strangely fulfilled by her proclamation she never loved that douche. And also a bit sad, because Jane is the type of woman who should experience whatever it is in those books that brings such a smile to her face.

She absolutely deserves something good. Because it's nothing but a pipe dream for me to hope I could be the one to give it to her, I firmly put it out of my mind and go back to reading the crime thriller in my hands.

CHAPTER 15

JANE

TODAY WAS A really good day, but it was painful too. I had an amazing time with Kyle, and I watched him come out of his shell more than ever as we acted like tourists. After coffee in the bookstore, we visited several local artisan shops and galleries. We then had a lunch of thick deli sandwiches and decided to drive Park Loop Road, which enabled Kyle to have a taste of Acadia National Park. The scenery, as always, was stunning and reinforced one of the many reasons why I continue to live in this area rather than go out and explore the world.

Kyle seemed to really enjoy the day. It's almost as if he "needed" to relax. Once he gave into it, I got to see more of his wit and humor as the day went on. Not to sound too cheesy, but he was kind of like a flower that bloomed under the sun.

But it was painful to me as well, because it only made me like him more. I had suspected there was more behind those walls he'd erected, and the more he showed it to me, the worse I felt because I'd never get to really touch the real Kyle. Because he's insisting we are nothing but friends, I'll only have him on the most basic and shallow level.

We catch the last ferry back to Misty Harbor. The sun is setting as Kyle drives his truck off the dock. I'm hungry and I'd like to suggest we go grab dinner, but I'm hesitant to do so. I don't want him thinking this is me pining for another date—which makes me look pathetic—and I have a feeling he's probably had about as much friendship frolicking fun as he can handle for one day. He's slipped back into his quiet mode, not having said much on the ferry ride.

So I remain quiet as we drive down Front Street, staring out the passenger window at the point where Misty Bay meets the Atlantic. The sky still has some pale pink up high, but the horizon is already purplish-gray, signifying dusk has arrived on the East Coast. The lighthouse comes into view, its revolving strobe winking at me on each half-turn. The lighthouse has always made me feel a little sad as it stands tall and alone, removed from the rest of the town because its duty is first and foremost to protect the incoming water vessels. It reminds me a little of Kyle, actually.

When Kyle turns onto Gray Birch Street, which borders the south side of my house and intersects with Cranberry, I reach to the floorboard and grab my purse, preparing to exit the vehicle after a quick and friendly goodbye. While in my very own romance novel, Kyle would pull me back and kiss the hell out of me, I know that's not going to happen because he's drawn a line in the sand, and it's not likely he'll cross it. He seems like a determined man in all things, and wishy-washy doesn't describe him at all.

Kyle pulls into my driveway. Before he comes to a complete stop, I grip the door handle, prepared to make flight. I'm totally shocked to inaction though when he shoves the truck into park and turns off the ignition.

What the hell does that mean?

"I'll walk you up," he says as his gaze rests on my front porch. "You didn't leave your light on."

Oh, okay. Safety. He's being a gentleman. A good friend, so to speak.

I don't respond, just open the door and hop out of his truck. My hands go into my purse for my keys. By the time I have them, I've rounded the front of his truck and we head to the porch steps in silence.

Kyle follows behind me, and even though I know he's merely being polite, my skin starts to tingle over the memories of our first kiss that occurred right here five days ago.

I don't have a screen porch door the way Kyle does, so I'm able to quickly unlock it and push the door open a few inches. With my hand still on the knob, I turn to Kyle with a hammering heart because if he's going to do something, now is the time.

"Well, hope you had some fun today," I say with a cheerful smile, but I'm sure with undisguised hope in my eyes.

Kyle's own gaze is soft, and I know he sees what I feel. He nods and gentles his voice for my benefit. "Yeah, I did. Thanks for inviting me."

I wait, because if he's going to kiss me, it should be now. But he only stares at me a moment more before tipping his head. "Good night, Jane."

My heart sinks in disappointment, because those words ring with finality. Still, I put on my bravest smile. "Good night, Kyle. See you around."

I get a long, thoughtful look before he gives me a small return smile. "Yeah, see you around."

Kyle turns and jogs down my porch steps. I step inside, close the door, and lean my back against it. Shutting my eyes, I let out a long-suffering sigh. I am all kinds of stupid to let myself get caught up with him. I reason to myself that it's only because he's intriguing, incredibly hot, and he'd be a great summer diversion, knowing those are all legitimate reasons to crush on someone. But if I'm honest with myself, I know it's because there's something about him that speaks to me on a deeper level. While he's still as much a mystery as he was the day I met him, I realized something about him today as I tried to unobtrusively observe him.

As I watched him loosen up, start to unwind, laugh a little more easily, I realized that Kyle was like a sponge, soaking up the goodness of a simple, yet ordinary day. We didn't do anything more than visit a few shops, eat some food, and drive around to look at scenery. It was low pressure and spontaneous, but it was just ordinary living. And as I watched Kyle soak it up... no, *savor* it... I realized that he's not had this in a very long time. Hell, maybe he never had it.

But I could see it written all over him.

He wanted it and he wanted it badly.

I open my eyes. With another sigh, I start to push away from the door.

Only to be really "pushed" away from the door as it opens up on me, some unknown force propelling me gently into my living room.

I spin around and see Kyle standing in my doorway, his hand on the knob. "You didn't lock your door," he says while staring at me with veiled eyes.

"I was just getting ready to—"

"You didn't invite me in," he says gruffly, and then steps inside my house.

My jaw drops open, because he knows damn well why I didn't invite him in. Because we're friends only, that's why.

Kyle shuts the door behind him, and then completely confuses me when he says, "Didn't even give me a chance to kiss you goodnight."

My head spins one full loop before I orient myself. Placing my hands on my hips, I narrow my eyes at him. "You know damn well why you weren't invited in."

He gives me a sage nod. Without taking his eyes off

me, he says, "You're talking about that whole friends thing, right?"

I roll my eyes. "Yeah... that whole friends thing. You were pretty clear about it."

Kyle doesn't say anything, but he never takes his eyes off me as he flips the lock on my door. Something about that *snicking* sound makes my legs feel rubbery. "Yeah, well, I changed my mind about that."

"What—"

But I don't get another word out because in one long stride, he's got both of his palms against my face, pulling me halfway up to meet his mouth as he tilts his head down. He strikes fast and hot, immediately seeking a deep, wet connection with our lips and tongues. And I know he likes it because he gives a half-groan of appreciation with a half-snarl of need for something more.

My brain starts to question whether or not this is a good idea, but my body already made the decision. My arms go tight around his neck, and I plaster myself to his frame. My tongue duels with his, greedy for more.

As if he's satisfied with my hold on him, he drops his hands and they go to my ass. His palms are huge and his fingers dig in against that crease that separates my butt from my leg. With an effortless heave, he picks me up. My legs automatically wrap around his waist, and then Kyle is spinning me toward the small hallway that leads to my bedroom.

To. My. Bedroom.

I tear my mouth from his and pant, "Wait."

Kyle immediately stops, but his hands grip my butt tighter. He peers down at me... eyes darkened with need and frustration.

"What are we doing?" I breathe out softly.

"We're going to fuck," he growls impatiently.

Admittedly, even though those words are crude, the way he says them hits me straight between my legs. I'm not quite sure what that says about me, but I give a slight shake of my head. "You said you only wanted to be friends. This isn't what friends do."

"I was wrong about the friend thing then," he mutters impatiently.

"So we're not friends?" I press him.

"Yes, we're friends," he says in exasperation. "And soon to be lovers if you're done questioning me."

"So is this a one-time only thing?" I ask, because even though he's trying to clarify things, I'm not sure I really understand, and that's because Kyle is so freaking complex and mysterious. I can't make any sense of my feelings, so perhaps if I understood where he's coming from, it would be a bit clearer to me.

"Jane," Kyle says gruffly. The heat in his eyes indicates perhaps more frustration than the sexual promise I'd seen there just seconds ago. "I don't know what the fuck this is. I just know I want you and I'm tired of fighting it, so I'm not going to fight it. I'm giving in and taking what I think you're offering. So do you really have to know more than that? Because if you do, you need to know I don't have the answers. I don't have the answers, so I'll just set you down right now and go home. We'll just be friends, and it will be fine."

Just the thought of him putting me down and walking out my door freaks me out, and I involuntarily clutch my legs and arms around him tighter while shaking my head. It's with no amount of urgency that I say, "No! Don't put me down. I don't need the answers."

That's an absolute lie. I so need the answers, but I'll just have to wait for them.

"My room's to the left," I say as I incline my head that way, because he's looking at me dubiously.

"Jane," he growls low. "I need to know you're okay with this. I'm not promising you anything but tonight and that I'll make it so fucking good for you, I swear. But that's all I know at this moment. Are you okay with that?"

My head nods up and down furiously, my arms and legs tightening even more. "Yes," I assure him breathlessly. "I'm okay with it."

Immediately, the anger and frustration melt from Kyle's face, and a look that I'd characterize as immense relief mixed with extreme hunger replaces it, and that causes flutters in my belly.

Kyle maneuvers me through the hall and into my bedroom, where his knee goes to the mattress and he lays me down. I release my hold on him and watch as he just stares down at me, one foot still planted solidly on the floor.

"I know exactly what I'm going to do to you," he whispers as his eyes start to burn hotter. His hand comes out and touches the side of my leg lightly, causing goose pimples to spring up. "I've spent so much time these last few weeks imagining what I'd do to you if I had you in this position that I know down to the fine details how this night is going to play out. And I swear to God, Jane… it's going to be so fucking good."

A cramp of longing hits me in two places at once. Right in my sex and right in the center of my chest. Those words and the promises of pleasure they held may have been the sexiest, most erotic thing I've ever heard in my life. The look of stark need on his face, and the reverent way he just spoke them, made my heart contract with hope. I know without a doubt Kyle has been missing something in his life by the way in which he's looking at me, and knowing I can fulfill whatever this void is gives me all the feels.

It gives me the best kind of feels, and I know after tonight, my life is not going to be the same. I'm pretty sure Kyle's won't either.

CHAPTER 16

KYLE

I JUST PROMISED Jane that I was going to make her feel good, and I intend to keep that promise. I'm rusty as fuck when it comes to giving a woman pleasure, but I didn't lie to her just now when I told her I've been fantasizing about this for some time. I've probably thought up a dozen different scenarios involving Jane, all while jacking off to said fantasies, so I know exactly what I'm going to do to her tonight.

She stares up at me... eyes wide and trusting. Mouth slightly parted to where I can barely see a peek of her teeth through those full lips that have starred in a few of those fantasies.

I have to resist the impulse to strip her quickly and take her hard and fast. It's the way I've fucked for so long that I've forgotten the nuances and pleasures of foreplay.

But tonight, I'm making a change. Jane is a different class of woman, and what I know about her I like. She deserves to feel good, and I want to be the one to give that to her. I want to own that about her.

I bring my other knee to the mattress and place my

palms down beside her shoulders. As I hover over her, I take in every tiny detail of her face. I've never seen green eyes as brilliant as hers. They are now as dark as emeralds, but I've seen them lighten to the shade of mint when she laughs. Even though she's a blonde, her lashes are fairly dark, which make her eyes stand out like beacons brighter than the lighthouse. Her nose is narrow but slopes upward slightly, making her look sassier than I know her to be. And well… those lips. Like I said, they've had top billing in a few fantasies.

Jane lies below me, completely giving herself over. She's placing a huge responsibility on my shoulders, but I've handled tougher burdens in my life.

While my fingers itch to touch her and I'm already hard as a rock, I need to start right with Jane.

So I dip my head down and touch my mouth to hers softly. While I had intended to go gently, the touch of her lips against mine is completely electric, and both of us groan in appreciation.

I press against her mouth harder before giving her my tongue. Again, she groans. A slightly rougher sound rumbles in my chest, filling me with an animal urgency that I know is going to be hard as hell to keep at bay. I want her so badly that I can feel my control already starting to slip, even though all we've done is shared the beginning of a hot kiss.

In my mind, I know I should slow things down, but Jane doesn't make it any easier by slipping her hands under my t-shirt and snaking them up my torso. The feel of her soft skin against my abs makes my head spin deliriously. She makes a tiny sound of frustration as she tries to push my t-shirt up, but doesn't know how to get it off.

Not wanting her to suffer, I push up, going to my knees. I peel my shirt off, loving the eagerness with which her eyes roam over my skin. She lingers on my tats and I know I'll answer for them at some point, but then I'm stunned when her eyes drop down to stare at the erection pushing against my jeans. I'm so hard it hurts, and her looking at it makes it hurt even worse.

Tentatively, Jane's hands come to the top button. She looks up at me for a moment, maybe for permission, I'm not sure. But my throat is so dry that all I can do is swallow hard as I stare back at her.

She must take my silence as tacit approval for she pops the first button. My cock jumps and tightens as she pops the next, revealing the head of my dick. I watch, mesmerized, as she slowly runs her thumb over the exposed skin.

Jane lets out a stuttering breath and pops the next button, giving some relief to the ache, but I can't stand this slow torture she's wreaking on me. In a burst of energized need, I bat Jane's hands away before reaching down and hauling her up with my hands under her armpits. I pull her right up to her knees so we're facing each other.

I note vaguely Jane's flushed cheeks and eyes glimmering at me darkly before I roughly pull her shirt over her head. I toss it over my shoulder as my gaze goes to her chest, and I get my first really good look at her breasts. They're fucking fantastic. Big and round with her nipples poking out hard against the lace of a pale blue bra. The cups sit low on the globes of her tits, pushing them inward and teasing me with cleavage meant to be fucked.

Which is funny as I'm not really a breast man. My ideal fuck is taking a woman from behind so I don't have deal with kissing her. Just bending her right over a piece of furniture—

—I walk back into the clubhouse and the scent of sex and pot smack me hard in the face. I'm buzzed as fuck from the joint I'd just smoked outside with Bridger, but I feel like getting really fucked up tonight. The pressure of maintaining this lifestyle, and the stress of being undercover, have made alcohol and drugs a necessary balm. While I can drink like a fish, I at least keep my drug use to a minimum, terrified that type of addiction could impede my long-term judgment. So I look for other ways to get relief, and the best I'd found so far was to fuck myself into oblivion. Luckily, there are enough club whores to keep my dick satisfied.

My gaze slides to the pool table. One of the whores is naked and bent over it, her legs spread obscenely and her torso tied down to the felt top so she can't move. She lays her cheek on the green baize that's covered with cigarette burns, a blissed-out look on her face. One of my club brothers is fucking her from behind, hips pumping furiously as he races to get off as fast as possible. After all, he's got several other guys waiting behind him to take a chance. No telling how many times this girl has already been fucked tonight, but she loves this shit and asked for it. My brother thrusts hard a few more times before pulling out, snapping the rubber off, and coming all over her ass. My other brothers all yell and cheer him on, and another one steps up—

A groan of disappointment slithers out of my throat, and I give a hard shake to my head to dispel that memory. No idea why the fuck I'd even think about that disgusting shit when I have the beauty of Jane in front of me. The disappointment is in myself, not only for thinking of that crap, but also because my dick went even harder. It didn't need to get harder because Jane was really all I wanted, yet it did as I thought about taking a woman from behind because that's how you keep distance.

A searing hot flash of doubt courses through me, and I almost push Jane away. But I'm sidetracked when her hands come to the clasp at the front of her bra. My eyes latch onto those delicate fingers with pale pink polish as they flick open the clasp and peel the lace apart.

And Christ... her breasts are so fucking perfect as they're revealed to me. Almost as if she's never revealed them to anyone else, or I'll choose to think of it that way, at least. She's offering me the most perfect gift in the world right now, and the last oily feelings of guilt for being sucked into that terrible memory vanish.

"Kyle?" Jane whispers, and my eyes snap up to hers. "You okay?"

"Yeah," I say in a rasping voice as I look back at her, but I'm still feeling a little off balance.

Jane must sense it, because she takes control. She takes my hands in hers and pulls them upward, pressing my palms gently against her tits.

And fuck… just…

"Goddamn… you're perfect," I mutter as I squeeze the flesh and her hands fall away. My thumbs graze over her nipples, and Jane's head falls back as she moans in pleasure.

Apparently, my dick wasn't as hard as it could get, because that moan right there slams into me with brutal force, making me swell so painfully hard I have to drop a hand and tear at the fly to release the remaining buttons to give me relief.

As soon as my dick springs free, I slip a hand to the back of Jane's head, the other moving from her breast to her lower back, and I pull her back to my mouth. I want to kiss her again, because it's Jane. She's not a woman who I ever want to face away from me.

Our mouths connect, teeth gnash, and our naked torsos press into each other. We kiss like savages, locked tightly against one another. I can feel her nipples pebbled hard against my chest, and my cock jumps as it's pressed into her belly. I can feel my pre-cum wetting her soft skin, and there's a very real possibility I might just spontaneously explode.

Needing a tiny bit of space so I can slow this down... so I can savor this a bit more, I pull my mouth away from Jane's and push her gently away from me. Her eyes open slowly and are glazed and feverish looking. Her lips are wet and swollen, and, fuck, I want them wrapped around my dick, but that's going to have to be later. I'd never survive her blowing me.

"Lay back," I order her gruffly, placing a palm in the center of her chest.

"Okay," she whispers in acceptance, letting her body drop gracefully back down to the mattress.

I scramble off the bed and remove my jeans, followed by a quick grab of a condom out of my wallet. I throw that on the bed and then look back to Jane, who is sadly wearing far too many clothes still.

My palms go to the mattress and I bend over her, placing a tiny kiss to her stomach. Her muscles clench in response. I look up briefly to find her head tilted back and her eyes closed. Without ever taking my gaze off her, I close my lips over her nipple and have to suppress a grin as her eyes shoot open. She groans, and I give a swift, hard suck followed by a gentle lick.

Jane's hands fly to my head, almost as if she has no

control, and she holds me to her breast.

"Just like that," she murmurs.

So I let my tongue, teeth, and lips explore the soft skin of her tits and the hard pebbled nipples that are balled tight in pleasure. Jane clasps my head, unwilling to let me go. She moans and writhes under me, but I find myself wanting more from her.

My hand slides down her belly. I feel her muscles once again leap and bunch under my touch. When my fingers hit the waistband of her shorts, Jane's body goes utterly still with anticipation. I lift my head up to look at her and find her watching me intently. I don't let my eyes drop, but hold her pinned while my fingers work at her button, then her zipper. I stare into those emerald orbs that are blazing with desire and slip my fingers into her panties.

Our gazes stay locked as the pads of my fingers skim through her hair before dragging lightly through her folds. Jane sucks in a breath and holds it deep, never once letting her eyes drop as she waits to see what I'll do. When I circle just the tip of my index finger on her clit, her hips shoot off the bed and her neck arches. She cries out, and that is just the fucking sexiest thing I've ever seen.

I want to see it again.

All of it.

"Help me get your shorts off," I order her as I start to pull the material down, along with her panties. She works one side while I get the other, and soon, I'm tossing the last of her clothing to the floor. I take a moment to let my eyes glide down her perfect body as I press my hand between her legs. I tilt my head to look at Jane, and I see she's watching me with dark eyes. I slip my middle finger into her, and I love the way her greedy hips arch into my touch.

I love it so fucking much that I could do this all damn night with her.

So I continue to use my fingers against her. In her. On her. She writhes and moans and her hand eventually wraps around my wrist to try to make me go faster. I indulge in her whims. Within seconds, she's starting to crest. I take her right to the apex, but before she can fall, I pull my hand away from her.

Jane's eyes shoot open, and she looks at me with utter need. "Why'd you stop?"

"Because I want you to come on my dick and not my fingers the first time," I tell her, my hand nabbing the condom from the mattress beside us.

Jane groans in response. I smile as I know that turned her on, but fuck if it wasn't the truth. I want to be inside her when she comes that first time.

I roll to my side, getting the wrapper opened with practiced fingers because I've used a lot of condoms in the last several years. I fucked a lot, but I always wrapped my shit tight.

After I get the latex rolled on, I turn back into Jane,

wrapping an arm around her waist. I pull her in close to me and graze my lips against hers. I'm a selfish fuck, but there's a very real possibility that this is indeed a one-time only event, and I want to preserve the best possible memory for myself to look back on. More importantly, I don't want to risk the possibility I'd lose control and hurt her, so I roll to my back, pulling Jane with me.

She settles into my body almost as if by designed purpose, her pelvis coming right over my cock to gyrate against it. My hands go to her ass, and I urge her movements along. Jane and I kiss like starved beings, moaning in pleasure and unfulfilled need. I skim my hands over every square inch of her body I can touch. She rotates her hips, rubbing against me, driving me mad with the need to come.

And then, finally, Jane pushes a hand in between our bodies and wraps those delicate fingers around my dick. I groan with immediate satisfaction followed by anticipation of what's to come. Or maybe it's misery because it's painful not being inside her.

Just when I'm at the point of begging Jane to finish me off, she rears upward, tossing back her glorious bounty of golden hair. Her eyes are still clouded with lust as she looks down at me, one hand squeezing my dick. My breath freezes in my lungs as she lifts up slightly to position herself over me.

And without giving pause or thought to her actions, while holding my eyes hostage upon her, she sinks slowly onto me. I watch, mesmerized, as I disappear into her inch by inch, and there's something almost poetic about it. While it's an erotic sight, it's also beautiful to me.

And Jesus fuck… the feeling. It's exquisite and torturous. I want to stop her. I want to propel her along.

When she bottoms out on me with a soft grunt of satisfaction, my hands go to her hips and I hold her firmly in place. Jane's head tilts as she looks at me curiously, her lips tipping into a gentle smile.

"Go slow," I tell her, because I don't want to lose control. Jane has the power to make me go out of my mind with desire and need, and I don't want to risk hurting her.

"Okay," she whispers, rotating her hips a little. That little sensation is almost too much, so I bite down hard into my lower lip and loosen my grip so she can move some more.

I resolve to myself I won't come until Jane does, and then after I come, I'll make her come again. But I need her to ride me slowly because I need to savor every second of this. It may be my one and only time with Jane because I know my conscience will get the better of me come tomorrow morning.

CHAPTER 17

JANE

I STARE DOWN at Kyle, his jaw tight but his eyes burning as if possessed by a fever. His entire body is coiled with tension as I sit atop him.

Full of him.

So damn full of him, and it feels amazing.

I'm not the most experienced girl when it comes to this, but I've had a healthy sex life and I'm an adventurous spirit. Kyle commanded me on top, and I wasn't about to back down from that challenge. But as I look down at him, I can see that yes... he's coiled with sexual frustration and the need for release, but he's also worried. I can see that clearly in his eyes, and I have to wonder why that is.

I mean, Kyle definitely knows his way around a woman's body, but I also sense that he's very lost right now and unsure of himself. Since I know that has nothing to do with sex since he's quite good at it so far, that must mean it has to do with me. He must be worried for me, or afraid of me.

This makes me sad.

It also makes me determined.

When I feel Kyle's grip relax against my hips, I press my hands to his stomach for leverage and push slowly upward to test his reaction. Kyle's jaw goes tighter and his eyes burn hotter.

When I reach the end of his length, I sink back down onto him, relishing the glide of his shaft within me and the pleasure it produces. When I press my pelvis back against his, a tiny shudder courses through me. Kyle lets out a soft hiss of breath.

"Like that?" I ask him in a low murmur. He asked me to go slowly, so that's what I'll give him.

"Yeah," he says in a hoarse voice. "Just like that."

I nod and start to rise again, but I falter when he slides one hand from my hip to where we are joined together. I watch almost hypnotized as his hand splays and he touches his fingertips to my lower belly. He moves his thumb inward and presses it against my clit, causing a tremor to race through me. I watch and wait for him to do something, but he doesn't.

My eyes slide to his, and he's smiling at me in amusement. "Go on, Jane. Fuck me."

I don't question him, but my body immediately rises. Kyle's hand moves with me so his thumb stays on my clit, and oh wow... oh, damn. I can feel the friction of his dick to my clit as Kyle presses down, and my eyes practically roll in my head. I lose track of what I'm doing, so infatuated with this new sensation that I start pushing down again before I get too far.

And oh my God... that feels even better.

"Kyle," I whisper with my eyes squeezed shut as I bottom out on him again. "I can't... when you do that... I can't..."

"Can't what?" he murmurs as his other hand, which is still on my hip, urges me upward again. My leg muscles cooperate and I glide up his shaft, but that pressure he keeps on my clit muddles my head. It's intense and overwhelming, and I know it won't take long for me to come.

My eyes fly open as I stare down at him. "I can't concentrate."

"Don't want you to," he says in a low voice. His hand on my hip guides me back down again. "I told you I want you to come on my dick, so that's what you're going to do. I'm just helping you along."

Oh, God.

Those words.

Those dirty, filthy words that have never been spoken to me before by a man and which would normally cause my nose to crinkle in distaste. But coming from Kyle, in this moment, while he's doing to me what he's doing...

My blood is racing and my clit is actually pulsing with agonized pleasure as he holds his thumb there to keep the friction going with my movements.

Kyle speaks very clearly, still with amusement

though. "Jane… baby… ride my cock and get yourself off. I want to watch you come."

"Oh, God," I moan as I practically fall back down on him again. The force causes him to go deep inside. His thumb presses tighter to me and stars start winking in my peripheral vision.

My entire body is as coiled as I noted his was a few moments ago, and I think I might go crazy if I can't release this tension. Suddenly, I become obsessed with having this orgasm, knowing it's going to blow me wide apart, and needing to give that to Kyle because that's what he asked for.

In the dirtiest of ways possible, he told me he wants me to come on his dick, and even as my face flames red, I start to move a little faster. I move up and down, my breath now coming in short, staccato bursts. I feel that lovely cramping feeling from deep inside as I coil tighter and tighter. I move faster, using Kyle's thumb and dick to create constant friction, and I can't even think about his pleasure right now. All I want is to give him exactly what he asked for.

"So fucking beautiful," Kyle murmurs, and I make the mistake of opening my eyes. Kyle's gaze is pinned to where we are joined, watching his thumb and his dick claim me. He looks rapturous, like he's never seen something like this before. Like I'm a mystery and a miracle all at the same time.

And I explode.

Just like that... because of the way Kyle is looking at me, I just burst apart.

I give out a cry that sounds almost inhuman and my entire body bucks from the pleasure as it ripples outward, tearing me to pieces. I fall unceremoniously back down onto him, his dick pressing in further than ever, but I'm almost incoherent as I'm overwhelmed with the force of my orgasm.

"Just fucking beautiful," Kyle mutters, and then he's rolling me to my back. I'm as limp as a rag doll, which means I'm pliant, and Kyle doesn't waste any time.

One hand goes under the back of my leg and he lifts it up. The other hand plants down hard into the mattress near my ribs to hold himself steady, and then he starts to move.

Hard.

And fast.

And rough.

I grunt when he thrusts in deep. While he doesn't stop moving, he does slow down. "You okay?"

I nod my head quickly. "Yeah."

"Too hard?"

I shake my head even quicker. "No. I liked it."

And I'm not sure if those were the right words or not, but Kyle's eyes flash in triumph. He raises my leg even higher, props it on his shoulder, and well... damn... didn't know I was that limber.

That position opens me wider and allows Kyle to

thrust deeper. He picks up the pace again and starts to really fuck me hard.

My hands go to his chest, not to help him in any fashion but to just feel him. I purposefully keep my eyes averted from the leering skull tattoo and the words of warning that I should fear this man. Instead, I watch his face carefully, his eyes almost completely fogged over with lust and passion as he drives into me. Sweat beads at his temples and he grits his teeth as harsh bursts of breath blow through them. He's almost in a frenzy, and every time he thrusts into me, I can feel another orgasm starting to build bigger. Every time he hits me deep, an animal sound of desperation rumbles out of my mouth.

I have never, ever been taken like this before. My entire body right now is completely enslaved to him, not only by his strength, but also by the way he's making me feel. It's not just the feel of him inside of me, but by how much he needs me in this way.

I watch in fascination, turned completely on, when Kyle pushes up to his knees, wrapping an arm around my leg to hold it tight to his shoulder, and then his other under my ass to lift me up so I can meet his thrusts. He drives into me over and over again. I groan and writhe and when my orgasm can't coil inward any further, when it becomes so painful for me to hold it off, tears start leaking out of my eyes.

Kyle doesn't see this as his own are closed and he's practically hurling himself into my body. His fingers are digging down into my thigh and ass, and I can tell he's completely lost to sensation right now.

He might be the most beautiful thing I've ever seen in this world. Right now, he's stripped down to his rawest form, and this is the closest I've ever been to the true essence of Kyle Harding.

"Jane," Kyle rasps out, almost as if he's in pain.

I can't even answer because he surges into me one last time as he throws his head back and roars out his release. It's spellbinding and erotic, the way he falls prey to pleasure, and it makes my own orgasm fire off.

"Ohhh," I cry out as I buck from the initial burst of pleasure. Kyle's head comes down and his eyes snap to me. They're still fogged, but they watch me in fascination as I tremble from the remains of another climax, my inside walls squeezing against his dick.

Kyle's fingers relax and he drops my leg down to the mattress before coming down to lay on top of me. He keeps his weight off by digging his elbows into the mattress, but he moves his face closer to mine.

"Are you alright?" he asks, his eyes solemn in their need for this information. My heart squeezes as it doesn't take a rocket scientist to understand he's worried he hurt me. I mean, he was rough and that was hard, but holy hell... that was the best I've ever had.

Who knew?

I raise a hand, placing my palm to his cheek. He sucks in a soft breath and leans slightly into my touch even though his gaze is pinned on me as he awaits my answer.

"I'm more than alright," I tell him with a reassuring smile. "I mean, I came twice, so yeah... I'm totally alright."

"You'd tell me if I hurt you, right?" he presses.

I bring my other hand to his opposite cheek, pulling him down to me. I place a light kiss on his lips. "I'd absolutely tell you if you hurt me, but Kyle... I loved that. That was amazing."

He lets out a relieved sigh and smiles back at me, and I'm glad to see that it's genuine. "Good. I just... I'm sorry if it was too rough."

"It wasn't."

Kyle's eyes hold mine for a moment, then he gives a little nod. "Okay."

I expect him to settle down for some post-sex cuddling, but instead, he pulls out of me slowly, which causes an embarrassing moan from me. Kyle doesn't seem to notice as he rolls right off the bed and walks out of my room. I hear the bathroom door close a few seconds later.

Rolling to my side, I curl an arm under my head and wait for him to come back. I assume he's coming back as I don't think he'd walk home naked.

Less than a minute later, Kyle's back in my bedroom. He walks straight to the bed, his face impassive. I push up to one elbow, aware and self-conscious that we're both naked now that the heat of passion has cooled. His eyes slide to my breasts for a brief moment before returning back to me. He sits on the edge of the bed, completely unfazed by his nakedness, and says, "We need to talk."

I let out a groan of frustration and sit up further. "Let me guess… this is the point where you tell me this was wrong, you shouldn't have crossed that line, and then you'll give me the let's-be-friends line again, right?"

"Wrong," he says quietly, and that gives me pause. His voice gets a little frostier though. "I did cross a line I didn't mean to, but I can't find it within me to be sorry."

"Oh," I say, completely confused by this. "Then what do we need to talk about?"

Kyle stares at me a long moment. I can see whatever he's getting ready to tell me is going to take some courage on his part.

I sit up straight and look at him with panicked eyes. "Oh, God… was I bad? And that's why you don't want to see me again?"

"Jane—"

I flop back down to the mattress and drape my arm over my eyes to shut the sight of him out. "Oh, this is humiliating. I just—"

"Jane—"

I remove my arm from my eyes just as suddenly and plead with him. "You just need to go, Kyle. We don't need to have that talk. I get it."

"Jane," Kyle snaps at me harshly, and I jerk from the tone of his voice. But then his hand reaches out and he slowly strokes my collarbone. He watches his hand draw a light pattern on my skin for a minute before looking up at me. "You were amazing. That... what we just did... was beyond amazing."

Pure, unfiltered joy pulses through me, and I grin at him impishly. "So we'll have sex again?"

"Maybe," he says slowly, and I deflate.

"Maybe?"

"Hence the reason we need to talk," he says pointedly.

"Okay," I say hesitantly, and I feel completely vulnerable. I sit up against the pillow but reach out to the edge of the comforter, pulling it over to cover as much of my body as possible.

But Kyle covers my hand with his and stops my movement. "Don't."

"Don't?"

"Don't cover yourself around me," he says gruffly as he holds my gaze. "Just... let me look at you as much as I can, okay?"

"So," I say slowly as I release my hold from the blanket. "You just want me to walk around naked all the time?"

"If there was a God," he mutters as his eyes slide down to my breasts for a moment. When he looks back up at me, he says, "I just mean don't hide yourself from me. You're beautiful like this. When we're together, don't hide it."

"When we're together," I repeat. "So this wasn't a one-time only thing?"

Kyle takes a deep breath and rubs his palm over the back of his neck, his eyes scrunching a bit in what looks like guilt, but I can't be sure. He focuses back on me and says, "Jane… I'm not going to stay here forever. In fact, I'll probably be heading out in a few months."

"Where will you go?" I ask softly.

"I have no clue yet," he tells me bluntly. "But when I do, it will be alone."

After what we just shared, after he called me beautiful, and after he said what we had was amazing… well, I'll have to admit this is a crushing statement to hear. I mean, it's not like I'm already planning my life with him, but his words are clear in their meaning that I am nothing more to him than a temporary measure.

A diversion, I guess, to while away his time.

"I get it," I say softly but with acceptance. "This is just a fling, so to speak."

"Label it how you want," he says gently, but there is no mistaking his commitment to what he's saying. "But you need to know I'm leaving soon and, because of that, this has an expiration date on it. If that's not something you want to get tangled up in, I'd understand that."

I hate this conversation, but I ask for clarification, "So we'll have a sexual relationship with an expiration date? I think what you're saying is that you're afraid my heart will get tied up in this, so you want to prepare me right off the bat that you've got nothing to give in that department, right?"

"Pretty much," he says bluntly, but then tempers it with, "But we're friends, Jane. That hasn't changed."

"Oh, you mean the type of friends who won't stay in contact once you leave, right?" My sarcasm is unmistakable.

Kyle doesn't respond, just stares at me guardedly. Yes, the blush of pleasure is gone and Kyle is down to business. Which means I need to pull my heart out of the equation right now. I have to give him some small measure of credit... at least he is trying to prevent me from getting hurt.

And I know Kyle could totally hurt me down the road.

For that reason, I need to use caution and careful, reasoned thought.

"Let me think about it," I tell him with truthful candor. "This is a lot for me to consider."

He blinks slowly as he takes in my words, and I can tell he didn't expect that. In fact, I can tell he fully expected me to open my arms to him and tell him I'm fine with him having sex with me for the next few months, then we'd both sort of ignore the fact I was falling hard for him. We both know that's probably how he thought it would go down because, let's face it... I'm the one who has pursued him from the start.

But I'm really not sure I can handle the limits he's put in place. While I've acted quite impulsively when it has come to Kyle, I need to heed his warning and think very hard about what it would mean to be involved with him and the boundaries he's laying down. It's not going to be an easy decision to make, and I'm going to carefully guard my heart throughout all of this.

CHAPTER 18

KYLE

I WALK INTO The Lobster Cage, and my eyes take a few moments to adjust to the dimness. There aren't any windows in this place; half the lights are burned out and the ones that are lit are on their last leg. The best illumination comes from the handful of neon beer signs hanging on the walls around the joint, casting glowing patches of red and blue depending on the brand of beer they advertise.

It's starting to get crowded as The Lobster Cage actually serves decent bar food. The single fisherman will eat here while pounding a few beers after a hard day's work.

That's why I'm here actually.

To get a semi-decent meal and pound a few beers.

Or forty.

It's been three days since I walked out of Jane's house and she said she'd think about what type of relationship she could handle with me. In hindsight, I'm probably a stupid motherfucker for even saying anything. What we had that night... what we did together... it was some

179

amazing shit unlike anything I've had before. I'm pretty sure it was the same for her. If I'd have kept my mouth shut, I'd probably be with her right now instead of in this dingy bar with twenty men who smell like salt and fish.

I take an empty barstool, and Gus meanders over to me.

"Haven't seen you around in a while," he says conversationally.

I don't respond to his observation because I'm not feeling conversational. "I'll take a draft beer and some nachos."

He grunts in acknowledgment, not in the slightest put out by my brush-off. He's used to dealing with all types of people, including the surly, anti-social types. He quietly pours my beer and sets it in front of me, then heads off to put my order into the back kitchen where I think his wife works the grill.

I watch the muted TV above the bar while I wait for my food. It's a baseball game, which isn't really my sport, but I watch it in silence and sip at my beer.

The nachos come and they're not bad. Much better than the plain ham sandwiches I'd been having. I have a second beer with my meal.

Then I have a third. And a fourth. And a fifth.

By the sixth, Gus takes my keys and I know I'm walking home, but that's fine by me. It just means I can add shots of bourbon with my beers. I'm feeling lose, relaxed, and completely not on edge when I think about Jane. In fact, one could say that the alcohol is sort of numbing the feelings of desperation that have been slowly mounting the past three days of not hearing from or seeing her. I mean, forget about the sex. I'm a little put out that I just haven't seen her, and that's been pissing me off.

I mean, really… what more does she want? I purposely did outside work the last three days around the cottage and lighthouse, giving her ample opportunity to see me and come talk. Yet not a peep out of her. Tonight, I realized I probably had my answer from her.

She wasn't going to accept my conditions on a relationship, and frankly, I can't blame her.

I hold my hand up to get Gus's attention. When he looks at me, I say, "Just keep them coming all night."

Gus gives a wry smile and nods, then turns his attention back to the customer he'd been talking to.

I stare at my beer, taking periodic sips and wondering when in the hell I'll be able to get out of Misty Harbor. Not for a few months as the trial wouldn't start until then, and I consider perhaps asking Joe to move me earlier.

Maybe to Puerto Rico or something.

"Here you go," I hear a female voice say, and another draft beer slides into my view. I look up and see Jane's friend, Miranda, standing on the other side of the bar. "Gus said you wanted to keep them coming, so here's your next one."

"Thanks," I mutter. My tongue feels like it's glued to the top of my mouth. I also note that unless I squint, there are actually two Mirandas in front of me, and because I don't think she has a twin, I know I'm on my way to getting stinking ass drunk.

"Why are you in here all by yourself getting shit-faced?" she asks as she rests her forearms on the bar and leans in toward me. She's grinning and cracking bubble gum.

I don't want to talk to her, and yet I can't seem to stop myself. "Your friend… Jane…"

She grins even bigger, chews her gum with exaggeration, and waits me out. She makes me deliver more information.

I give a careless wave of my hand toward the direction I suspect is Jane's house, but I'm not sure. "She's trying to decide if she wants to have a sexual fling with me or not."

Miranda raises an eyebrow, but she's still amused. This means she knows what happened between Jane and me. It also means she knows Jane hasn't given me her decision, and by that inaction, I'm choosing to believe I know what her decision is. So I just bend my head over the bar and sullenly stare into my beer.

"She doesn't know what to do," Miranda offers me, and my head snaps up. A rush of dizziness hits me, and my hands slap to the bar to keep my balance on the stool.

"She tell you that?" I ask... well, maybe slur. I hope to God I remember this conversation tomorrow.

"Well, of course she told me that," Miranda says, then blows a bubble with her gum. I watch as she sucks it back in and says, "She tells me everything."

"Everything?"

Miranda leans in closer to me and nods her head. "Everything."

My mind races. She clearly knows I've put out some boundaries with Jane, but does she know about that amazing, hot, beautiful, and mind-blowing sex we had? And if she does, does that help or hurt me? Would Miranda help Jane make the decision to stick with me while I'm here?

You're such a selfish fuck, my conscience screams at me. Because I'm trying to be a good guy where Jane is concerned, and make sure that I do everything in my power not to hurt her, I bend my head back over my beer and decide to ignore Miranda. It's not going to do any good to get her involved, and besides that... I'm drunk. I have no business doing anything but getting my ass home and into bed.

Except, I do need to finish this beer.

"Want my advice?" Miranda asks.

"Nope," I say without looking up at her, because if she gives me that knowing smirk like she's privy to Jane's innermost secrets, I might continue to engage her.

"Suit yourself," she says as she pushes away from the bar. "I'll keep an eye on your beer."

I watch her walk away, telling myself not to call her back so I can pick her brain about Jane. She heads out from behind the bar and starts clearing a table, and I turn back to my mug, taking a huge sip. Yeah… I think I need Joe to get me out of here. My testimony is important enough and my acts of service for my government should easily get me relocated. I'll call him in the morning, he'll get me transferred somewhere far away, and I can put Jane Cresson out of my mind.

Someone bumps into me before I feel them slide into an empty stool on my right. I don't bother to look, preferring instead to finish off my beer and perhaps order another, but my hand freezes halfway to my mug when I hear Jane say very softly, "Hey, Kyle."

Her voice is gentle and her eyes are knowing. I hate she's seeing me like this. This makes me pissy. "What do you want?"

She nods her head slightly, as if she's not surprised by my attitude. But then, she nudges my shoulder with her own and says, "You're supposed to say, 'Of all the gin joints in all the towns in all the world, she walks into mine'."

I blink at her, my brain feeling like sludge. "What?"

"*Casablanca*," she murmurs. "1942."

"Never saw it," I mutter and pick my beer up.

It's stopped by her hand on my wrist with a gentle

pressure. I turn to look at her, and she leans in to whisper in a voice so low I can barely hear her, "Come on. Why don't you let me take you home? You've had enough to drink."

"Why are you whispering?" I ask her with narrowed eyes.

She pulls back from me quickly, dropping her hand from my wrist. "I don't know. I just didn't want you to make a scene."

"A scene?" I ask, confused. "Why would I do that?"

"Well, you're drunk," she points out. "And Miranda called me when she first came on shift to tell me you were here and drunk, and figured you could use a lift home."

"Yes, I am drunk, but I'm sure I can walk out of here just fine without falling on my ass," I tell her, pleased that actually came out sounding semi-coherent. "And I can walk home just fine too, so no worries I'd 'cause a scene'."

"I'm not worried about *that* type of scene," she says in exasperation. "I didn't know if you'd be pissed I came or that I asked you to leave."

I give her a sardonic smile and lean toward her. "Well, you don't have to worry. I'm not pissed you asked me to leave."

She gives me a relieved look. "Alright. Then let's go."

"Not leaving either," I tell her adamantly. "I'm enjoying myself right here."

"Kyle," she says hesitantly. "Let me take you home, get you to bed. Sleep it off, and then we can talk about this tomorrow."

Oh, now she wants to talk?

"Nothing to talk about," I say stubbornly, ignoring the small cramp in my chest when I see her face fall in disappointment.

"There's not?" she asks softly.

"Nope. Nothing to talk about at all," I confirm, ignoring the cramp as it gets more painful. I know I'm being a dick, but really… it's best to cut this off right here and right now. Jane will never be able to handle all the ways in which I can break her. I don't consider for a second that she could break me.

Liar.

Jane's eyes search mine, trying to reveal my true feelings. I hold her gaze and remain silent.

Her shoulders slump and she gives a small nod before sliding off the stool. "Alright. Take care, Kyle."

My chest feels like it's caving inward as I watch her walk away from me. She heads over to Miranda, who is standing near the door, and they talk quietly. Miranda looks over at me once and glares, then turns back to whatever Jane is telling her.

A hand slides up my spine, startling me, and fingers curve around the back of my neck. Lips touch my ear and a sexy voice says, "Kyle… baby. It's been a long time since you've been in. Want to have a little fun tonight?"

Leaning to the right to pull away from her, I give her a brush-off. "Not interested, Barb."

She pouts at me and hops on the barstool Jane had vacated, putting her hand on my thigh and sliding it upward to my crotch. "Come on, sugar. You know I got what you want."

My hand clamps on her wrist, stops its ascent up my leg, and my gaze cuts over her shoulder to Jane. And fuck... she's staring right at us, eyes wide and face pale. Then she shoots me that look... the one that says I'm an unbelievable asshole, right before she turns around and jets out the door.

"Christ," I mutter as I throw Barb's hand off me and lurch off the barstool. I almost career into a small table where two patrons sit closely together, but gain my balance for a fraction of a second before I stumble toward the door.

Miranda meets me there, and I growl at her. "Don't even think about trying to stop me."

"Wouldn't dream of it," she says with a wink as she opens the door for me. She gives me a hearty pat on my shoulder before shoving me forward. "Go get her, tiger."

Fuck, I'm drunk. I practically fall through the door, immediately going down to one knee on the concrete, which hurts like a son of a bitch. I manage to catch a glimpse of Jane as she walks quickly toward her car.

"Jane," I call out to her as I push myself up. "Wait."

She walks faster so I take off after her, intent on

running her down.

Except... I'm really fucking drunk. I stumble and crash right back down to the sidewalk again.

"Fuck," I yell at the top of my lungs as I roll to my back and stare at the sky and stars above me. It might be my imagination, but I think the moon is mocking me.

And then Jane's face is pushing into my field of view above me. She looks down at me with guarded concern.

She came back for me.

"Are you alright?" she asks hesitantly, crossing her arms protectively over her chest.

"Yeah, I'm fine," I assure her as I roll to my side.

"Well, okay... good," she says as she turns away and starts walking back to her car.

"Wait," I call out, hoping my voice doesn't sound as pathetic as I feel. She stops, and I manage to get up on one knee. "Jane... I could actually use a little help."

Slowly, she turns to face me, her face closed off and filled with distaste.

"I'm sorry," I tell her... well, slur. What can I say? I'm drunk. "But I'd gladly take that ride to my house now if you still wouldn't mind."

She takes a few steps back toward me. "I'm sure Barb would give you a lift."

"I don't want Barb to give me a lift," I grit out as I stand up. I sway to the left, then to the right, and finally seem to steady myself for a bit. "I want *you* to take me home."

never once would have thought Kyle was the snuggling type. Even after we'd had sex the other night, I never expected him to get back into bed and cuddle with me.

I knew he wasn't that type of man.

Or perhaps I'm wrong about that.

Regardless, I'm content to lay here for just a few moments and feel what it's like to be wrapped up securely in his arms.

Eventually, though, my need to pee outweighs my desire to cuddle with Kyle, so I attempt to break free of his hold. This takes some doing and isn't easy, as he's still clearly passed out and not helping matters. Somehow, I manage to get his arm around me to loosen and I'm able to slither out. I roll off the bed and look down at him sleeping. His face is so peaceful looking, so anti-Kyle, that I have to just watch him for a bit, which I'm sure isn't as creepy as it sounds.

But then my bladder calls out to me, so I walk quietly down the hallway to his little bathroom where I do my business. I have no intention of going back into Kyle's room because I had not intended to sleep in the bed with him last night. However, once I got him in the house and managed to get him into his bedroom, he had fallen backward on his mattress and passed out cold. He had mumbled something in the car when I woke him up about "hoping he didn't get sick," and that worried me enough that I felt compelled to stay and make sure he was okay. I couldn't handle the thought of him drowning in his own vomit or something, so I reasoned to myself that I was being a good neighbor by lying on the bed next to him in case he needed help.

I certainly hadn't intended to fall asleep.

Not bemoaning that fact either, but there's no reason to stay now. Kyle is fine, and there's really nothing that needs to be said. He made that clear last night at the bar. The icing on top was Barb Privett coming onto him—in a very familiar way that made it clear she had carnal knowledge of Kyle. That thought right there causes acid to surge in my stomach, and I walk quickly through his house to the front door. There's not a doubt in my mind that had I not showed up last night, Kyle would have gone home with her. In fact, I'm not really sure why he came after me, because he'd told me not two minutes before that there was nothing to talk about between the two of us.

Yes, it's best I get home and leave Kyle far behind.

Too much trouble.

Too much drama.

Not enough of the real Kyle to keep me interested.

♦

I'M STARTLED SO much by the banging sound that my paintbrush slips a little in my hand, but not enough to ruin the stroke. I tilt my head to listen. It seems to be coming from my porch. It's definitely not a knocking on my door, but something is definitely striking wood.

Bang, bang, bang.

"What the hell?" I mutter as I stand up from my stool and arch my back to loosen it up. I've been sitting in front of my easel for the last three hours—ever since I left Kyle's house—and my muscles are screaming at me.

I follow the banging sound, which leads me from my back room/studio, through the living room, and to the front door. I open it up and see Kyle kneeling on the first porch step closest to the ground while he bangs a nail into the top step, which he's replaced with a new board.

I step out and watch dumbfounded as he pulls a nail he's holding in between his lips and hammers it in.

Three strikes. *Bang, bang, bang.*

"What are you doing?" I ask, and his head slowly rises.

He pulls the last nail out of his mouth. "Penance."

"Penance?" I say with a furrowed brow.

"Yeah, for getting drunk and acting like an ass last night," he says sheepishly. "And I noticed the top step was weak the other day, so thought I'd replace it for you."

"So fixing my step is penance?"

"No, hammering nails when my head is already pounding is the penance part," he corrects me, and then to prove his point, he drives in the last nail while grimacing the entire time.

"Did you take any aspirin?" I ask.

He stands up and shakes his head. "Nope. Got up,

showered, and went straight to the hardware store to get the materials to fix your step."

I shoot him an exasperated look and jerk my head toward the door. "Well, come on inside. I've got some aspirin, and I'll cook you breakfast too."

I expect him to decline because Kyle never seems to want to accept anything from me, but to my surprise, he merely climbs the porch steps and says, "Thanks."

Kyle sits down at my kitchen table while I pull eggs and bacon out of my fridge. It's closer to lunch than breakfast, but this is an easy, fast meal.

"I've got aspirin in the medicine cabinet if you want some," I tell him as I put the pan on the stove and turn the heat on.

"I'm good," he says, and I can feel his eyes on my back as I lay slices of bacon in the pan.

While they start to sizzle, I pull some orange juice from the fridge, a glass from the cabinet, and take them to the table to set down in front of Kyle. As I turn back to the stove, Kyle grabs my wrist, halting my momentum.

I look at him questioningly and he merely nods to the chair. "Let's talk."

"I've got to cook breakfast," I say, suddenly not wanting to have a talk with him. He sounds far too serious at this moment.

"It won't take long," he says solemnly.

Hmmm. A quick brush-off. Quick is better than drawn

out.

I step to the stove after tugging my wrist away from Kyle and turn the burner off. I then pull out the chair adjacent to Kyle and sit down. Clasping my hands, I place them on the table and give him a polite smile.

He doesn't smile back, but I'm stunned when he says, "I'm sorry."

Tilting my head to the side, I ask, "For what?"

Because I truly have no idea what he's apologizing for. I'm thinking there are several things, but I couldn't prioritize them.

"For last night," he says softly. "For getting drunk and telling you there was nothing to talk about. That wasn't true. I only did it because I was frustrated and pissed off I hadn't seen you in a few days."

My heart swells a bit, feeling warm and bubbly.

"Pissed off you hadn't seen me?" I shamelessly fish for a compliment.

He gives me a pained smile, dropping his eyes to the table briefly. When he looks back up, I've never seen such a clearly genuine look in his eyes. "Jane... I like you, and, apparently, I really like being around you. So yeah... I was a little pissed you were absent for so long, when prior to that you'd been all up in my business constantly."

I try not to beam in pride that he liked me being so pushy, so I merely nod in understanding.

"But things changed the other night," he adds on.

"When we had sex?" I ask to clarify.

He nods stiffly. "We crossed a line that changed things. If I was a stronger man, I could have resisted you, but now that I've had a taste of you, I can't regret what I did."

I have no clue what any of that means, so I hold my tongue, figuring he'll get to his point.

Kyle swallows hard, and I know whatever is coming next is hard for him to say. "I still stand by what I told you that night. If we continue, it has to be with the knowledge that I'll be leaving and this will eventually end."

That happy, warm, bubbly feeling falls completely flat.

"But," he says softly. "I also have to let you know that I'm a selfish motherfucker, and I really am hoping you'll accept what little I can offer you. I'm leaving, but I'd really like to spend my days here with you as much as possible. So I'm not sure if you've made your decision, but I wanted to let you know that I do care what your decision is. I didn't want you to think after last night... what you saw in the bar... that I didn't want you, or didn't care what you decided to do."

It's at this point I realize I've been holding my breath, and it comes out in one forcefully long exhale. He watches me carefully, and I note his shoulders are stiff with tension. I know my decision is important to him. This makes my heart start to warm back up because that is a big admission from a man who pretty much told me the other day that it was "his way or the highway."

And that's not going to quite work for me, so I have a counter proposal.

"I accept your boundaries," I tell him, and there's immense satisfaction that courses through me when I see his shoulders drop with relief. "But with a caveat."

Kyle's eyebrows draw inward in consternation. "What caveat?"

"I'm good with us moving forward. We'll see each other, sleep together, whatever you want to do to spend time with me. And I promise I'll have no expectations of anything from you when you leave."

His eyes narrow dubiously. "But?"

"But you have to promise that you won't have any expectations that you'll actually leave as you said you're going to. I think you need to leave open the possibility that you might want to stay."

Kyle's eyes immediately darken with obvious pain. It's right there... clearly written on his face. I've just asked him to do the most impossible thing in the world, and I know he believes that right down to the very fiber of his being. For whatever reason, Kyle deeply believes he has no choice but to leave, and this confuses me, because there's always a choice.

But rather than deny my request, he gives me a small smile and lies right to my face. "Okay... I'll keep the possibility open."

CHAPTER 20

KYLE

I HAVE NO clue if Jane believes what I just told her, but her expression is sweet and accepting. It's all the affirmation I need because I want to seal this sort of deal we just made in the only way I know how. I push out of my chair and haul Jane out of hers, sweeping her up into my arms. She huffs out in surprise, but her arms immediately wrap around my neck as I start heading toward the hallway that leads to her bedroom.

I know I should be overwhelmed with guilt because I'm asking a lot of Jane and not giving anything in return, but fuck if I can muster up an ounce. It was no lie when I told her I was a selfish motherfucker. At least I feel some redemption about the fact I'm being up front and honest with her that I'm leaving.

Of course, that redemption is completely negated because I did just lie to her when I told her I'd keep an open mind about staying. That's just not an option, even if I wanted to. When I leave, I'm heading straight for a criminal trial that will last weeks. I'll probably be sequestered for safety purposes, and if all is right in my world, we'll ultimately get convictions on all the defendants. After that, I'll be taking the tiny scraps left of my life and the ghost of my former self, and I'll try to figure out how to live again. How to take a fresh start and try to make something of it.

Fresh start.

Funny I'd even think I'd deserve something like that after the things I've done.

I enter Jane's room with her clinging tightly to me, seemingly okay with me just dragging her back here like a caveman. I take a moment to actually look around, something I didn't do the other night when I fucked her, and a smile tugs at my lips. I hadn't noticed before, but in the bright light of day, her walls are a buttery yellow and white lacy curtains grace her window. Her bed is old-fashioned looking, made of brass and covered with a multitude of poofy pillows and a flower-embroidered spread.

It's so Jane and I can't wait to lay her—throw her— on that perfectly made bed and mess it up. Part of me wonders if I'm a sick bastard for that... for wanting to dirty her up a bit.

Tilting my face so I can look at Jane, I find her eyes shining with equal parts of hope and determination that I said I'd keep an open mind about staying, but, more to my satisfaction, they're shimmering with desire. That I can deal with.

With great restraint and counter to original plans, I

lower her slowly to the floor so she gets her footing. Her hands come to my chest, fingertips pressing in slightly. She's so damn gorgeous and earnest in her desires that I know I'm not worthy, but she is also standing before me because she wants to be here.

"You do want this, right?" I press her, because while her eyes may tell one story, I know the heart can be trickier.

Jane slides her hands up my chest and clasps them behind my neck. She steps in closer to me and tilts her head back a bit. "Kyle… I want this. I know and understand your terms. I'm a grown woman and I know the risks. So yes, I want this, but what I also want is for you to accept that so we don't have to have this conversation each time. Frankly, it's a downer."

Relief courses through me, along with a tremor of amusement. I can't help but chuckle. "A downer, huh?"

She grins and nods. "Total downer."

I bend in and brush my lips against her jaw. "Let's see if I can rectify that, okay?"

Jane presses in closer and whispers. "Sounds like a fantastic plan. I've never had sex like this in the middle of the day and so spontaneously."

I jolt because this surprises me. While on one hand Jane is definitely a wholesome type of girl, I personally know she's got spunk and adventure within.

She just shrugs at me with a sheepish grin. "What can I say? Craig wasn't all that creative."

I wince, because I don't want to think about her with another guy. In fact, I want to obliterate that douchebag from her memory, and it's time to start that process.

My hands come up to frame her face, and I bring my mouth down to hers. She's waiting for me, open and accepting, and the minute our tongues touch each other, every cell in my body becomes electrified. It's a sensation I've never experienced before. I've fucked a lot of sexy women. Done a lot of dirty fucking. Had women bend over backward to please me.

But never has one touched me like this on a cellular level. Only Jane has managed to make me feel something so unique and mysterious that I almost doubt what I'm feeling in this moment. I deepen the kiss. The tingles of need sweeping through my body magnify, and yes… it's mysterious, but it's real.

She's more real than anything I've ever known before.

"Yoooo-hoooo," I hear a woman's voice calling out from Jane's living room, and my body freezes. A slight moan of disappointment slides from Jane's mouth into mine before I break the kiss.

Jane lets her head fall forward onto my chest, only to lift it back up and bang it softly there a few times in frustration. My hand automatically curls around the back of her neck, and I give her a squeeze of understanding.

"Now that's a downer," she mutters, then looks up to me with apologetic eyes and explains, "You're about to meet my mother."

"Fuck," I mutter back, then look hopefully over her shoulder at the frilly white curtains. "Can I sneak out the window?"

She snickers and takes my hand. "You're funny."

"Wasn't being funny," I tell her truthfully as she leads me out of her bedroom. With my free hand, I adjust myself down below and hope her mother maintains eye contact with me.

Jane holds my hand all the way into the living room and doesn't release it when she says, "Mom... what are you doing here?"

Her mom is standing just inside the doorway, holding a large grocery bag in one arm. A set of keys is dangling from her other hand. With wide eyes, she stares at me but addresses Jane, "Oh, dear Lord... I guess I should have knocked, huh?"

Jane squeezes my hand. "Mom... you remember Kyle, right?"

"He took you to dinner a while back," her mom says as she nods at me with a smile.

A big, smug, knowing but happy smile.

Yes, she looks oddly pleased that her daughter is leading me out of her bedroom. In fact, I'd say she was actually basking in that knowledge, which is totally fucking weird in my book. If her mom really knew who I was deep down, she'd be screaming at her daughter to run in the opposite direction.

Jane makes a disapproving sound in her throat, and I look down at her. She's shaking her head at her mom and has a chastising look on her face. A teacher's look. I bet many a student has cowered from that look from Miss Cresson.

"Mom," Jane says with censure. "Kyle was fixing that rotted windowsill in my bedroom."

Her mom doesn't move, but her smile gets bigger… more knowing. She doesn't buy Jane's lie at all.

"Surely you saw his tool box out there on the porch," Jane points out, and I have to marvel at her quick thinking.

Jane's mom raises her eyebrows and smirks at her daughter. It's clear she's still not buying it. To prove that, she says, "Yes… odd place to have a tool box if you're fixing something inside."

I duck my head and hide my smile. I see where Jane gets her snark and quick wit.

Jane sighs in capitulation, and her mom moves across the living room, stalking toward us like we're prey. She shoves the grocery bag at Jane and sticks her hand out to me. "Hi, Kyle. It's nice to officially meet you. I'm Meredith Cresson."

In addition to her sass, Jane clearly got her looks from her mom. Meredith has the same golden hair and meadow-green eyes, and she is strikingly beautiful like her daughter. I take her hand and shake it. "Nice to meet you."

She gives me a squeeze and a wink. "I'm so glad to see Jane getting back into the dating world."

"Mom," Jane says on almost a whine as she shifts the grocery bag in her hand. "Kyle and I aren't—"

"She's been living like a monk, I tell you," Meredith says with relish, and I can tell she's taking some pleasure out of embarrassing her daughter.

Jane tries in vain to set her mom straight. "We're not—"

Meredith ignores her and tugs on my hand, leading me toward the kitchen. "Kyle... she needs to get out more. Experience new things. All she does is teach her kids and paint, not that that's bad, you know, but she needs more, right?"

"Mom," Jane says in exasperation as she follows us. "Please don't—"

"Now, Kyle," Meredith says as she pushes me toward the chair I'd vacated not five minutes ago. "I want you to tell me all about yourself."

I do the mannerly thing and sit down, actually enjoying Jane's discomfort a little bit. She's always so annoyingly confident about everything that it's actually funny to watch her be a bit discombobulated. I want to make her that way, and I have a very good idea on how with my mouth, but that's clearly not going to happen right now.

Meredith sits down in the chair next to me and waves a hand over her shoulder at her daughter.

"Honey… there's an apple pie in there I made. Why don't you cut us some slices and make some coffee?"

"Mom," Jane says with even more frustration. "This isn't a good time."

Meredith ignores her daughter and looks at me with avid interest. "So how long have you two been dating?"

"Mom," Jane snaps, and her mom gives a little jump as she turns to look at her daughter. "We are not dating."

"You're not dating," her mom repeats disbelievingly, and my chest tightens when I see the brightness of Jane's eyes flatten just a bit.

"What she means is we're not dating seriously," I say much to my surprise, but then figure—what the fuck— I'm going with it. "And by that, what she means is that it's pretty new, but it's exclusive."

Meredith turns back to look at me and levels a dazzling smile of relief. I can see this is a woman who loves her daughter very much.

I return her smile confidently, but then my gaze slides past her to Jane. She looks back at me with narrowed eyes, probably wondering what in the hell I'm doing by stringing her mom along like that. But fuck… what was I supposed to do? Tell her mom we were just temporary fuck mates?

Because no… that is not what Jane is to me.

I mean yes… there will be fucking and lots of it, I hope, but that is not all there is. In fact, there's so much more.

But I said it right. We're dating. It's not serious. It made her mom happy and wasn't an outright lie. This is a small town and we are probably going to be seen around, as I intend to take Jane out to dinner, perhaps for beers at The Lobster Cage, and maybe even back to Bar Harbor for some more sightseeing.

Those are all things we'll be doing over the next few months, and I find myself looking forward to every bit of it. And when I leave, I'm sure Jane will figure out something plausible to tell her mother, but in the meantime... I don't see why everyone can't just be happy about the way things are right in the present.

CHAPTER 21

JANE

M Y EYES FLUTTER open, and I wait for them to get accustomed to the darkened room. I'm wide awake and feel strangely refreshed. I turn my head to look at my clock and note it's just shy of three AM.

I turn my head back to the right. In the moonlight streaming through my windows, I can see Kyle's face partially lit. Again, he looks so peaceful and relaxed, despite the harsh angles of his cheekbones. He's lying on his side, his head inches from mine and his arm resting lax across my naked stomach. We've been asleep for several hours.

I don't move for a moment, instead staring at my ceiling that has become more revealed in the natural ambient moonlight. There's a rusty ceiling fan that rattles when I turn it on, so I don't really use it, afraid it might fall on me.

As I lay there, I think about the naked man sleeping beside me.

And the things he did to me tonight with his mouth and his hands and then with his...

My skin tingles at the memory, and an ache of need forms low in my belly. It's a need for sure, because what Kyle showed me tonight made me realize what I've been missing.

He left my house after having a slice of apple pie and making small talk with my mom, carefully avoiding any personal information about himself, much the way he's done with me. He did this masterfully by diverting my mom with questions about our family and me. After the pie, he made his excuses to leave, saying he had some things to do, not even bothering with the pretense of "fixing" my window. I walked out on the porch with him where he wrapped a hand around the back of my neck and pressed a kiss against my temple, promising he'd get up with me later. I offered him my cell number, but he shook his head, stating he didn't even own a cell phone. I should have found that odd, but if there's one person in the world who I could see shunning a cell phone, it would be Kyle.

I spent the afternoon shopping with my mom where she talked incessantly about how handsome Kyle was. Not long after I returned in the early evening, Kyle showed up at my door. Within moments, we were in my bedroom and naked.

While the clothes may have come off fast, he kept the pace of things very slow. As I remember the details of last night, the ache drops from my belly to between my legs. He positioned his face in between my thighs and stayed down there forever. Long enough to have me writhing and moaning and calling out his name. He made low sounds in his throat as his mouth worked me, almost as if he were savoring a fine sip of wine. I came twice, only then did he put a condom on and fuck me.

It was once again fast and rough, and God help me... I loved it like that. His fingers dug deep into my flesh, his hips slammed against mine, and Kyle made animalistic sounds of pleasure with his face buried in my neck. And there's no describing how it felt when he lifted his head up as he surged in deep one last time, his eyes locked on mine, and said in a rough, low tone one word.

Jane.

A tiny shiver of pleasure skitters up my spine over that memory, and I smile into the moonlit room.

I can tell Kyle is deep asleep by the pace of his breathing, but I feel like I'm ready to take on the world.

Energized.

Filled with spirit and creativity.

There's only one thing for me to do.

♦

I HAVE A bad habit of sticking my tongue out the side of my mouth when I'm concentrating really hard, and while painting is normally something that tends to flow naturally, I've been playing with new techniques, so it's requiring some attention to detail. My art forte is definitely watercolors, but I've been playing with mixed media lately. I hope to start working on it with my high school students soon. Tonight specifically, I'm working on a piece I started with a basic drawing done with my graphite pencil, and then filled in with acrylics.

The drawing is simple and slightly abstract. Two cats with elongated necks and triangular heads that make them look slightly alien. I'm painting one in gray and the other in black, and I think it's turning out nicely. It's far too modern for my personal tastes, but Miranda loves stuff like this, so it will be a gift to her.

I put a slight dab of white into the iris of one of the cat's eyes so as to create reflective light. Turning to lay my brush on a side table, I jolt with fright over the figure standing in the doorway of my studio. I immediately recognize Kyle there, actually leaning casually against the doorjamb as he watches me, but my heart is still thundering. I know that has to do with the scare I just had, but it continues on because of how hot he looks in just a pair of jeans hanging low on his lean hips and his muscular and tattooed expanse of abs and chest for me to behold.

"How long have you been standing there?" I say almost breathlessly as I press my fingers to the center of my chest.

"Not long," he says and pushes off the doorjamb. He walks into the room and looks around. It is mostly filled with finished paintings and a few easels, rows of shelving on one wall to hold my supplies, and a tiny desk against another wall where I do stuff like reconciling my bank account or surfing online on my laptop.

"I'm sorry if I woke you up," I murmur as I watch him prowl around the edge of the room, taking a moment to pause by the shelves and peruse my paint supplies.

"You didn't," is all he says without looking at me. Instead, he picks up a brush, inspects it briefly, and then puts it down. I find this reserved attitude a bit disconcerting. I mean, it's always sort of awkward that next morning after some amazing and intimate sex, but I wasn't ready for him to invade my little studio that is sort of like a haven for me.

He turns to me, his eyes sliding to my canvas where the cats are almost complete. "Nice pussies," he says with a smile.

I roll my eyes, but I'm immediately relieved to have him joke with me. "Juvenile," I chastise.

Kyle chuckles as his gaze slides to me. "Nowhere near as nice as yours."

I blush hot, which means my cheeks are probably blazing red. He smirks, which means he notices, and then adds on in a low voice. "I know without a doubt they don't taste as good as yours."

My face gets hotter, but I manage a snappy retort. "Acrylic paint tastes terrible."

Kyle grins at my rejoinder and turns to my desk. To my surprise, he grabs the small wooden chair nestled underneath and pulls it across the floor to sit right behind my stool. He takes a seat and his long, jean-clad legs frame the rear of my stool on either side.

"What are you doing?" I ask curiously.

"Going to watch you paint," he says.

My entire body tightens at the thought. "I don't think—"

Kyle's hands go to my hips. He turns me on my stool, so I'm facing my canvas again. "Paint," he orders.

"Kyle—"

His chin goes to my shoulder, and he softly repeats, "Paint."

A tiny spasm of adrenaline rockets through me at his seductive tone, but also because he wants to watch me do something that's a part of my very being.

"Okay," I whisper, and Kyle lifts his chin.

I continue using white to add highlight and contrast shading along the body of the black cat, my own body in a state of hyper awareness of Kyle's just inches behind mine. I swear I can feel heat radiating off him.

"Where do you get your ideas from?" Kyle asks, and I give a little jump to feel his breath on the back of my neck. I'd piled my hair up when I'd quietly slipped out of bed, only bothering to put on my panties and the t-shirt I'd been wearing.

I give a tiny shrug. "I'm really not sure. Sometimes I'll see an object that will spark an idea, or I'll read about a scene in a book and feel compelled to paint it."

"The colors in this are deeper than your watercolors," he observes astutely.

I nod as I continue with my brush strokes, feeling more at ease as we talk. "Good eye, and that's the benefit of acrylics. I'm not used to painting with this, but I'll get better with practice."

"Why are you using them if it's not what you're used to?" he inquires.

I draw a thin white line of paint along the jawline of the gray cat. "I like learning new things, and I need more than just watercolors to teach my students."

"Makes sense," is all he says.

Kyle's silent as he watches me for a few moments, and just as I start to really relax into my work, his hands come back to rest on my waist. I can hear him scoot the chair forward until it bumps against the back of my stool. He leans forward and presses his chest to my back, his chin coming back to my shoulder.

My brush freezes on the canvas and my breath goes still within my lungs.

Kyle's hands slide down over my hips to my outer thighs. His roughened palms cause goose pimples to rise as he strokes them along my legs.

"I have to say, Jane," he says gruffly, his lips mere inches from my ear. "You sitting here in that t-shirt and just your panties, hair all piled up and that little tongue sticking out the side of your mouth... Well, I had nefarious intentions walking in here."

Kyle's hands pivot and his fingers glide over the insides of my knees. With very little pressure needed at all, he pulls my legs slightly apart and then starts sliding his hands up my inner thighs. I go dizzy from his touch, his sexy voice, and perhaps the fact I'm still holding my breath. As his hands slide higher, my legs press in a little just from the nervous anticipation.

"Relax, baby," Kyle whispers as he puts pressure on my legs so they open again.

My breath comes out in small, stuttering huffs, and I suck another lungful in as his fingertips skim the elastic edge of my panties.

"Want to know what my nefarious intentions are?" he teases me as he runs just one finger along the edge.

I nod frantically but no words come out.

"Let me show you," he murmurs, his hands falling away from me briefly.

I almost call out in distress over the loss of his touch, but then he's banding an arm around my stomach, pulling me back so my ass presses against his crotch. His other hand glides slowly down the front of my panties, his fingers sliding through my wetness before pressing inside of me.

My hips buck hard against his delicious invasion, my head falls back to his shoulder, and my paintbrush falls from my hand. It slaps against my thigh, leaving a white paint streak and landing on the floor, but I don't care one tiny bit.

"Don't stop," I moan as he finds my clit, circling his finger around it gently.

"Just getting started," he assures me as he continues tracing lazy patterns.

"More," I demand greedily, planting my feet into the floor hard and pressing my hips up.

Kyle gives a low groan of triumph. "That's my girl."

My heart constricts hard over those words.

My girl.

"Lift up a bit," Kyle demands of me, so I do, raising my ass off my stool. Kyle quickly dispenses of my panties, leaning to the side a bit to push them down my legs. Once he frees one foot, he ignores them and straightens back up in his chair before once again pulling me back against him.

He brings a palm down in between my legs, cups me intimately for a moment as he again leans to the side.

I'm confused when he says, "Watch."

Kyle dips his fingers inside me briefly before dragging them upward to reveal my clit. He pulls back on the tiny hood covering it, and I'm enthralled by how swollen and needy it looks.

Then I'm absolutely stunned when I see that Kyle has one of my paintbrushes in his other hand. He must have nabbed it off my supply shelf, but it's one that has luxuriously soft bristles.

I suck in my breath and watch as Kyle takes the brush and swirls the bristles along the inside of one thigh. I jerk because it tickles and laugh nervously.

But my laugh dies down when he slowly drags the brush in between my legs, and ever so gently swipes it right up my center. My hips fly upward. Kyle's arm holds me tighter as he uses his other hand to hold me open.

"Watch, Jane," he murmurs, his voice thick with wonder and lust.

And I watch as he uses the damp bristles to circle around my clit, and the sensation is indescribable. My entire body starts to tremble as I watch him getting me off with my paintbrush. He carefully dips the tip inside of me just marginally... enough to get it wet, and then he makes light strokes against my clit, over and over again.

My body trembles harder and my hands turn into claws that I sink into his thighs.

The strokes are so feather light, and he's purposely going slowly to draw this out, whereas I only want to come and come and come.

"God, this is sexy as fuck," Kyle mutters in my ear as he twirls the brush around my clit, going a little faster. My entire body goes tight. "We need to try this while I'm fucking you."

And just like that, I explode.

I groan out my release as he continues to swirl the brush around, whispering words of praise and encouragement, and when I don't have any more to give, he tosses the brush to the floor and merely places his large palm over my crotch to gently squeeze me possessively.

"Kyle," I murmur in repletion, still dizzy from that climax.

"Get up," Kyle commands me gently, his hands going to my hips to push me up from the stool. The minute my legs straighten, he's turning me to face him. My hands go out to his shoulders for balance, and I watch as he quickly unfastens the fly on his jeans. He lifts his hips a little, pulling them down just enough to free himself. I watch with wide eyes because that part of him is just as beautiful as the rest, marveling at how quickly he gets a condom out and rolls it on.

I give a tiny gasp of surprise as Kyle's hands go back to my hips and he jerks me forward. He looks up at me with fevered eyes and admits something I think shames him by the tone of his voice. "I can't get enough of you."

Before I can even respond, he surges out of the chair and spins me toward the nearest wall, right beside my desk. He pushes me right up against it, my breasts flattening and my heart racing with his forcefulness.

Kyle's mouth comes to the side of my neck and he bites me gently before giving me a soft lick. His hands pull my hips backward and I feel his body bend, then he's pushing inside of me.

Straight inside, one long, fluid stroke.

"Ooohhh," I moan as I turn my head and place my

heated cheek against the cool wall.

Kyle grunts in pleasure before he pulls out and thrusts back in hard. My body jars against the wall as he starts a steady rhythm, and I realize... this is new as well. So many things that Kyle is showing me that in my totally boring previous sex life had seemed like pretty good stuff.

But now... now that I know this...

I think I might be ruined for anyone else after Kyle leaves.

CHAPTER 22

KYLE

I PULL A small cooler from the back of my truck, keeping half an eye on Jane as she spreads out a navy-blue blanket on the grass. She'd suggested a drive over to Acadia again. When I picked her up, she surprised me by coming out of her house with a picnic basket. She announced as she jumped in the truck that we'd have to stop for some drinks, and so we graced a rundown-looking mini mart before we hit the ferry and purchased a cheap Styrofoam cooler, a small bag of ice, and a six-pack of Coke.

Here I am, a man in hiding, having spent the past several years selling my soul to the devil, getting ready to sit down with the sweetest, sexiest woman I've ever known to have a motherfucking picnic.

I feel like I'm in the Twilight Zone.

It's felt like that for the past two weeks since Jane and I have been regularly seeing each other. And by seeing each other, I mean there's been a whole lot of orgasms dished out, intermixed with what you could call "dates," I guess. That included going on a double date to dinner with Miranda and some dude she's banging, but it's totally not serious. It also included a trip to the county fair where Jane screamed and dug her nails in my leg during every ride, except for the Ferris wheel, where we made out like teenagers at the top. We then gorged ourselves on corn dogs, cotton candy, and elephant ears until my stomach hurt so bad I didn't think I'd be able to fuck her that night.

I did, however, persevere.

Jane also convinced me to go to dinner at her parents' house one night. This was something I internally balked at, as I genuinely liked Jane's mom, Meredith, and didn't want to string her along by letting her think this was something lasting with her daughter. I had a hard time sitting at a woman's table, eating her food and knowing I was probably going to hurt her daughter in the long run.

Didn't matter that her daughter knew that going into this and had agreed to it; it still made me feel bad. I only agreed because Jane sensed my reluctance before I could even accept the invitation, and she quickly backpedaled. I saw the clear disappointment and sadness in her eyes that I couldn't give her this little bit of normalcy in this crazy relationship we had, and even as she was saying, "Never mind I asked. I'll come up with a good excuse for my parents," I was saying, "Of course, I'd be glad to go."

Turns out, it was nice and her parents are great, but it only served to remind me how different my world is from Jane's. She adores her parents and has a natural and easy relationship with them. I can't imagine how that might be affected if they knew what was really going on between their daughter and me.

I carry the cooler over to the blanket. After setting it down on a corner so it's not lifted by the breeze, I take a seat on one side as Jane removes items from her basket.

"I made some fried chicken and potato salad," she says as she pulls out some paper plates. "And I was going to make some cookies but decided to buy them instead at the bakery. No sense in ruining this outing for us."

Chuckling, I take a plate from Jane and put a piece of chicken onto it. It smells phenomenal. There's something about the fact that Jane made it that makes me believe it will be the best chicken I've ever had. Today will no doubt go down as one of the best days ever, which I seem to think a lot when I'm around this woman.

As Jane dishes me some potato salad, I take a bite of the chicken and groan. Her eyes snap to me.

"That's fucking amazing," I mumble around my food before chewing.

She ducks her head almost shyly, which is not like Jane, but I've come to find out that she actually doesn't take a compliment very well. She's almost embarrassed when I do. I find that charming and sad at the same time. I suspect that's because she's not had a lot of genuine accolades from men before, which is totally odd given how amazing she is. Also odd is the fact that I hand out compliments to her. Never been that kind of dude, but she brings it out of me and I can't fucking help myself.

"Miranda's thinking about dumping Jim," Jane says off-handedly before licking a bit of potato salad off her thumb.

"The guy who went to dinner with us a few nights ago?" I ask, then take another bite of chicken.

Jane nods as she selects a drumstick from the container of fried, spicy goodness.

"Thought his name was Tom," I say after I swallow and put my chicken down on the plate. I reach over into the cooler to pull out two Cokes, popping the top on one before handing it to Jane.

"Was it?" she asks as she accepts the Coke and takes sip.

"Yeah," I tell her, and then try a bite of potato salad. "And damn... that's amazing too."

"The secret is to add a little poultry seasoning in it," she says with a nod down to the container before looking back to me. "Tom, Jim... whatever. The point is she wants to dump him."

"Didn't care for the guy anyway," I say as I continue to eat. "And I could totally tell he wasn't Miranda's type."

Which also seems to say something about how I've integrated into Jane's life since I've even gotten to know her best friend quite well. I've been around her enough to know that she needs a good guy with a strong hand who won't take her bullshit. Apparently, though, she either gravitates to assholes with low self-esteem or wimps who like to kiss her ass.

Jane snickers. "He so was not Miranda's type. And that thing he did with his nose…"

"That snuffling noise whenever he finished a sentence?"

"What was that?" She laughs.

"No fucking clue, but it was driving me batty," I commiserate.

"Oh, my God," Jane says as she continues to laugh. "Can you imagine them in bed together? 'Oh baby, that feels so good.' Then that god-awful snuffling sound."

I watch, chicken poised halfway to my mouth, as Jane laughs with abandon. With such radiance. Green eyes shimmering whimsically. Completely in the moment… with me… sharing something that we both found funny as hell.

Sharing something with me that I don't remember having in forever and a day.

I drop the chicken to the paper plate and reach across the expanse of the blanket. I lean toward Jane at the same time I cup the back of her head to pull her toward me, and I lay a swift but soft kiss on her mouth before I release her.

Her eyes are wide with surprise when I pull back,

because I'm not the most spontaneously affectionate person.

"That was different," she says.

"It was?" I ask, feigning ignorance.

She nods. "You usually only kiss me when you... well, you know... you want sex."

That would be true. I love kissing Jane, which leads to fucking ten times out of ten.

But that wasn't my intent just now. Hell, I'm not even sure what my intent was, but I was filled up with a gloriously warm, euphoric feeling that was due solely to the woman sitting across from me and, before I knew it, I was giving her a kiss.

I try to play it off though. Looking around at the picnic area, I casually say, "Who says I don't want to have sex here?"

Jane rolls her eyes at me, and I grin. Crazy how easy my smiles have been coming the last few weeks.

Like this picnic.

I couldn't imagine doing something like this... all normal and romantic. It's a completely foreign concept, and yet I'm drawn even stronger to these things with Jane. My curiosity about this laid-back, normal way of life is stirring, and perhaps I'm even remembering a bit how to live this way.

It's hard to describe to anyone what it meant for me to go undercover with Mayhem's Mission. Hell, it's even hard for me to understand it at times. But in order to do it, I had to let go of every bit of my humanity, and I had to embrace a life bankrupt of any morals, decency, or kindness. My Mission brothers were a ruthless gang involved in serious criminal enterprise from drugs and illegal guns to sex slavery. And that was only the tip of the iceberg. It was the "business" part of what they did.

But there was another part.

A darker part.

It was where I had to convince them that I was cut from the same cloth. I had to do terrible things to people that, without the immunity the government has provided me, would land me in jail for the rest of my life. I have so much blood on my hands that it won't ever come off.

So yeah... I get why she was surprised by this little act of affection on my part. Given my past, I'm just as surprised.

But goddamn... she is crawling under my skin, invading my senses, and turning me inside out. She makes me laugh, which is a practically unheard of accomplishment. She's witty and funny and full of personality. Jane is a force of nature that has the strength of a hurricane, and fuck if she didn't roll right over me.

Hell... even sex with Jane is fun. I'd thought she might be a little shy or reserved, but she's not. She's an incredibly sensual woman who perhaps needed just a little encouragement to explore more of that side of herself. Once she understood that I found it incredibly erotic for her to be vocal about what she wanted, the sex became even better.

Not to say she couldn't throw me off my game every now and then.

Just last night, I thought I'd nearly have a heart attack when Jane demanded I fuck her from behind. I think I actually missed a stroke, but I quickly had her flipped over before I plunged back in. It was then that I realized we were facing the large mirror on her dresser and Jane was watching us with dark, lust-filled eyes as I rode her hard. It made my balls tighten and the need to come was almost painful. My hand pushed into her long hair and I gripped it hard, and that got her attention. Her glazed eyes slid to look at me in the mirror, and we held each other's gaze for just a brief moment. Then her lips curled upward and a mischievous glint sparkled back at me. She then turned to look back at herself, and, in an imperious voice—while I was still fucking her hard—she said, "Magic mirror on the wall, who is the fairest one of all?"

I came to a dead stop rooted deep within her, and her eyes slowly raised to focus back on me.

She grinned at me and panted, "*Snow White and the Seven Dwarves*, 1937. Now get back to business, baby."

And I couldn't help it. I fucking threw my head back and busted out laughing. I laughed so hard that I collapsed on top of Jane, and then rolled us to our sides. Jane laughed with me as I wrapped my arms around her tight, that orgasm I was so close to completely forgotten—although, admittedly, I was still hard as a rock.

We started talking about movies.

Just like that, I went from fucking Jane to leaving orgasm city behind and talking about movies.

I was fine with that because it was real, and it was Jane, and just having that with her appealed to me on a level I didn't realize I needed.

♦

THE RINGING PHONE startles me awake. For a brief moment, I'm disoriented. Then my eyes land on the mantle with Jane's painting above it, and my heart immediately settles. I sit up quickly from the rust-colored couch where I'd been laying down and immediately grab the burner phone from the oval-shaped coffee table.

"What's up?" I answer when I connect to Joe on the line. I stand up from the couch and walk to the front windows, peering through the blinds toward Jane's house. It's completely dark, but I'm not surprised. She was having a "girls" night out with Miranda, which, according to Jane, meant that she had to make sure Miranda didn't get into too much trouble.

I'm hoping Jane will come over here after she gets home.

"I've got some bad news," Joe says, and my body tightens over the ominous tone of his voice.

Pulling back from the window, I open the front door and walk out onto the porch. I sit down on the top step and stare at Jane's house. "What is it?"

"One of our servers has been infiltrated. The tech team just found the breach, and they were able to shut it down fairly quickly." Joe's voice trails off slightly.

"But…" I prompt Joe, because I can tell he's walked me up to the cliff.

"Your information was in there. New name and current address. It doesn't look like that information was compromised, but we can't rule it out just yet."

"Fuck," I bark into the phone and run my hand over the stubble on my head. "Why the fuck was that in there?"

"Come on, Kyle," Joe chastises. "You know we have to have accountability somewhere. It takes funds to set up this type of thing, and we have to answer for that. But Camden has his top techs working on it right now."

Bart Camden is Joe's boss—and technically mine, for that matter, since Joe and I were effectively partnered up the last several years.

"There is some good news though," Joe adds on. I let my eyes drift from Jane's darkened house over to Front Street where her parents live a few blocks down. Such normal people who have no clue about me.

"What's that?" I ask.

"A few of the Mission higher-ups have reached out to the prosecutor about cutting some deals," Joe says, and this causes me to sit up a bit straighter. This is surprising because there's a code among the members of Mayhem's

Mission. You never rat out your brothers, but if you do, be prepared to die for that action.

This is good news indeed. It means convictions will be easier to secure. It could mean a domino effect with the rest of the defendants who were indicted, and perhaps this will go away faster.

"Do I have anything to worry about at this point?" I ask as my eyes cut back to Jane's house. I don't care about myself, but if someone's coming for me, I am not going to put her in danger. I'll pack my shit up tonight and hightail it out of town.

"We believe you're good for now," Joe says. "Like I said… it doesn't look like your information was compromised, but I wanted to let you know because nothing's ever one hundred percent. If you want to relocate, we'll make it happen."

My gut twists, not knowing if I'm making the right decision. I'm hoping to fuck the feds have my back because part of this decision is for my own needs. "I'll stay for now. But if you find out that the breach went as far as my information, you let me know immediately."

"Will do, buddy," he assures me. "Talk later."

"Later," I say before disconnecting the call.

CHAPTER 23

JANE

"HONESTLY... I JUST couldn't stand one more night of that snuffling noise he made with his nose," Miranda grumbles as she sips at her coffee across the table from me.

Kyle—who's seated beside me—lightly knocks his leg against mine in solidarity of amusement, and I have to restrain myself from laughing.

Miranda and I didn't get home until after one in the morning, and this came after a very messy breakup with her "snuffling" flame. She was extremely drunk, and well... she was extremely honest with him. She did not let him down gently, but her decision was at least ratified somewhat when he said, "I can't believe you're that shallow, Miranda, as to let something like that bother you." Then he snuffled.

Miranda pointed at him and said, "See. You just did it again. I can't take it."

It was not a fun night for me, not only because of Miranda's drama and drunkenness, but mainly because I would have rather spent the time with Kyle.

Tick, tock goes the clock on our relationship.

We're having breakfast this morning at Tillie's Shiny Diner and at the invitation of Kyle. He showed up bright and early at my door, waking both of us up—Miranda had passed out on my couch—and offering to buy us breakfast. I was all over that, because even though I'd had only about six hours of sleep, I wanted to spend whatever time I could with Kyle.

He said he was leaving at some point and I believe him, despite the fact we seem to be getting closer.

Tillie's is a popular hangout and is indeed a shiny diner. The outside is done in bright, reflective silver aluminum, and the inside has red vinyl booths, a black-and-white tiled floor, and a long counter with spinning stools. There's a vintage jukebox on one end that carries music from the 40s, 50s and 60s. Tillie serves breakfast at all hours, and she makes a killer fried egg.

"Miranda," I say with a bit of brutal honesty myself. "All bodily noises aside, you need to stop getting charmed by a man's pretty face and take closer stock of what they bring to the table."

"You got sidetracked by Kyle's pretty face," she retorts at me, and Kyle actually snickers even though his head remains bowed over the newspaper he's reading. "Actually, if I recall… it was his body. You were going on and on about how hot his abs were while he was pressure washing the lighthouse."

"Miranda," I exclaim indignantly at the same time

Kyle's head whips my way. I don't bother looking at him as I glare at my best friend. She grins right back at me.

"Thought I was hot, huh?" Kyle says, and I turn my head to look at him.

"Oh, shut up," I snarl to mask my total embarrassment. "You totally know you're hot."

Kyle's eyes crinkle with amusement, and if I'm not mistaken, a little bit of pride. He shakes his head and goes back to reading his newspaper, but his hand slips under the table to rest on the top of my thigh. It's a bold move, but it's equally sweet, and there's nothing but a gentle intimacy to the action. It's something that Kyle has apparently been getting more comfortable with, as evidenced also by the spontaneous kiss he gave me yesterday during our picnic.

"Anyway," I say as I turn back to Miranda. "Don't you think it's time you started looking at what's underneath the hood rather than the exterior?"

Miranda snickers, totally reading my words as dirty rather than metaphorical. "I can't help it, Janey. I love me a hot man, and it's even better if he's a bad boy. I personally don't care about anything past that other than snuffling. I can't deal with that apparently."

I sigh. I love Miranda so very much, but I don't think she'll ever grow up. I'm pretty confident she'll never settle down, and I'm outright positive she won't get involved with a guy seriously. After what her parents went through and the public spectacle it made, she's about the most anti-commitment person I know.

Well, other than Kyle.

"For example," Miranda says dramatically and nods her head at something behind me. "That guy right there totally needs to be warming my bed."

I roll my eyes but turn in the booth to look behind me. There's a man sitting at the end of the counter, drinking a cup of coffee and looking right back at Miranda. He quirks a pair of sexy lips and nods at her. I can feel Kyle shift in the booth as he looks back as well.

We both turn back, Kyle's head tipping down again to read the newspaper and me rolling my eyes at Miranda. "Seriously?"

Miranda is still staring at the guy and her look is blatantly inviting. Without taking her eyes off him, she addresses me, "Oh, come on, Jane. I get you got your own hottie sitting next to you, but that guy is perfectly delicious. Leather jacket, goatee, tattoos. Total biker badass, and that is right up my alley."

"He's no biker," Kyle says in a low but authoritative voice, never looking up from the paper.

"Excuse me?" Miranda says, her eyes now sliding over to Kyle with curiosity.

He looks up and shrugs. "He's not a biker. Not like what you're thinking. All rough and dangerous and slightly criminal. Sure, he might ride recreationally, but he's not the type of badass you're looking for, if that's really what you're looking for."

Miranda harrumphs and her eyes go back to the guy, not willing to let Kyle rain on her parade.

But now my curiosity is piqued. "How do you know that?" I ask.

He turns toward me in the booth, his arm going around the back where his fingers brush against my shoulders. He gives a slight, nonchalant shrug. "I've hung around my fair share of bikers."

His smile is open and his words are light, but I see something deep in his eyes that troubles me. I have no doubt he's hung around his share based on how confident he sounds and I hear the ring of truth, but I get the feeling that his experience was far from good.

"Did you ride with a gang or something?" I ask.

A dark, painful flash in Kyle's eyes, but before he can answer me, a cell phone ringing pierces the air around us. My eyes immediately drop down as Kyle leans to the side, extends a leg, and fishes a small phone out of his front pocket. It's not a smartphone, not even a flip phone, but a small, plain black unit with a digital screen big enough to only hold perhaps a phone number.

He brings the phone to his ear as he starts to slide out of the booth. "Talk to me," is how he answers.

My hand shoots out and I touch his forearm, my head tilted and my gaze questioning. Kyle tells whoever is on the other line, "Hold on just a sec."

Then he covers the phone with his hand and raises his eyebrows, indicating he's waiting for me to ask a question.

Sliding my gaze to the cell and then back to him, I say, "I thought you said you didn't have a cell phone?"

There's no pause, no stutter, and no guilt in his eyes. He simply says, "Just got it the other day."

"Oh," I murmur, accepting it, but wondering why he didn't tell me or give me his number.

"I gotta take this call," he says, and then leans over and kisses me on the top of my head. "Be right back."

Kyle turns and walks out of the diner, the phone back to his ear. I watch as he heads down the sidewalk a bit, one hand tucked in his pocket while he listens to whoever is on the other end.

"Does that bother you?" Miranda asks, ever observant of me. She knows me all too well.

I shrug. "Maybe a little. I wonder why he didn't tell me."

"Did you see how basic that thing was?" she says as she comes to his defense. "He's clearly not a techie type of guy, and I'm betting he prefers to just walk over to your house to talk to you."

That's all true. He comes over whenever he wants to be with me, although I haven't quite had the guts to just meander over to his because I want to see him. Yes, I get that's contrary to the fact that I regularly showed up on his doorstep back in the day when we were first getting to know each other, but now that sex is involved, I guess I'm just being a little old fashioned. I'm not sure I'm ready to march over there with a "do me, baby" type of come-on, although I'm sure Kyle would definitely take me up on it.

"Hell yeah," Miranda murmurs in a low, sexy tone of appreciation. She's looking back over my shoulder. Before I can even turn to see what she's looking at—presumably the hot-biker-not-actually-biker type guy—he's at our table and Miranda's sliding over to let him in.

I try not to let my jaw drop as he turns slightly to face her, completely ignoring me, and says to her, "I'm Steve. And you are too beautiful for me not to come over here and let you know that."

I roll my eyes, which I can do because neither one of them is looking at me.

Miranda flutters her eyelashes and holds her hand out. "Miranda."

Steve pulls it to his mouth and kisses her knuckles, and I shake my head. I've seen enough *Sons of Anarchy* and I can tell you for sure that Jax Teller would never do that. He's totally not a biker like Kyle says, but Miranda eats that shit up and doesn't see it for what it is... just a way to get into her pants.

To my surprise, Steve releases her hand and reaches across the table toward me in an invitation to shake his hand. He holds it out palm sideways and says in a more businesslike tone, "And you must be the wary best friend. I'm Steve."

I shake his hand, a little mollified that he wants to

impress Miranda by seeking my approval. "Jane."

Steve gives me a quick shake and lets me go as he asks, "Hope your boyfriend isn't going to be pissed I came over here like this," he says as he nods out the window to where Kyle is still talking on the phone. "Not going to kick my ass, is he?"

This guy Steve has a decent build. Might even be an inch or so taller than Kyle. But if he was truly a badass biker, he would not be worried about anyone kicking his ass. Seems Kyle totally called that one correctly.

I give Steve a reassuring smile. "No ass kicking. He's cool."

Although I know without a doubt that Kyle would not be cool if Steve's attentions were directed my way. Kyle may not be a long-haul type of man—a thought which saddens me with each passing day—but I do know he's proprietary. He's given the evil eye to a few guys who have looked at me a little too appreciatively when we've been out and about.

Steve turns back to Miranda. "I'm in a bit of a rush to get to work, but I was wondering if I could call you sometime?"

Miranda's eyes, which are surprisingly clear despite her drunkenness last night and thanks to Visine, sparkle with interest. "Only if you promise to use it to call immediately. I am on the prowl for my next boy-toy after all."

"Good grief," I mutter under my breath, but both of

them ignore me.

I sip at my coffee, my gaze wandering to look out the window at Kyle. His back is to me, but his posture seems stiff and defensive. My imagination runs wild as to who it could be, since while we've been very intimate with each other, about the only real thing I've seemed to glean from him is that he has no real family and no close friends. This should make me happy because I am what I believe to be a friend to him, but I not only find it sad, I find it to be disconcerting as well. I know no one who is that much alone in life.

Miranda and Steve exchange contact information, and after Steve promises to call Miranda that very night after he gets off work, he makes his exit. Five seconds later, Kyle is sliding back in the booth beside me.

"What did that guy want?" he asks as he looks at Miranda, and I'm surprised how keenly aware he must have been of what was going on inside the diner while he was on the phone.

"My body," she says pertly and gives him a wicked grin over the edge of her coffee cup. "And he just might get lucky tonight."

I actually expect Kyle to say something at this point in the way of a warning, because she's my friend and I assume he'd be a little protective of her. I'll, of course, read her the riot act later, but it will fall on deaf ears as it always does.

But Kyle doesn't say a word. Instead, he reaches into

his back pocket for his wallet as he asks me, "You about ready to go?"

"Um, yeah," I say guardedly as I sneak a quick glance at Miranda.

She shoots me a small shrug, and then looks over at Kyle. "What's your rush, big guy?"

Kyle slides from the booth, grabs the check the waitress had left about fifteen minutes ago after we'd eaten and were enjoying more coffee, and then holds his hand out to me. I take it, and he pulls me from the booth as he grins down at Miranda. "Appreciate you letting me in on that little secret that Jane was lusting after my body," he tells her with a mischievous gleam in his eyes. "She's been a little shy with me so far in bed, and I think now is the perfect opportunity to let her explore a bit."

"You... you..." I sputter with embarrassment as I yank my hand away from his. "You did not just say that to her."

Miranda, at this point, is laughing, clearly enjoying my torment. I'm not anywhere as sexually liberated as Miranda is, and I tend to let my partner lead. Now, granted, a flush of excitement went through me when he said I was going to get to explore, but I didn't want him to make a billboard announcement about it.

"Come on, Jane," Kyle says huskily as he takes my hand again and brings it up to his lips. He grazes the back of my knuckles, and I realize my perception may be wrong about bikers. I can totally imagine Kyle in a biker gang, but that soft kiss on my knuckles was not in the slightest bit out of place.

I kept my swooning sigh internalized, and I gladly let him lead me out of Tillie's Shiny Diner and back to his house.

CHAPTER 24

KYLE

"*Y*OU HAD TO *know I'd find you,*" *I tell the man who stares at me with terror from where he's lying on the floor. One eye is already purple and swollen shut. There's a cut on his left cheekbone that's bleeding profusely and the area along his jawbone is swollen. My knuckles on my right hand are shredded from the repeated blows I delivered but, unfortunately for him, I'm just getting started.*

"*Please,*" *he begs, a bubble of blood forming on his lips.* "*Not in front of them.*"

I shake my head slowly, denying his words as I look down at him. "*It has to be in front of them. Otherwise, the lesson won't be appreciated.*"

A strangled sob sounds behind me, but I don't bother looking. I already know I'd see his wife and son huddled together on the linoleum floor of their kitchen that's now splattered with his blood.

"*He's just a little boy.*" *The man begs me, hoping to appeal to any bit of humanity within me.*

I reach my arm backward without taking my eyes off the man. My hand is immediately filled with the smooth wood of a baseball bat that's passed to me from one of my brothers. Zeke ordered me to impart this particular message, but I didn't ride alone tonight. He wanted witnesses along to make sure I did the job and did it right.

"And now, that little boy is going to watch his daddy pay the consequences for double crossing Zeke," I tell him quietly. "Consider it a learning lesson for him. It will probably even save him some pain of his own in the future because it will teach him that you keep your word."

The man coughs and more blood bubbles from his mouth because his ribs took a pounding from my boots as well.

He wheezes and, as I raise the bat, I hear his little boy start to cry. The man raises his hands defensively and begs one more time, "Please."

It falls on deaf ears as I bring the bat down hard on his kneecap. The man shrieks, and his wife starts to cry piteously. I don't turn to look at her. Instead, I mark my target for his other knee and bring the bat down hard. The man screams again, clutching at his knees with bloody foam frothing out of his mouth.

"Learned your lesson yet?" I yell as I bend over him.

"Yes," he moans as he curls inward. "Yes, yes, yes."

It sounds genuine to me, but I know every detail of this will be relayed to Zeke, so I'm nowhere near able to quit. I'm expected to make this painful, but more than that... I'm expected to truly prove my loyalty to the club.

I raise the bat and bring it down again, this time

against the man's ribs. His back arches, and then he curls inward again, trying to shield himself as best he can as I rain down blow after blow upon him.

Sweat is pouring down my face from my efforts, and my Mission brothers behind me are egging me on harder. I only stop swinging the bat when he loses consciousness.

The kitchen goes silent, and I wipe my forehead on my sleeve. I drop the bat on the floor behind the man I just beat to a pulp, perhaps even killed. I'm satisfied that it will get me full privileges into Mayhem's Mission.

It's just a job, I tell myself. I have to do this for the greater good. I'm doing this to bring this club down.

I turn away from the carnage to walk out of the kitchen, my eyes sliding past the wife and son still huddled on the floor, knowing I won't be able to bear looking at them.

Just as my boot hits the threshold of the doorway that leads out, I hear the small, terrified voice of the little boy ask, "Did you kill my daddy?"

Bile roils within my stomach, rises quickly up my throat, and, for a brief moment, I think I may compromise this whole undercover operation by spewing vomit all over. Instead, I swallow it down, harden my heart, and turn to look at the little boy. His brown eyes swimming with tears, he looks at me pleadingly to tell him that it will all be okay.

I shrug my shoulders. "Not sure, kid. Maybe I did."

I vaguely hear the wife's sobs, but I'll never forget the way that little boy looks at me, tears now spilling down his cheeks. Eyes accusing me, hating me... fuck, I don't know *what they're doing, but to me, they're condemning me.*

Turning my back on the little boy, his sobbing mother, and the carnage I created, I walk out of the house and resign myself that if I hadn't before, I'd just earned my one-way ticket to hell no matter if this mission is ultimately successful or not.

My body flies straight up on the bed, a silent scream held still in my throat. I'm frozen for a moment, not disoriented but completely still immersed in the memory.

A soft hand touches my back, and Jane sits up in bed beside me. "Kyle… what's wrong?"

I shake my head and give a little cough to loosen my vocal cords. Still, I'm practically croaking when I tell her, "Nothing."

"You're soaking wet," she murmurs, her hand sliding up to my shoulder. She shifts in the bed, comes to her knees, and brings her palm to my forehead. "You're not running a fever though."

Jane is naked in front of me in the moonlight, her breasts full, her stomach flat, her hips rounded. I should want to push her down onto the bed and fuck away my misery, but all I want to do is bury my head in her chest and cry.

Jane's hands come to palm my face as she leans in to whisper, "Baby… what's wrong?"

I shake my head again, and my voice is a little clearer

when I admit, "Bad dream."

She tilts her head. While I can't exactly see the depth of the sympathy she has in her eyes, I can feel it when her arms come around my shoulders and she presses her body into mine, locking herself in tight. I've never needed consolation before. Shunned it, actually.

But with no shame in me, I band my arms around her and pull her down into my lap. My face goes into her neck, and we just hold onto each other for an infinitely long time. Her naked skin on mine, the sweet scent of her hair, and the even more delicious scent of us combined together.

My heart rate slows and the image of that little boy finally disappears.

Finally, Jane's fingers slide up, and she massages my scalp gently as she observes with blunt honesty, "This isn't like you, Kyle."

"What's that?" I mumble into her neck, but knowing damn well what she means.

"Being vulnerable," she says simply and doesn't elaborate. She doesn't need to. She hit the nail on the head, and I also know Jane well enough to know that she won't belabor her observation either. She's the type who wouldn't want to embarrass me for what I'd perceive as a weakness. She won't push at me to know what woke me up in a sweat, and she won't seek details unless I give her some reason to believe I want to share them.

So she just lets me hold her in silence.

She leaves it up to me what to do.

She opens the cage to the restless, dangerously disturbed animal, and she waits to see if it will walk out and take a little bit of freedom.

I pull Jane back down into the bed, rolling so we come to rest on our sides, facing each other. Before she settles fully, I throw an arm back and lean toward the lamp so I can turn it on. When I roll back to Jane, her eyes are squinted slightly as she adjusts to the light, but with absolute acceptance in her gaze for whatever I want to give her in this moment.

It's not much, but I want to give her something.

Scooting close to her, I slide a hand over her waist and hold her there lightly. I don't pull her into me because we're going to talk and I want to see her face.

Her gaze is trusting and patient.

"My life... before I came here," I begin with all the vagueness in the world. "It was brutal."

Jane's fingertips come to the skull tattoo on my chest and stroke the ink. It confirms to me that she suspected what little I'm getting ready to share.

"I've done things that are heinous," I tell her. "Unforgivable, really. If you knew who I was, Jane, you'd despise me. You'd be disgusted, and you would never look at me the same way again."

"Not possible," she whispers in disbelief.

I won't debate it with her. I'm never going to give her details because I don't want her to have the same nightmares that I do. But after my talk with Joe today, when he called me while I was enjoying a normal breakfast date with a woman who I've come to care more about than I ever thought was possible, I knew it was time I had to move on.

Joe's information wasn't clear or overly revealing. He'd advised me that nothing had been found to believe my location had been compromised by the ATF server breach. This was heartening. However—and there was always a 'however'—the few members of Mayhem's Mission who had been previously clamoring to explore plea deals in exchange for testimony have now all of a sudden clammed up. Not just one or two of them. Every single one who was in a plea deal negotiation suddenly put the brakes on everything.

This was suspicious.

This was more concerning than a breach into the ATF server.

This meant that those men who were running scared and wanted to avoid decades behind bars with a plea deal were now suddenly feeling confident.

And Joe's concern was that if they were feeling confident, that probably meant I'd been found.

Now it's time for me to pave the beginning of the roadway that will lead me out of here. I knew tonight would be my last night with Jane, and I spent the last several hours making love to her until we fell into an exhausted sleep not long ago.

I guess my nightmare was an internal sign from my consciousness that I needed to start my break.

Rolling Jane to her back, I settle myself between her legs. While I hold most of my weight off her, I give her enough of it so that we're touching everywhere possible that we can for now.

I give her a soft kiss and rub my nose briefly against hers. When I lift up, I look into her beautiful green eyes and I give it to her straight. "I'm sorry I can't be completely honest with you about who I am. You know me so much better than anyone, and yet, you don't know all the important things."

"Kyle," Jane says with such sweet empathy that my chest starts to ache.

I shake my head, silently letting her know that she needs to hear me out. "I'm leaving—"

"No," she says adamantly, cutting me off as her eyes flash with defiance.

"Jane… baby… I have to," I cajole.

I expect her to argue, cry, lament, plead, beg, and negotiate with me.

Instead, her head lifts from the pillow, one hand goes to the back of my head, and she pulls me to her for a kiss. A hot, wet, passionate kiss full of desperation and need.

I don't resist.

This I cannot resist.

Jane ensures this conversation is put on hold as her

other hand slips between our bodies and she grabs onto my cock, which had already started to harden when her lips touched mine.

Jane shifts her hips, widens her legs a bit, and strokes me swiftly. My body reacts, and I groan into her mouth.

She kisses me like she's never done before, pouring every bit of passion laced with misery over my declaration that I'm leaving. I try to pull my head up, just so I can look into her eyes and see how badly she's broken despite what she's doing to my cock right now.

But Jane isn't having any of it. Her fingers grip into the muscles of my neck, and she shifts again, tilting her hips under me. With a rough tug of her other hand, she pulls my dick right to her entrance and rubs the tip of me through her wetness.

"Christ, Jane," I growl into her mouth, because that felt goddamn amazing. Her soft skin against mine with nothing in between, a sensation I've never felt before. My head swims with confusion and my body rages with lust. I manage to grit out, "Let me get a condom on, honey."

Her answer is to kiss me harder, growling into my mouth and pulling me into her. I slide a fraction of an inch in, and, for a moment, my heart actually stops beating as I take it all in.

Jane desperate to make our bond closer.

My need to separate from her.

The unbelievable feeling of having every single barrier between our bodies removed, even if I'm keeping one firmly in place around who I really am.

"Please," Jane begs as she pulls slightly back from my mouth. "Fuck me, Kyle. Right now."

I want to tell her it won't change anything, but because I'm selfish and I want this memory of her more than anything, I give into my basic urges and fall deeply into Jane's body.

One push.

A surging force into all that sweetness.

Totally claiming, although it could never be a permanent one.

She's the best thing I've ever felt in my entire fucking life. For a second, I think I might actually have been forgiven by God for all my sins since I've been given the most perfect gift I'll ever receive.

CHAPTER 25

JANE

M Y FISTS CLENCH in hard anger as I stomp across the dewy grass of my front yard, leaving the grass of Kyle's behind me. Just half an hour ago, Kyle and I shared something I've never given to another man—my unprotected body. I know it was a first for him because he told me so after we'd come down from the high of what I felt was the most euphoric lovemaking I had ever experienced in my life, and would probably never experience again. Kyle knew I was on the pill as he'd seen them in my bathroom. For some reason, despite the fact he's held a huge part of himself in reserve from me, I trusted him not to hurt me and never had a qualm about taking him inside me without a condom.

Stupid, stupid, stupid.

To think that experience would change anything with him.

I was desperate, no doubt. He said he was leaving and it was imminent. I was grasping at straws, literally grasping his dick and trying anything I could to make him understand he simply couldn't leave me behind.

I thought for sure... just absolutely for sure, that while he was inside of me, moving so slowly and whispering words he'd never said to me before, that it would be okay. That he realized I was more important than wherever it was he felt he had to go.

I was so wrong.

As my foot hits my first front porch step with what feels like the force of a sonic boom, I can feel my anger continue to rise rather than dissipate as I put distance between us.

A half an hour ago, I'd been thrown from the summit of Mount Hopeful down into the abyss of Crushed Dreams. And Kyle was the one who threw me down there.

Stupid, stupid, stupid to have ever believed he could give me more than what he'd promised me.

I had orgasmed twice before Kyle joined me, and it was so beautiful and so deeply intimate that I felt completely fulfilled. There were several long moments that he stayed inside of me, holding me tight and running his lips along my shoulder and jaw. It was all going to be okay.

I stomp up the remaining steps of my porch and throw a viciously angry look over my shoulder at Kyle's house, which is ablaze with lights.

He's packing up his stuff, after all, and needs to see what he's doing.

That's right.

Kyle pulled out of my body and, with his semen leaking out of me, told me that he was leaving right then.

He told me I had to leave his house so he could pack.

He told me he wasn't going to discuss it when I tried to question him.

He wouldn't even look at me as we dressed.

And most humiliating of all was the light kiss he gave me on top of my head right before he said, "Trust me on this, Jane. This is what's best for you."

Stupid, stupid, stupid for ever having given an ounce of my heart to him.

That was it for me. I tore myself away from him and ran out of his house. He called after me, but I didn't stop, because I never wanted to see him again as long as I lived.

I'm so proud of myself that not a single teardrop has fallen, and I expect that's because I'm so mad that my body is shutting down. I angrily jam my house key in the lock and storm into my house, intent on perhaps throwing some glass items and easing my frustrations that way.

Instead, a large hand clamps over my mouth. A jolt of fear rips through me so forcefully that every bit of anger and betrayal I'd been feeling toward Kyle immediately vanishes.

A gun appears before my eyes, and my intruder says to me, "I'm going to move my hand from your mouth, but if you scream, shout, or do anything contrary to what I tell you to do, I'm going to put a bullet in your brain. Got me?"

I nod my head furiously, despite the fact I seem to be paralyzed in terror. I can't fathom someone in my house with a gun. I have nothing of value here except... myself.

Immediately, tears fill my eyes and start to leak down my cheeks as he removes his hand from my mouth. His hand goes to my shoulder and he turns me to him. It's dark and I can't make out much except he's large. I don't know if I can fight him off, especially since he has a gun.

"Turn on that lamp," he orders me with the gun pointed straight at my face.

I do as he requests. When the glow of light hits him, I gasp in recognition.

Steve. From the diner yesterday.

Steve, who asked for Miranda's number.

"What do you want?" I manage to push the words out past my throat, which is constricted tightly in fear.

"I want your boyfriend," he says simply with a nod of his head toward Kyle's house.

"What?" I ask, dumbfounded.

"Call him," Steve—if that's his real name—says as he waves the gun toward my front door, beyond which lies Kyle's house across the street.

"What for?" I ask.

Stalling maybe, I don't know.

"Call him," he barks at me. He swings the gun back my way, the hole of the barrel looking ominously big as it sits less than a foot away from my nose.

"I don't understand. What do you want him for?"

"I want him to come over here, and I don't want him to suspect a fucking thing. I want him walking in here unprepared and unarmed, and you're going to call him right fucking now and get him over here."

"I can't," I say on a sob, my life literally flashing before my eyes.

Steve moves faster than I could have ever imagined, and he lunges at me. Grabbing a handful of my hair, he viciously yanks my head back and pushes the barrel of the gun to my forehead. "I'm not going to fucking tell you again... call him."

"I don't know his phone number," I cry out. This is absolutely true. I only found out he had a cell phone yesterday morning, and I never did get a chance to ask for his number. *And the jerk never offered it to me either*, I think bitterly, but even if I knew it, I wouldn't ever call him. I would never ask Kyle to come over here into unsuspected danger.

And oh, Kyle... what have you gotten yourself, and now me, into?

"How can you not know his fucking phone number?" he snarls at me, yanking my head back further. I can feel hair ripping from my scalp.

I cry out in pain, but I manage to stammer, "He just got the phone. I hadn't had a chance to get his number."

This doesn't enrage him as I suspected it would, but

it doesn't pacify him either. With his fist still gripping a hunk of my hair, he shoves me viciously away from him, causing me to go crashing to my floor.

"Fuck," he curses in frustration, and, for once, his gun points downward and away from me as he seems to be thinking up an alternate plan.

I suppose I'll never know how Kyle knew what was going on or how to capitalize on the fact that the gun was no longer on me, but to both my astonishment and Steve's, Kyle comes bursting through the door, bellowing in rage and charging at my attacker.

I watch, horrified, as Steve swings his hand with the gun toward Kyle, but he's not quick enough. Kyle barrels into him—his shoulder to Steve's chest—with one hand locking around Steve's wrist. They go crashing backward over my couch in a tangle of limbs, and Kyle actually yells out to me, "Get out of here, Jane."

But I'm frozen in place as they disappear from my sight, hitting the floor with such force the house seems to shake. I hear grunting, cursing, a scuffling sound, and then the crack of a gun going off.

I scream and push myself off the floor, disregarding Kyle's order to run and scrambling around the couch instead. I'm immediately relieved to see Kyle pushing up to his knees, the gun now in his hand with a dark red stain of blood spreading across Steve's chest. His eyes are closed, and he's not moving at all.

Kyle stands. His eyes roam over me, head to toe,

before he asks, "You okay?"

"No," I say in a shaky voice.

"Are you hurt?" he asks with concerned eyes as he steps toward me.

I hold my hands out to fend him off and take a step back. Shaking my head, I tell him, "Not hurt."

Kyle gives a sad smile of acknowledgment and tells me, "Dial 9-1-1. Tell them you had an intruder who has been shot and killed. Tell them there's an armed ATF agent in the house when they arrive."

"An armed what?" I gasp in surprise, but Kyle ignores me, instead pulling his phone out of his pocket.

I watch as he dials a number and puts the phone to his ear, completely shocked by what has occurred and not understanding a damn thing. He walks to the window, gun still in his hand, and looks out into the darkness. When someone answers on the other side of the phone, he says, "I've been found. I need you to get here now."

Kyle's eyes cut to me, and then he covers the mouthpiece of his phone. In a firm voice, he says, "Call the police, Jane. Now."

This jolts me somewhat... the businesslike calm he's exhibiting despite the fact I think he just killed a man. I pull my own phone out of my pocket with a shaking hand and call the police like he asked me to do.

◆

"I DON'T GIVE a shit what you say," I growl at the cop who's been sitting with me for the past hour. "I'm done. I'm going home, and you can't stop me."

"Miss Cresson," the man says patiently. "Your house is still being processed. You can't go home."

I have no clue who this guy is with. I've got local police, state patrol, FBI, and ATF. I swear I even saw people walking around with jackets that said Homeland Security.

I give the man a sarcastically sweet smile and tell him, "Well, I guess it's a good fucking thing my parents live within walking distance of me, huh?"

I push up from the table, the chair scraping on the tile floor. I've been in this room longer than the hour this man has been talking to me. I was brought here in the back of one our local police cruisers, driven by Chance Dawson, a total goober I went to school with who I'm sure had never seen a dead body before. He acted like he was driving a celebrity or something to the station when he was told to bring me there by an FBI agent who showed up on the scene not long after I called the police and Kyle had finished talking to whoever was on the phone.

We had been immediately separated, each being interviewed by men who had clearly identified them- selves as FBI, although I was told vaguely that I'd be interviewed later by ATF. I have no clue what the fuck is going on, but I notice with an odd sort of detachment that Kyle didn't seemed wigged out by any of this.

Not that I was held at gunpoint.

Not that he killed a man.

Not that he was surrounded by flashing police lights and was telling his story to the FBI. In fact, he had been casually leaning up against one of the unmarked cars with his hands in his pockets, cutting short glances of worry at me. I glared back at him, because the one thing that had become patently clear to me is that Kyle had been beyond deceitful. I mean… I'm not stupid. I knew he had secrets he was keeping. But I didn't know they involved murder and law enforcement and Jesus… will I be able to get the blood out of my carpet when I get home?

"Miss Cresson, I urge you to please wait," the man says. "I know Agents Kizner and Sommerville want to speak to you."

"I have no clue who those men are, and I don't want to know," I snap at him as I walk for the door.

"They're ATF and they're heading up this entire investigation," he says as my hand closes around the knob.

"Well, good for them," I sneer as I jerk the door open. "I wish them the best of luck."

I step out of the small room I'd been put in at our dinky Misty Harbor police department and run smack into Kyle. His hands come out to steady my arms, and I immediately tear free of him.

"Don't touch me," I snarl.

He flinches slightly, but his face hardens into stony resolve. "We need to talk."

"You need to go to hell," I hiss at him, so angry by his duplicity that I can barely look at him.

"Agent Sommerville," the man who had been sitting with me says to Kyle from behind me. "I tried to keep her in place."

"It's okay," Kyle says to the man, but he doesn't take his eyes off me. "Clear the room so I can talk to her."

I narrow my eyes at Kyle and practically spit out my disbelief. "Sommerville? Agent Sommerville? Who the fuck are you? Is your name even really Kyle?"

With each of these questions, my voice gets more hysterical.

Kyle takes my arm. My immediate reaction is to pull away, more in disgust than anything, but I'm also far too curious to find out the exact reasons Kyle had been playing me.

And ultimately, almost getting me killed.

I let him direct me back into the room. Luckily for him, he releases me the minute we're inside. I don't bother taking a seat because I don't plan to be here long. As soon as he closes the door behind us, I whirl on him and demand. "Speak and speak fast. I want to get out of here."

Kyle nods in understanding, and then completely stuns me when he says, "Your parents are out in the waiting room. I called them."

"You called them?" I ask in disbelief.

He doesn't answer. Instead, he walks away from me to stand in front of the window that looks out over the darkened parking lot of the police station. With his hands tucked in his pockets, he almost knocks my feet out from under me when he says, "I was an undercover agent with the feds... ATF to be exact. I was deep undercover with a very dangerous biker gang for a few years, and just about nine months ago, we brought them all down."

"Those tattoos," I murmur, the very first thing coming to mind. I could never reconcile the man I'd come to know with such an evil-looking skull on his chest and a warning that he should be feared.

"Part of my cover," he provides. "Since we made arrests, I've been laying low because I'm the key witness to all of it. The trial will start the month after next."

My jaw, which had previously dropped down to my chest, draws upward and I ask, "Like witness protection?"

"Sort of," is all he says as he turns to face me. "The man in your house tonight was sent to put a hit on me. I assume he was going to use you to draw me in."

"How did you know he was in my house?" I ask.

"I didn't," he says flatly. "I knew you were hurting. I went to see if you were okay."

"Is your name even Kyle?" I ask in a pitifully small voice.

"Yes," he says gently and takes a step toward me. I take a step back, but he continues. "It's Kyle Sommerville, and most of what little I told you about me personally was true, except for the fact that I have a sister named Andrea. She has no clue I'm even alive, as my death was faked when the arrests were made."

My eyes fall to the tile floor, unable to look at Kyle anymore. Of all the things I thought he might be, it was never law enforcement. But it explains his reticence to get involved with me and his continued resolve that he was going to be leaving at some point.

Still, I feel so… so… deceived. Even though he told me he was leaving, he deceived me about why. And yes, I get that even his sister was kept in the dark, but what we had was different. We shared the deepest of intimacies, and he surely had to know that I'd never have given him up.

My nose starts to sting at the realization that Kyle would have never trusted me, and I use every bit of my willpower not to let my welling emotions turn into tears. I square my shoulders and look back up at him. He's watching me carefully… warily.

I lift my chin. "Is there anything else I need to know?"

Kyle sighs and takes a few steps until he's standing in front of me. "Only that I'll be relocated tonight and held somewhere until the trial starts. Technically, you're not supposed to know any of this, but I insisted that they let me tell you the truth—"

"The truth?" I practically shriek at him, my anger overtaking my common sense. I step into him and jab a finger in the middle of his chest. "Why tell me the truth? Is it because you trust me, Kyle? Is that it? Because you didn't trust me enough just a few hours ago when you were fucking me. Why do I get the truth now?"

Kyle's hand comes up, perhaps to touch my face, but I knock it away, too enraged to even give him a chance to mollify me. "I'll tell you why you're giving it to me straight now," I say in a low voice seething with accusation. "Because you're leaving and you know you don't have to look at me again. You can leave this all behind with a little salve to your conscience that you finally came clean with poor little Jane Cresson who spread her legs for you while looking at you with starry eyes?"

"Jane, that's not—"

My hands come up, slam into his chest, and the tears fill my eyes. My chest heaves as I lay it all out. "I cared for you, Kyle. I mean, I really, really cared for you. And you not only used me, but you also put me in danger. You got your rocks off while hiding out… just biding your time."

"It's not like that," he grits out in anger.

"It's exactly like that," I say softly, suddenly completely defeated and feeling wiped out.

"No," he says harshly as his hands come to my

shoulders. He holds me tightly in place and puts his face near mine. "I care for you too, Jane. More than you could ever even imagine. I was leaving tonight because my partner had alerted me that my location may have been compromised, and I didn't want you in danger. But what I've just told you... about me being undercover? That doesn't even scratch the surface of my story, and if you knew the things that I had to do to achieve my objectives in this operation, you'd be disgusted by me. You'd despise me."

"I despise you for not being honest with me," I rasp out through the tears clogging my throat.

"You'd despise me more if you ever knew the real me," he tells me flatly. "All of this that happened tonight... what I've told you so far? That's not me. It's got nothing to do with the reasons I held myself back from you. Why I never fully gave in to you. There are things that your beautiful soul could never comprehend about me, and be it cowardly or not, I could never bear to see the look of hate you'd have for me if you really knew it all."

For the first time since I arrived here at the police station, my anger toward Kyle vanishes. It's simply gone. In its place is an apprehension that feels almost ominous in nature. Kyle's still keeping deep secrets from me, but he talks about them as if they're so horrific that they will change everything. It will mar completely the way I feel about Kyle, and while I know it's over, and I know I've been betrayed, there were some very beautiful moments with this man. I don't want those to turn ugly. I can't stand it if they were to be tarnished.

And suddenly, I don't want to know anymore. I want Kyle to keep his secrets, and I want to leave this room, go to my parents, and let them take me home where I know they'll baby me. Miranda will come over, and she'll hold me while I cry for my losses. I don't want to know the deep, ugly truths about Kyle. Instead, I want to hold onto my anger for his deception. I truly believe if I do that, I might just be able to heal my broken heart with time.

My eyes focus in on Kyle's, and I lock them there tight. I take one last look at him, trying to be strong so I don't dissolve in front of him, and I tell him from the bottom of my heart. "Good luck to you, Kyle. I wish you the best."

Kyle's face crumbles, but I can't let it deter me. I turn and walk away from him without a backward glance.

CHAPTER 26

KYLE

Two months later…

THE GRAVEL CRUNCHES under the tires of my rented sedan as I pull into the driveway to my sister's house. She has no idea I'm coming, but she won't be overly astonished at seeing me alive. After I was pulled out of Misty Harbor that night Jane got attacked, I insisted Andrea be told what had happened. The trial wasn't very far away and, after fucking things up with Jane so bad, I just couldn't go another goddamned day with my sister thinking I was dead. It was one lie I simply had to rectify. So I had Joe visit her, because telling her I was alive after she'd mourned me was not something that could be done over the phone.

From that point and until the trial started, I was seriously sequestered away, but Joe arranged for me to talk to Andrea and we've had a few conversations. They've been short and have focused on nothing but good stuff, which includes mostly her joy I'm alive and my joy that she has a baby on the way.

That all changes as of today, for I am now a free

man.

The trials did not go all the way as expected. I was called as the first witness and my testimony lasted four full days. It was solid enough that attorneys representing defendants asked the judge for a half-day recess so they could "discuss things". Within just a few hours though, Zeke Powell, the president of Mayhem's Mission, was accepting a plea deal that would give him a shot at parole in thirty years versus life in prison with no possibility of parole. For that deal, he gave up Senator Latner, and from there, all the dominoes started to crumble.

The only thing left unresolved was proving who put the hit out on me. The man who broke into Jane's house who I subsequently killed wasn't any known killer for hire. There had been a cash deposit into his bank account for five thousand dollars two days before he showed up in Misty Harbor, but it couldn't be traced anywhere. There's no doubt in anyone's mind it was Senator Latner who was behind it, and it was a pitiful attempt to snuff me out. But none of it matters because Latner will be spending the rest of his days behind bars.

The final plea deals were all executed and approved by the judge just two days ago. The day after the deals were finalized, I gave my notice to the ATF that I was quitting. While my actions were vile and inhumane much of the time I was undercover, I know deep in my heart I've ultimately saved lives by completing my mission and, for that, I'm proud.

But despite that, I really need to leave it all behind. The scars run too deep, the memories are nothing but bitter, and I don't have a passion for justice anymore.

As soon as I exit the car, the front door of the stilted beach cottage that belongs to Andrea and her husband Wyatt flies open. They live right on the sandy dunes of the Outer Banks in North Carolina, and it's hot as hell even though we're breaching the end of September.

Andrea trots gingerly down the steps, one hand on the rail and the other holding her swollen belly, but her eyes are pinned right on me.

"Jesus Christ, slow down, Andrea," I hear from the top of the stairs, and I look up to see Wyatt coming down behind her. I've only been around him twice, but he's a decent dude. Works for the local police department while Andrea practices law. Ironically, they met while on an undercover assignment when Andrea was working for the FBI prior to her moving here.

I don't bother to look at Wyatt again though, because I only have eyes for my sister. So like me with the same blond hair and blue eyes, and even our predisposition to work in law enforcement. But we're different in that she's always had the sunny, bubbly personality and I've always been more circumspect about things. Over the past few years, while Andrea has been settling into married life and setting her eyes on raising a family, I'd been running drugs, guns, and selling women into slavery. Her sunny disposition has only gotten brighter, while my glass runs less than half full and mainly has a thick layer of sludge on the bottom.

"Even though I'm seeing you with my own eyes," she says softly as her flip-flops hit the gravel and she walks into my arms, "I'm just having a hard time believing you're really alive."

I engulf her, pull her as tight as that pregnant belly will let me, and lay my cheek on the top of her head. My voice is gruff with emotion when I tell her, "Believe it, sis."

We stay like that for several long moments until I feel Wyatt's hand on my shoulder. I lift my head and turn to find him looking at me with respect and appreciation. I've talked to him a few times on the phone as well these last several weeks, and we've talked about the sacrifices that had to be made while working undercover.

Andrea is the first to pull away, and her eyes are shining with happy tears that she unabashedly ignores as she smiles at me. "I hope you packed a lot of clothes so you can stay for a really long visit."

"Got nowhere else I need to be," I tell her.

And that's the sad truth.

◆

"ALL THOSE YEARS," Andrea murmurs as we sit on her back deck the next morning, watching the waves roll in. It's just dawn and the sun is peeking over the horizon.

She found me out here about twenty minutes ago, and we shared our coffee together as we watched the sun rise, turning the sky pink, orange, purple, and then blue. "And I never knew you were undercover."

"Isn't that the point?" I say, my tone matter of fact.

"Well, of course," she admits freely. "But I was FBI. I should have known. I'm trained to know those things."

I reach over and pat Andrea's knee to commiserate. I had told her last night the long and involved story about how I became an ATF agent, and what led me to go undercover. She knows that I joined the ATF with the sole purpose of infiltrating Mayhem's Mission, so she was purposely kept oblivious to it all.

"Did you love her?" Andrea asks, and the question should feel awkward because we've not been close in years. I absolutely could not let us be close because I never wanted Zeke or anyone in that club thinking they could use Andrea against me if things went south.

But her asking me if I loved her isn't awkward, and I answer her with brutal honesty.

"No," I tell her softly. "But I cared for her a great deal."

The "her" is Jacqueline Martin, a woman I'd dated for several months while I was working the oil fields in eastern Wyoming. It was good money and I was able to work on my criminal justice degree at night. I was close friends with Jackie's brother, Darren, who was a local deputy sheriff. It sort of naturally happened that I started dating her and, because she and her brother were close, we all hung out a lot. While I wasn't in love with her, I cared about her deeply.

When she went missing, it hit me hard, but it hit Darren and his parents harder. She was a dental hygienist and had gone to work one morning, left at her normal time, and never made it home. Three months after her disappearance, when the local law enforcement ran out of leads, a miraculous turn of events happened. The ATF showed up with some loose information they had about a notorious biker gang known as Mayhem's Mission, who were suspected of numerous criminal activities, one of which was sex slavery. There was some consideration thrown around that Jackie could have been kidnapped by them.

"I can't tell you how that made me feel," I tell Andrea as we stare out over the ocean. She knows I'm talking about Jackie's disappearance. "But there I was… sitting with a degree and no real direction in life, and I just knew… when Darren told me about the ATF's involvement, I just knew that I had to join in on it."

"You thought you could save Jackie?" Andrea asks.

"Not really," I admit with a heavy heart. "I had accepted that if she'd been taken, she was probably long gone from the area. But I hoped I could find answers that could lead to her. More than anything… I wanted to bring them down."

Andrea turns her head and looks at me. "All those

years of your life… committed to that one cause."

"Wasn't easy," I say as I reach out and take her hand. We both turn back to look at the ocean, and it fills me with some measure of peace. "I had to get on with the ATF first, and because Darren had always kept me involved with the investigation of Jackie's disappearance at the local level, I was no stranger to it when the ATF got involved."

"Was it your idea to go undercover?" she asks softly, and I sense the hesitation in her voice. She's asked the question, but I can tell part of her doesn't want to know the answer.

"Yeah," I admit to her. For a woman I didn't love, but did care for, I hatched a plan to try to achieve justice. "I presented it to them and offered to do it. I had to take their entrance exam and make the cut as an agent, just like any other. But after my initial training, I immediately went undercover."

"It's when you relocated out to Jackson, Wyoming," she says in remembrance. "You told me you wanted to be a motorcycle mechanic."

"Well, that was sort of the truth," I say with a chuckle.

She's silent for several moments, but then she gives my hand a squeeze. "I'm proud of you, Kyle. I honestly cannot imagine the horrors you've faced. And I know that you had to sacrifice yourself to get the job done. You ever want to talk about it, I'm here. You want me to mind my own business, it's done. I'm here for whatever you need."

I squeeze her hand back in grateful acknowledgment, and my lack of words tells her clearly I'm not ready to talk about any of it.

Except, well… maybe one thing.

"I met someone while I was living in Maine this summer," I say in an abrupt change of subject.

Andrea sits up straight in her deck chair and turns to me. Her eyebrows are aimed high as she gives me a smirk. "Really? Tell me all about it."

I shrug. "I was in hiding. Using an alias. Couldn't be truthful with her."

"Not exactly the right time to get involved with someone, right?" she asks.

I laugh, because damn if that wasn't the entire problem. "She got under my skin," I admit to my sister. "Just kept pushing at me, and finally… well, I just sort of went with it."

"What's her name?" she asks, and I hear that dreamy, romantic tone in her voice. Wyatt admitted to me last night after Andrea went to bed and we were sucking down a few beers that she was operating on pure hormones these days, which means whatever emotions she was feeling were intensified.

"Jane," I say softly, and I'm truly surprised that it hurts as much today to think of her as it did two months ago when I walked out of her life.

Andrea settles back in her chair, and I release her hand. I slouch down, propping my feet up on the railing that runs the length of her back deck.

"Tell me about her," Andrea prompts me.

And while I have no desire to ever tell Andrea about the horrors of my life while I was in deep with Mayhem's Mission, I'm oddly okay with spilling my guts to her about Jane.

Maybe because I have nothing to lose at this point.

"She's an artist," I begin my story. "A good one at that. Mainly watercolors. I have one of her paintings in the backseat of my car. No clue where I'll end up settling, but that will be the first thing that gets hung."

Andrea smiles, her tone sounding dreamy again. "I can totally see you with an artist. I bet she's quirky, isn't she?"

"So quirky," I admit with a sad smile. "But she also reminds me a little of you."

"Of course she does," Andrea says with a huff. "I'm fabulous, after all. Tell me more."

And I do.

I tell Andrea every bit of it.

The initial and swift attraction I tried to fight.

The way Jane pursued me in that incredibly sweet way, inching her way under my skin.

The attempt at friendship when we both knew that would never work.

Vaguer details about the intimacy we developed.

Shamefully admitting to Andrea that I never intended to make anything permanent with Jane and that I used her.

And finally, the self-hatred I've been bearing these last eight weeks that I brought danger into Jane's life and almost got her killed. I admit to my sister that I couldn't get out of Misty Harbor fast enough after all of that went down. Jane rightfully reacted badly to being attacked in her own home and then finding out that I'd been lying to her all along. She had every reason to push me away, and when she did, I took the opportunity and ran. I let the government hide me away, and I tried to put her out of my mind.

"You are so totally gone for this girl," Andrea murmurs when I finish.

"I am. But I fucked it up too badly," I tell her. "Ruined it."

"You don't know that," she offers helpfully.

"I do," is all I say. I can recall with keen detail the look on Jane's face when she found out the truth about me, and it wasn't even the entire truth. She didn't know about any of the bad stuff.

"You don't," she pushes back at me. "You haven't even had a meaningful conversation with her to know that. You absolutely cannot assume you know her feelings just based on that one interaction after it all went down, at a time, which I'll remind you, must have been incredibly stressful for her."

"What are you saying?" I ask guardedly, trying to keep any hope from filtering into my reasoning. It's self-preservation, really.

"I'm saying that you need to go to her and talk," Andrea says as she turns to look at me. She shifts in the chair, reaches out, and puts a hand on my shoulder. "Kyle... you deserve something good. She's the thing you deserve. But you're going to have to go after it."

CHAPTER 27

JANE

"**I**'M ALREADY SO sick of pumpkin spice and it's only been out one week," I lament quietly to Christa as I make a pumpkin spice latte at the espresso machine.

Christa snickers as she wipes down the counter. "I told you... come October 1st, people seem to just go rabid for the stuff. But don't worry... in another month, you'll be sick of peppermint mochas."

I'm sure that's true.

The morning rush is over, and I look around the small coffee shop where I've been working as a barista for the past month. It had been my hope to get a teaching job when I'd moved to Boston, but I'd not had any luck yet. So I was doing what I could to make ends meet, working at this boutique coffeehouse during the day and painting by night. I'd set up an online shop to sell my art, but it's been tough getting it up and running. I haven't quite figured out yet how to get visibility.

"Any plans for this weekend?" Christa asks as she leans a hip against the counter. I finish off the pumpkin spice latte and hand it across the counter to the customer, who doesn't even give a simple "thank you." I've found that people in the big city aren't nearly as friendly as in Misty Harbor, and I think that's because everyone is just in too much of a rush to get places. I've been completely overwhelmed by this transition from small town to big city life, but it was something I had to do.

There was simply no way I could stay in Misty Harbor after Kyle blew my heart apart. Everything I always equated to happiness in my hometown was stripped away when he left, and I felt completely disconnected. That warm, settled feeling that kept me tied to Misty Harbor was gone, and it was because it was the place where I fell in love and then was left far behind.

Granted, I know I reacted harshly to Kyle that night. I was completely wigged out by being attacked, and I'd felt completely deceived by him. But then the person who is always my voice of reason sat me down and gave me a strong talking to.

Miranda had finally said to me, after another evening of listening to me vilify Kyle, "Jane… get your head out of your ass. The man was a fucking undercover agent who infiltrated a dangerous biker gang and he was in hiding. Don't you think that's something he had a right to keep secret from you?"

I'd stammered and tried to argue with her, but she held her hand up and I snapped my mouth shut. Then her eyes softened and her voice was uncharacteristically kind when she said, "I know your heart is broken. Maybe his is too. Ever think of that?"

And well, no… I hadn't thought of that. I was too mired in my own misery.

So it was all Miranda's fault that I started to think hard about it. About how unlucky Kyle and I were in our timing, and how things might have been different with just a slight change in circumstances.

Then that got me thinking of a change in circumstances, and I realized that I couldn't sit back and wait for happiness and love to find me again. I had to go out and make my own way, because one thing was for sure… Kyle wasn't coming back to Misty Harbor. That was one thing he had been honest with me about from the start.

The move to Boston saddened my parents, because they not only lost me, but also Miranda as well. No way she was letting me go on my own because, in her words, "You need protecting, Janey. You're too naïve."

This was true.

Miranda got a good job bartending and makes way better money than I do. After we split rent and utilities fifty-fifty, she has money left over to do fun things with while I have enough to get maybe one cup of pumpkin spice latte if I was so inclined to drink one.

"Hello?" Christa calls out to me, and I blink my eyes rapidly, realizing I'm staring at the empty counter space where the customer had been waiting for his latte. "Earth to Jane. Come in, Jane."

"Sorry," I say as I focus in on her. "What were we

talking about?"

"I asked if you had any plans for the weekend, Space Cadet?" she says with a grin.

I give a small laugh back. I hit it off amazingly well with Christa, and we're a lot alike in our humor. "Um, by plans do you mean do I intend to splurge on Velveeta Mac and Cheese over the powdered Kraft?"

"Those were most definitely not the type of plans I'd been asking about," she says as she wrinkles her nose. "But I'm going to go see a friend of a friend of a friend who plays in a band Saturday night. Want to come?"

If I'd let my conscience answer for me, I'd tell her I most certainly didn't want to go. I was far more comfortable hiding out in my small apartment when Miranda was gone for the evening bartending. While I had hoped to bust out of my box a little by moving to the big city, I'd become even more introverted due to how overwhelming everything was. My monstrous plan to leave little Misty Harbor behind to find my happiness wasn't quite panning out for me.

And who was I kidding? I really missed it back home. I mean, I really, really missed it. I missed my mom and my dad, and my students, and my little house that overlooks the lighthouse and ocean. I missed knowing everyone and receiving friendly smiles and being able to walk safely down Main Street at night.

But I had to push past that. That was what I left behind to seek something better for myself. So I square my shoulders and tentatively ask Christa, "Is where they're playing far from here?"

"About three blocks," she says with excitement. "So you'll come?"

"What's it cost to get in?" I ask, mentally calculating whether I can even afford to do this.

"We'll get in free since we know the band," she says confidently.

"You mean the friend of a friend of a friend?" I ask with an eyebrow cocked.

Christa laughs and waves a hand at me dismissively. "Relax. We'll get in and it will be a blast. Think Miranda will want to come?"

This was an odd invitation as Christa and Miranda don't get along all that well. I think Miranda is jealous that I've developed a friendship with Christa, and Christa is just plain intimidated by Miranda.

"She's got to work," I say, knowing that will immediately put her at ease.

And yup… I see her shoulders relax and lines of tension ease from her face as she lies to me, "Well damn… that sucks. I bet she'd be a lot of fun to hang out with."

I snort. "Only if you want to make sure she doesn't strip on the stage with the band or throw up on you at the end of the evening."

"She's wild, huh?" Christa asks, but I know she's already suspected this about Miranda, who blatantly and aggressively hits on any single-looking man when she comes to hang out at the coffee shop.

"She's wild alright," I say fondly, because I love Miranda just the way she is. With no other customers to attend to, I decide to replenish some stock items, so I turn for the swinging pass-through door that leads to the back storage. "I'm going to organize for a restock. You good out here by yourself?"

"Yup," she says cheerily. "Got you covered, so you can take a break from the pumpkin smell."

Chuckling in agreement, I head into the storage room and begin to work. Most of the coffee materials are purchased in bulk, so I line up large bags of coffee beans and jugs of flavored syrup, mentally calculating which bottles and canisters I'll need to fill up front. I grab some plastic-wrapped tubes of coffee cups and the accompanying lids from another box. I do all of this while letting my mind wander and wondering if I'm really doing the right thing for myself by being here.

This has been an adventure for me, and not one that I've enjoyed overly much, but something positive has come from it. I've grown over the last few weeks as I've learned to exist in a very different atmosphere than what I'm used to. There's a doubtful part of me, however, that wonders if I truly needed this type of growth. Wasn't my life damn good back in Misty Harbor?

The answer is clearly "yes" BK.

Before Kyle.

After Kyle, things were complicated, and maybe I'm just running from painful memories.

♦

"DO YOU WANT Chinese or subs for dinner?" Miranda asks as soon as I walk in the door.

I'm starved, so the answer is easy. "Chinese."

"Shrimp lo mein, pot stickers, and hot and sour soup," she says in confirmation, proof we are the best of friends because she knows my Chinese food preferences.

Still, I can't afford all of that, so I tell her, "Just lo mein."

Miranda ignores me. She'll order everything I like and she'll pay for it, claiming that she wanted to have some too.

"I'm going to go put on some LuLaRoe and take my bra off," I tell her, which is unnecessary really since that's my habit every evening. I get in my comfy clothes, we eat dinner together, and Miranda heads out to her bartending job.

My bedroom is small, but we were extremely fortunate to find a two-bedroom place in a fairly decent part of the city and, best of all, only a few blocks from where both of us worked. I get undressed quickly and change out of my work uniform, then I head into the bathroom to wash my face. I'm bent over the sink, rinsing my face off and fantasizing about pot stickers, when Miranda calls out to me.

"Jane," she yells from what sounds like the living room, and I jump slightly because her voice startles me.

I grab the small hand towel hanging by the sink and press it briefly over my face to dry it. When I pull it away, I yell back, "What's up?"

"Need you to come in here," is all she says.

With a sigh, I hang the towel back up and walk out of the bathroom. The hallway that leads into the living room is short, with a small efficiency kitchen just beyond. I see Miranda standing there, looking at me with an odd look on her face, but I pause only briefly on her. For right beside her is someone I'm not prepared to see.

A ghost.

A figment.

A man who should not be standing here right now.

God, he looks good. Different, but really good. His hair is growing in, and it's blonder than I had realized. He's also started a beard, which he has neatly trimmed, and he seems to have filled out a bit or it could be that he's just wearing tighter shirts.

He looks at me warily from across the room, and I can see him swallow hard before he says, "Hello, Jane."

I just stand there... completely unable to do a damn thing. I can't speak. I can't move. I can't decide what it is I want.

I never thought I'd see Kyle again in my life, and I went through a mourning process for him. And now I'm inundated with all these different emotions ranging from anger to relief to bitterness to joy to love to hate to…

"What are you doing here?" I manage to whisper as I cross my arms over my chest protectively, not because I'm braless, but to protect my heart from this man who is provoking my world into chaos again.

Kyle's eyes cut to Miranda, who just stands there looking back at him as if he's a strange phenomenon, but they slide right back to me, seemingly uncaring that he has an audience. His voice is low and rumbling when he says, "I came to see if I could make things right with you."

My limbs go weak with confusion and my heart pounds erratically. Miranda's head snaps my way to see what I'll do, and I know if I look at her, I'll buckle. She's been a rock and an immense support to me over the last several weeks, but she's also been clearly on Team Kyle, because as she kept reminding me, "There were extenuating circumstances that you have to consider, Janey."

An irrational fear takes root in the middle of my chest as I remember the pain of him lying and leaving, and I know I can't go through that again, despite the fact that Miranda seems to see this in a much clearer light.

So I tell the brutal truth in a soft whisper. "There's nothing to make right. I understand why you couldn't share things with me, and I've accepted that. So honestly, this was probably a wasted trip to come here to see me."

Kyle winces. I wait a terrifyingly long moment to see

if he'll leave, but he doesn't. Instead, he says, "There's still a lot you need to know. That I want you to know if you'll give me just a little bit of your time."

CHAPTER 28

KYLE

THERE WAS A time months ago… just before we took Mayhem's Mission down… that I thought the president, Zeke Powell, was on to me. He looked at me a little different and, with that sneaking suspicion I had, I braced myself for imminent death. If Zeke thought in any way that I could have possibly betrayed him and his club, he would have put a bullet right between my eyes.

So there was a period of weeks where I waited for it, trying to act like nothing was wrong and yet completely resolved that I was going to die. It was a wretched feeling mainly because at that point, I wasn't in control of my own destiny.

It's how I feel right now.

All I can do is tell Jane the things I'd been keeping from her, and then it's out of my hands. She'll either tell me to go to hell, which would be the ultimate death for me and a far worse fate than Zeke could ever bestow, or she'll forgive me, which will at least keep that spark of hope alive that Andrea planted in me three days ago.

Luckily, that spark hasn't diminished in the three

days it's taken me to get to her. With promises to Andrea that I would come back soon, I left the day after our talk and headed to Misty Harbor via plane. I had two layovers. The last leg was on a small prop plane, but it was the quickest way there.

I was completely stunned to find her little house empty and abandoned with a "For Rent" sign placed at the end of the driveway. My immediate fear was that something bad had happened to Jane. Without another thought, I jumped into the rental car and drove the three hundred yards to her parents' house on Front Street because it was faster than running. I know I scared the shit out of Meredith and Allen when I banged furiously on their door, but I was immediately settled and relieved when Meredith smiled big at me the minute she saw me.

"I knew you'd come back for her," she said, beaming at me proudly as she opened the door wide and invited me in. She clearly had known something I had not.

I went in gladly and was prepared to do whatever sucking up I had to do with her parents so that I could find out where she was. Turns out, I didn't have to do much. I only had to tell them the truth of who I was, what I'd done, and what I wanted with their daughter. They accepted my intentions at face value, and, for reasons I cannot even begin to fathom, they put their trust in me that I could make Jane happy.

I received their blessing along with Jane's new home and work address in Boston. It was too late by this time to make the trip, and they kindly invited me to stay in their guest room. While I very much like her parents and felt comfortable enough with them, that was just a little too awkward for my liking. I declined, instead choosing to get a room at the one and only motel in the area, The Misty Slumber Inn.

I took off before the sun was up the next morning and was parking my rental car a few blocks away from the coffee house where her parents said she worked by ten-thirty. I didn't approach her though, as I knew we'd need privacy to talk. So I just waited it out, watched her walk home from work, and made my move.

She stands before me, looking as confused as I am terrified, and more beautiful than I could have ever remembered. Doesn't matter she's wearing some funky-looking leggings that are electric blue with big, yellow saxophones over them or a threadbare New England Patriots t-shirt. She is simply the most gorgeous creature I've ever known, and there is no other for me. There was a time I didn't believe I deserved her, but I'm tired of that way of thinking. Tired of living my life without happiness, hope, and ambition for my future.

"Will you give me some time?" I ask her softly. "Just to talk."

My heart skips a mad beat when I see her actually stiffen up at my suggestion, but then, just as quickly, she lets out a long breath. I'm not surprised when she looks to Miranda. I can see the questions written all over her face as she silently communicates with her best friend.

Should I listen?

Will he hurt me?

Is this even real?

Why should I trust him?

Miranda gives her an encouraging smile before she says, "Listen… I'm going to head into work a bit early and grab a bite to eat there. Let you two have some privacy."

Jane and I both watch in silent acceptance as Miranda grabs her coat from a hook by the door and scampers out, leaving us very much alone and facing off from opposite corners.

With an awkward gesture toward the couch, Jane says, "Do you want to sit down?"

It's a legitimate offer considering this will be a very serious discussion that could take a while, but I don't think I can even wait the few seconds it would take us both to get situated. So instead, I walk right up to her, putting my hands on her shoulders and tipping my face down to hers, so she's looking me dead in the eye. "I am so sorry for deceiving you, leading you on, and taking advantage of you. I should have told you the truth from the very beginning."

To my surprise, Jane shakes her head. "No, Miranda's right. You had to keep those secrets. You were in hiding and didn't know me well enough to trust me with that."

My grip tightens on her shoulders slightly, not because I'm afraid she'll pull away but because I want her to understand how serious I am about this. "But I did know you, Jane. From the first moment you left me your horrible muffins on my doorstep, I knew exactly who you were. I knew you were sweet, and kind, and persistent. You kept after what you wanted, and I'm just hoping you'll remember... there was a time you wanted me. A time you wouldn't give up."

"Kyle," she says on a shaky breath as her eyes soften.

"But first," I say cautiously, because this is really where I'm putting everything on the line. "I have to tell you everything about me."

Jane's eyebrows furrow. "What do you mean?"

"I mean, I have to tell you some bad stuff about me," I tell her. The one thing I know for sure is that I can't hold anything back with Jane from now on.

She gives me a tiny smile as if she knows something I don't. "Oh, I know about you being undercover. You had to play the part to get into the motorcycle club. Agent Kizner told me all about it."

"No, Jane," I say a roughly. "It wasn't a part. It wasn't an act. I did despicable things of my own free will."

"I'm sure—" she starts to say, but I just can't have her taking my goodness at face value. For her to accept I'm good, she has to understand the depths from which I've climbed back up.

"The first bad thing I did," I tell her without any preamble, "was sell heroin to a pregnant woman. No clue how many months, but she was huge. Probably close to giving birth."

Jane's eyes go round, and she blinks at me in astonishment.

"But that wasn't enough to develop the type of trust I needed to get into the club," I continue before she can stop me. "That night I woke up beside you... bad dream and all, it was about this man I beat nearly to death. In fact, I might have killed him. I'm not sure. But I did it while his wife and little boy watched."

Jane makes a small sound of distress. I hold onto her tighter, so she won't run away until I can make sure she understands I had absolutely no boundaries I wouldn't cross to get my job done. My voice cracks when I tell her the most brutal truth of all. "Jane... I would have done anything that I was told to do by that club. Think of the vilest thing you can imagine, and I'm telling you, baby... I did it. I did it all."

Jane doesn't respond for a moment, still staring at me with owl-like eyes and just blinking. I look at her, trying to read into her expression, wondering if she's so disgusted she literally can't say anything.

Then she surprises me when she puts her palms to my cheeks and says, "You did a job to save people. I don't need to know the details, but if you want to unburden yourself, I'll gladly take them. But all I really need to know, Kyle, is that you did something for the greater good. You did something that you believed in with such passion that you gave up your entire life to see it through. Now, you may be mired in guilt and maybe you're feeling the need for penance or something, but you're not going to get that from me. Just like you said you know who I am… well, I know who you are too. You are a good man. You're the best kind of man, really."

My body reacts so quickly that I'm not even sure what I'm really doing. Before I know it, I've snatched Jane to me and I'm wrapping my arms tightly around her as relief courses through me. Relief that she doesn't despise me for my transgressions.

"Kyle," Jane says softly, and I pull my face back so I can look at her. "I've talked to Joe a lot since that night you left. He told me stuff about your undercover operation. Why you volunteered, the risks you took, and how your life was in danger every single day."

I shrug because none of that will ever assuage the guilt I have for the things I did.

"He told me about Maggie," Jane says softly, and the air in my lungs freezes. "You saved her."

I bow my head and close my eyes, thankful for that one bright shining spot in everything. I had indeed saved her. After over three years of doing despicable things to maintain my cover, I risked it all to get one single female out of the clutches of that club, knowing it could mean my death.

"You saved her," Jane repeats.

"Saving one doesn't absolve—"

"You saved hundreds," Jane interrupts me. "Hundreds of women from being sold into slavery. Hundreds of men, women, and children who won't die by illegal guns. Hundreds of lives saved by taking a drug supply line out of commission. You did one of the bravest acts you could for your fellow citizens. Laid your own life on the line. Gave up all your dreams to make better lives for others. I don't believe there's a tit-for-tat type of system out there. No, 'I did this one bad thing so I need to at least save this many lives.' It doesn't work like that."

"Then how does it work?" I ask, my voice clogging with emotion.

"It works when you realize that once you forgive yourself, you can start to move on with the rest of your life," she whispers before stepping into me and laying her cheek on my chest. I know she can hear the thundering of my heart, yet I can't will it to calm down.

"You always find the good in people," I murmur as I wrap my arms around her, lifting her from the floor.

"I'm glad you came after me," she says quietly. "I missed you so much."

"I'm not even sure I deserve you," I mutter, more to myself as I'm still a little confused that she's accepting me back, which makes me ask as I loosen my hold so I can look at her. "Why? Why are you standing here letting me hold you?"

She doesn't answer, just turns the tables quickly on me. "Why did you come track me down?"

The answer is absolutely crystal clear. "Because I love you."

"Yes," she agrees softly with a smile. "Because I love you."

My fucking heart swells and expands, ripples with warmth, and I feel unbelievably light in my soul. Joy radiates through me, and it feels like a rebirth.

I feel new.

I feel immensely grateful for every possibility before me right now.

"I'm going to do this right," I promise her as I let her slide down until her feet touch the floor.

"How so?" she murmurs.

I hook her by the back of the neck with my hand and give a slight squeeze of possession. "I am going to make you feel like the most precious thing in the world every day for the rest of your life, because what you're giving me is beyond precious. You've given me another chance, and I'm never going to forget the value of that. Every day, I'm going to earn your love. Every fucking day for the rest of my life, I'm going to give you the very best I have to offer this world. It will all be for you."

Jane lets out a quavering breath. "God, that was poetic, and I'm completely turned on."

"I'm serious, Jane," I say, giving her another squeeze.

I know what I just said to her was really intense, but fuck... my feelings are really intense, and I need to get them out there. I also know she's trying to make light of it so I don't feel awkward, but fuck the awkward.

"Jane," I say as I lower my face toward hers. "Tell me you get everything I just said to you and you know it's from the bottom of my heart."

Her eyes get shiny. I feel like shit because I didn't want to make her cry, but then she smiles at me so brightly that I'm almost blinded. "I'm never going to forget a single word of what you just said because it was the most beautiful thing in the world."

My lips find her in a searching kiss, both of us seeking to validate our words and our emotions now with touch and physical intimacy. My body comes alive at what this means as I kiss her more deeply.

Jane's hands slide up my chest, and she gives a slight push that breaks our kiss. She gives a quick lick to her lower lip, which is sexy as hell, before she asks, "Are you going to move here to Boston?"

"I'll move anywhere in the world you want to," I assure her. "I quit the ATF, so I'm extremely mobile."

"What about Misty Harbor?" she asks tentatively.

"They still need a light keeper?" I ask with a grin.

"Quite possibly," she says with a laugh.

"Then Misty Harbor it is," I tell her, the decision absolutely made.

But first...

I sweep Jane up into my arms and turn toward the hallway that I'm assuming leads to a bed. We have other things to do right now.

EPILOGUE

JANE

Two years later...

I WALK IN through the open bay doors of Tinker's Garage, quickly scanning the area, but I don't see Kyle or anyone else for that matter. There's a car up on one of the lifts. I suspect that was Kyle's project today, although he's more than likely in the office doing paperwork.

Kyle has pretty much taken over Tink's business, as the old man is finally considering retirement. He's been spending more time in Pennsylvania with his daughter and grandkids, and I know he and Kyle are in talks for Kyle to buy him out so he can "officially" retire. I asked him if he would change the name of the garage to maybe "Kyle's Garage" or even "Sommerville's Garage," but he just grinned and shook his head. "Baby... Tink's is an establishment in this area. He's had this business for over forty years in Misty Harbor. The man deserves his name on the garage for eternity."

And that's my man.

He's completely settled into life here as if he'd been born here. It took him a while to figure out what he wanted to do for a living, but when he saw that Tink was looking for part-time help, it all just sort of made sense to him. He was a good mechanic, and he liked working with his hands.

Oh, dear Lord, did he like working with his hands. He was so good with them last night that he made me scream.

A delicious shiver runs up my spine just remembering last night, and so many of the other nights I've spent with him. He told me many, many months ago that it was his job to earn me, and he does... just so very naturally.

I know everything there is to know about Kyle. He's told me every single sordid and inhumane thing he did while undercover, and he did it while we laid in bed with his head resting on my chest and my fingers in his hair, which he'd let grow a bit longer than his buzz cut. I can't extinguish all of his guilt, but I make sure he knows every day how proud I am of what he did and the sacrifices he made.

Honestly, I wish I'd known that Kyle or had a peek of him. Not because I'm curious or there's a thrill knowing he used to be a dangerous biker criminal. No, I'd like to have known him just a bit so I could see how much he's changed. I can only suspect because of the way he was when we first met, but it warms me to know that he's very happy with his life right now. I know this because he tells me almost every single day.

I head into the back office and immediately see Kyle through the glass window cut in the wall. He's bent over some documents on the desk. The minute I step into the doorway, his head pops up. The minute he recognizes me, his face transforms.

Eyes crinkle and shine.

Gorgeous lips now framed in a sexy goateed smile.

Husky voice that says, "Hey, beautiful."

I force myself not to preen under his compliments that cause pure elation to run through me. You'd think after two years that the romance would wear thin, but far from it. I get as much of a thrill from seeing Kyle today as I did back then. Maybe even more so… particularly today of all days.

"What are you doing here?" he asks as he sets the pen he held in his hand down and pushes the pile of papers back to give me his attention. "I thought you were getting your hair done at Miranda's?"

"I am, but you forgot the lunch I packed." I hand him the brown paper bag I'm carrying. He takes it from me with his left hand, and I smile when I see the pale line of skin across his ring finger. He never wears his wedding band at the garage because he doesn't want it to get caught on something and ruined. I just don't want him to lose a finger.

Kyle takes the bag and gives it a questioning look. "You didn't bake anything, did you?"

I laugh as I lean against the doorjamb. "No, smartass.

Just a tuna fish sandwich and some chips. If you want baked goods, you'll have to go over to Margie's Bakery."

Kyle throws the bag on the desk and pushes his chair back. Opening his arms, he says, "Don't you have a kiss to go with that lunch?"

"I do indeed," I say with a grin, and then I'm straddling his lap and he's kissing me.

When Kyle's hands go to my ass, I swat them away and pull my lips from his. "Stop it."

His hands go right back as he grins up at me. "C'mon, baby. Little lunchtime nookie."

A throbbing forms between my legs because that sounds amazing indeed. And it would not be the first time I'd gotten it on with my husband in this office. Just a few weeks ago, he bent me over that desk and...

Shaking my head, I reach over to the desk and grab the bag. Handing it to him, I say, "Eat your lunch."

He ignores it, hands gently squeezing my ass. "Not hungry for that."

I shove the bag against his chest and insist. "Eat. Your. Lunch."

He again ignores me, sitting up straighter in his chair so he can bring his mouth to my collarbone. He gives it a light kiss and, damn it all to hell... I moan.

But then very quickly, I regain my senses. "For Pete's sake, Kyle... will you just look in the damn bag?"

My husband's body goes still as he lifts his head to look at me with curious eyes. I give a little push on the bag against his chest, and he finally takes the hint. Scooting back a little on his lap, I watch expectantly as he opens the bag and looks inside.

His brow furrows because there's no sandwich or chips in there—only a box.

He pulls it out. When he realizes what it is, his lips start to tip upward at the corners. He opens the flaps on the end—which had obviously already been opened by me and refolded back—and pulls out the little plastic stick.

Turning it over gently with his fingers, as if he was holding the most precious thing in the world, he locks his eyes right onto the positive sign in the digital window.

His head slowly rises, and his gaze is filled with wonder. "We're pregnant."

I nod quickly, unable to contain it anymore. Bouncing slightly on his lap, I clap my hands and practically squeal. "We're pregnant!"

"Holy fucking shit," he barks out before he tosses the stick over his shoulder and jerks me to him for a huge hug. We wrap our arms tightly around each other, and I can feel his heart hammering against my chest as I bury my face in his neck.

After a few moments, Kyle pulls back and looks at me mischievously. "We are so going to have sex right now to celebrate."

"But Miranda's waiting on me," I point out. And

yes, Miranda moved back to Misty Harbor right along with Kyle and me. She was my maid of honor at our wedding, and yes, her top came off at the end of the night as she danced on the tabletop.

"You would seriously rather go get your hair cut than let me lay you out on this desk and eat that gorgeous pussy of yours?" Kyle asks as he pushes up from the chair with his hands supporting me under my ass. He turns and sets said ass on the edge of the desk, his hands going to the button of my jeans.

"To hell with Miranda," I sigh as I lean back and let him do his thing.

But his hands go still and his eyes turn serious. Kyle's voice is rough when he says, "I can't tell you how happy this makes me. I've felt that I'm so complete since you came into my life, but now this… this just makes me feel like there's more."

"There is," I murmur at him with a smile. "So much more for us."

"I wouldn't have it without you." His eyes soften as he smiles at me knowingly. "You have this gift where you bring out the best in others, and if you struggle to find it, you help them create it. That's what you do for me."

"Oh, baby," I say on a sigh, my heart melting even more for this man. My hands go to his face, and I kiss him sweetly. "I love you so much."

His return kiss is just as sweet, but only for a moment. One of his hands fist in the back of my hair and his kiss deepens. He pulls back and practically growls at me with hot eyes. "Now I'm going to put my mouth between those sexy legs of yours and make you scream my name."

I wiggle my hips on the desk and tell him, "Go ahead. Make my day. *Sudden Impact*, 1983."

"Jesus, you're a dork," he says with complete adoration. "It's a good thing I love you."

"And I love you," I assure him, but then look down pointedly at my zipper. "But you mentioned celebratory oral sex and I'm ready for it."

"Me too, baby," he says before he kisses me. "I'm ready for everything with you."

THE END

Want to know a little more about Kyle Sommerville? You can find appearances from Kyle in the following previously released books, which can be read as stand alones:
Shaken Not Stirred (Last Call, Book #5)
Wicked Bond (Wicked Horse, Book #5)

And if you want to know more about Kyle's sister, Andrea Sommerville, you can read her story as a stand alone:
With A Twist (Last Call, Book #4)

If you enjoyed *Finding Kyle* as much as I enjoyed writing it, it would mean a lot for you to give me a review on your favorite retailer's website.

CONNECT WITH SAWYER ONLINE:

Website: www.sawyerbennett.com
Twitter: www.twitter.com/bennettbooks
Facebook: www.facebook.com/bennettbooks

OTHER BOOKS BY SAWYER BENNETT

THE OFF SERIES
Off Sides

Off Limits

Off The Record

Off Course

Off Chance

Off Season

Off Duty

THE LAST CALL SERIES
On The Rocks

Make It A Double

Sugar On The Edge

With A Twist

Shaken Not Stirred

Last Call Series Complete Boxed Set

THE LEGAL AFFAIRS SERIES
Legal Affairs Sneak Peek (FREE)

Legal Affairs

Confessions of a Litigation God

Clash: A Legal Affairs Story (Book #1 of Cal and Macy's Story)

Grind: A Legal Affairs Story (Book #2 of Cal and Macy's Story)

Yield: A Legal Affairs Story (Book #3 of Cal and Macy's Story)

Friction: A Legal Affairs Novel

STAND ALONE TITLES
If I Return

Uncivilized

Love: Uncivilized

Sexy Lies and Rock & Roll

THE SUGAR BOWL SERIES
Sugar Daddy

Sugar Rush

Sugar Free

THE COLD FURY HOCKEY SERIES
(RANDOM HOUSE / LOVESWEPT)
Alex

Garrett

Zack

Ryker

Hawke

Max

Roman (releasing 2/21/2017)

4 Book Bundle – Alex, Garrett, Zack, Ryker

THE WICKED HORSE SERIES
Wicked Fall

Wicked Lust

Wicked Need

Wicked Ride

Wicked Bond

ABOUT THE AUTHOR

Since the release of her debut contemporary romance novel, Off Sides, in January 2013, Sawyer Bennett has released more than 30 books and has been featured on both the USA Today and New York Times bestseller lists on multiple occasions.

A reformed trial lawyer from North Carolina, Sawyer uses real life experience to create relatable, sexy stories that appeal to a wide array of readers. From new adult to erotic contemporary romance, Sawyer writes something for just about everyone.

Sawyer likes her Bloody Mary's strong, her martinis dirty, and her heroes a combination of the two. When not bringing fictional romance to life, Sawyer is a chauffeur, stylist, chef, maid, and personal assistant to a very active toddler, as well as full-time servant to two adorably naughty dogs. She believes in the good of others, and that a bad day can be cured with a great work-out, cake, or a combination of the two.

CPSIA information can be obtained
at www.ICGtesting.com
Printed in the USA
BVHW031558060421
604207BV00013B/550